Falling for the Fake Lumberjack

OTHER TITLES BY SARA NEY

Campus Legends

How to Lose at Love

How to Win the Girl

How to Score off Field

Accidentally in Love

The Player Hater

The Mrs. Degree

The Make Out Artist

The Secret Roommate

Jock Hard

Switch Hitter

Jock Row

Jock Rule

Switch Bidder

Jock Road

Jock Royal

Jock Reign

Jock Romeo

Trophy Boyfriends

Hard Pass

Hard Fall

Hard Love

Hard Luck

The Bachelors Club

Bachelor Society

Bachelor Boss

How to Date a Douchebag

The Studying Hours

The Failing Hours

The Learning Hours

The Coaching Hours

The Lying Hours

The Teaching Hours

#Three Little Lies

Things Liars Say

Things Liars Hide

Things Liars Fake

All the Right Moves

All the Sweet Moves

All the Bold Moves

All the Right Moves

Stand-Alones

The Bachelor Society Duet: The Bachelors Club

Jock Hard Box Set: Books 1–3

The Pucker Next Door

Not Your Biggest Fan

Biggest Player

SARA NEY

Published by Montlake, Seattle

www.apub.com

EU product safety contact:
Amazon Media EU S. à r.l.
38, avenue John F. Kennedy, L-1855 Luxembourg
amazonpublishing-gpsr@amazon.com

ISBN-13: 9781662536007 (paperback)
ISBN-13: 9781662536014 (digital)

Cover design by Letitia Hasser
Cover Image © Michelle Lancaster PTY LTD; © teddyandmia / Getty;
© Alona Horkova / Getty

Printed in the United States of America

Falling for the Fake Lumberjack

Chapter 1

Harris

I know relaxing isn't in your DNA, but you owe it to yourselves to try—you assholes need it, some more than others.

Coach's voice carried through the locker room when he made his announcement a few weeks back, half joking—about sending the team on a retreat.

Retreat?

What are we, ten years old?

Management always gets what it wants, and what they want is all the guys on my line sent on a *team-building retreat.* Don't know who pissed in their Cheerios, but it looks like I'm gonna be stuck in some rando lake resort near the mountains for some "well-deserved" R & R and other nature-inspired bull crap.

As if throwing a bunch of competitive maniacs in the wilderness were going to help us unwind and bond and shit.

I mean. What does one *do* at a lake?

Kayak? Not interested. Go boating? Last time I boated, it included beer and wakeboarding, and we've been told not to embarrass ourselves by drinking. Can't swim—too cold. And have I mentioned I loathe getting touched by things I cannot see beneath the water? Seaweed and such?

Uh, hello—have you heard of the Loch Ness Monster?

Don't fish. *I refuse to.* Since I went fishing with my Grandpa Walt the summer I turned nine and got hooked in the ear by one of his errant casts, I will not fish, and you cannot make me. *The grudge game is strong with this one.*

"Fishing is a state of mind, bro," my teammate Dex declared after discovering our destination was a mountain town. "It's you, your worm, and—"

I cut him off. "I'm not touching worms."

He shrugged. "You can use fake bait. Some of them have glitter."

"No fishing."

"Fine." He sneered at me, disgusted by my lack of masculinity. "Don't come crying to me when you're bored out of your mind."

Bored?

Yeah, I probably will be bored; at least I'll have my own space.

I was lucky enough to score my own little cottage (thanks to my seniority), which is more than I can say for half the linemen on my team, crammed together in the massive lodge at the top of the hill.

Granted, it has a full staff and full amenities. And room service. And a spa . . .

I double-check the address on my phone before pulling into the gravel driveway of my little rental, happy to have finally arrived after a three-hour-long drive from the city. Cut the engine and sit gazing at it several moments, taking in the peace and quiet.

Not a peep, unless you count the birds.

I listen harder.

Huh. Maybe this wouldn't be so bad.

I step out of the truck, pea gravel gritty beneath my boots, and retrieve my overnight crap. With the press of a button, the hatch in back lifts. I grab my bag and heft it over my shoulder, glancing around me at the trees and stuff.

The resort has cottages scattered near the lake, a long stretch of water and shoreline in the near distance. Pine trees line the edge of the property, their needles crunching under my feet along with the gravel, branches swaying softly in the wind.

I raise my nose in the air and sniff; the faint smell of woodsmoke lingering, mixing with the scent of pine, crisp and fresh.

"Ahhh."

Not bad at all!

Beyond the cottages, a vast lake glistens under the sun's rays, with dozens of docks stretching out with an invitation to dip your toes into the cool water or jump in—something I will *not* be doing.

My assigned cottage isn't big by any means, but the charm makes up for its size. Window boxes. Two matching rocking chairs. I squint at them, trying to picture myself sipping coffee out here like the sort of calm, reflective guy who drinks coffee by the lake.

News flash: *I am not that guy.*

A stone path leading up to a door painted a muddy shade of green—the same color as the patches of moss that cling to the sloped roof in a way that feels more quaint than neglected.

Best of all?

No roommate.

I drop my bag on the porch with a satisfying thud and stand there, soaking in the silence. No teammates bitching at each other. No Coach blowing his whistle like we're about to storm the beaches of Normandy. Peace and quiet.

Solitude.

But no key.

Why did I throw out the welcome instructions?

"'Cause you're an idiot."

Whatever—I can figure this out. The key must be here somewhere.

"Great start," I mutter to myself. Nothing says *relaxation* like breaking into your own cabin.

I glance around like the key's going to magically appear in front of me. Maybe it's under the doormat or something—people do that, yeah?

After a few moments of awkwardly patting down random surfaces like a cop at airport security, I spot a little wooden plaque by the door with a cheery **Welcome!** sign.

Behind it?

The key.

"Wow. Great fucking hiding spot. Took all of three seconds," I grumble, fitting it into the lock and pushing through the door. "I'm definitely going to be murdered in my sleep."

Inside it's exactly what you'd expect: small, cozy, and decorated like it belongs in a catalog for people who use words like *vintage hygge* unironically.

Dinky entryway. Little living room. The stone fireplace practically screams *"roast marshmallows here!"* Small kitchenette with a stove straight out of the '70s and—wait for it—a plaid couch.

Of course there's plaid. Nothing says *lake retreat* like plaid furniture older than my grandmother's perm.

Cute, though.

I dig it.

I toss my bag onto the couch and give the place a closer look. It's not terrible. Not luxurious by any means, but it's got a rustic, woodsy vibe people lose their shit for on Instagram. Vintage. Cool.

I wander over to the kitchen, then open a cabinet or two.

The cupboards? Empty.

No surprise there. The last thing management would do is stock us up on snacks, God forbid—it would cost too much money. They probably expect us to *forage* like wild animals, which would force us to bond with nature.

"Bet Dex is already having the time of his life." I picture the asshole enthusiastically untangling a fishing line while I'm here trying to figure out the Wi-Fi password.

I plop down on the couch, pull out my phone, and check for service. Two bars. Not *great,* but better than expected for a place that looks like it hasn't been updated since the invention of the internet.

"Well, at least I won't die of boredom."

Then, something catches my eye that I did not notice on my initial walk-through.

Tacked to the fireplace mantel is a sheet of paper. Dangling there, as if waiting to impart some critical lake-living wisdom. Knowing my luck, it's probably a list of chores or instructions on how not to burn the place down.

I push myself off the couch and walk over, eyeing the paper, already irritated by its big, bold letters.

Welcome Sentinels and Staff to your team-building retreat! Super, more fake enthusiasm. I skim the next part: **Below is a list of activities designed to help you bond with your teammates and foster a deeper connection.**

Deeper connection? With Dex and Jude?

Ha!

I've heard them both letting it rip and heard them shitting and routinely have to listen to them complain about fractures, pulled muscles, and concussion results. I do NOT need to go deeper.

Daily Group Hikes!
Morning Yoga by the Lake!
Fishing Derby!

Translation: forced fun, which is the worst kind.

Why the hell are there so many exclamation points? Who wrote this fucking thing, the cheerleading coaches?

"You have *got* to be kidding me," I mutter, resisting the urge to crumple the paper and toss it into the fireplace as kindling.

Morning yoga? Who in their right mind is going to participate?

Unfortunately it doesn't end there. I groan, reading further.

Team Building! Talent Show Night!

"Talent show? *What the actual fuck . . .*" I groan. "Apparently we're in summer camp now."

And the cherry on top? **Trust Exercises!**

I roll my eyes so hard I think I might sprain something in my brain. Trust exercises? With these guys? The same guys who steal my bath towel during a shower, then snap me in the dick with it.

I walk back to the couch and flop down dramatically.

"I am not doing a talent show." They can't make me. Football is my talent—what more do they want from us?

I didn't participate in the talent show the one summer my parents forced me to attend camp to socialize with regular kids, who weren't obsessed with sports the way I was. It was the kind of camp where you canoed, swam, and tie-dyed shirts in the craft shack.

I remember how my pottery looked like a blindfolded toddler had painted it, and chucking it in the trash so my dad wouldn't see it.

Also me: The evening of the camp talent show, I had faked a stomachache and was sitting in the corner while the other kids embarrassed themselves singing off-key renditions of popular music. When I was pushed to join them, I miraculously "lost my voice." Then, during the hiking trip, I claimed I twisted my ankle and spent the rest of the day on the bench, sipping watered-down Bug Juice.

Now here I am, years later—a grown-ass adult—in the exact same nightmare scenario.

Only this time with my teammates.

The same guys who think burping and smashing beer cans on their foreheads are talents.

I look at the paper again. **While participation is not required, it is strongly encouraged—top scores will be rewarded with various prizes and acknowledgment!**

"Hell. No."

No thank you, Coach.

If management thinks I'm getting up on a stage and doing anything remotely close to performing, they've got another thing coming.

Why do they think we need team-building exercises to begin with?

I see these assholes on a daily basis—there is no escaping them. Between practice, the locker room, conditioning, and the occasional party, I'd say we're pretty goddamn bonded, *fuck you very much*.

Apparently, some genius in the business office decided we needed a "retreat."

I twiddle around with my phone a bit longer, the service bars suddenly disappearing, and swing my gaze to the lake.

It glistens under the setting afternoon sun, calm and still, like a scene straight out of one of those cheesy brochures they use to convince people this kind of place is relaxing.

Hefting myself up, I sigh. "Maybe if I go out to the end of my pier, I'll get my signal back."

I've sat around long enough.

Clutching my phone in my hand like a lifeline, I head out the back door, trudging down the small path to the dock. The boards creak under my feet as I walk, the lake lapping softly against the posts, all peaceful and serene—exactly the opposite of how I feel right now.

When I reach the end, I hold my phone up, as if added elevation were going to magically bring those bars back.

It does not.

I check again, praying for at least one measly bar, but nope—nada. As I'm about to give up and accept my fate, I glance around and notice some familiar faces on the piers nearby.

A few of my buddies are scattered along the shoreline, talking so loudly I can hear them planning something that will surely end with someone in the water—or covered in mud.

It's like they're already in some survival mode.

"Hey, nut sack, you made it!" Two docks over, Quinton Wallace throws his middle finger up in greeting, grinning like the asshole he is. "Was hoping you wouldn't!"

"Fuck off." My voice echoes across the lake, bouncing back at me with perfect comedic timing.

Fuck off . . . off . . . off . . .

I can hear Quinton laughing and see his head thrown back as if my echo is the funniest thing he's heard all day. His laugh roars back at us, too, ricocheting from tree to tree, the water an acoustic portal.

"Careful, dude—the lake is listening!" I shout.

"The lake is the least of my problems." Quinton was busted for possession of marijuana before his rookie year began. I'm no saint, but I know not to do shit like that.

I'm about to turn back to my cottage when I hear footsteps on another pier. One of my teammates—Elijah—is strolling barefoot, his always-present grin on his face because nothing bothers this dickhead.

He stops at the edge of his pier, clutching a coffee mug in his hand as if it weren't too late in the day for caffeine. If I was drinking coffee right now, I would be wide awake until two in the morning.

"Sup, bro." He yawns.

I point in the direction of his mug. "It's almost dinnertime. You trying to pull an all-nighter?"

He shrugs, taking a sip like it's no big deal. "Helps me wind down."

Wind down? *Coffee?*

I resist the urge to laugh.

"Beautiful, isn't it?" I gesture toward the lake. Mostly because I have no idea what else to say. I suck at conversation.

Elijah looks out over the water, nodding thoughtfully. "Yeah. Makes you appreciate the little things, you know?"

He sounds so profound. Like Yoda.

We stand there in silence for a minute, the sound of the water gently lapping against the pier, and for a second, it actually *is* kind of peaceful. Then Elijah, without any warning, takes a giant gulp of coffee and turns toward me. "You gonna make it to yoga tomorrow?"

I stare at him for a second, processing the question. "Uh. Wasn't planning on it."

He shakes his head. "Seriously? It's a team-building activity." He stretches one arm above his head and groans. "Sunrise yoga by the lake."

I snort. "There's no way in hell I'm waking up at the crack of dawn to do downward dog with you idiots."

Elijah shrugs—and I can hear him slurping his coffee from here. "Suit yourself. Coach says it's mandatory, though. Something about flexibility improving performance."

"He said it was *strongly encouraged*—not mandatory. And I'm *so* sure flexibility is the only reason he wants us there." I roll my eyes. "Not because the photos would be good PR."

Elijah grins, unbothered. "Hey. I don't make the rules. I show up." He stretches his arms behind his head, twisting his body to the right, then to the left, like he's already warming up for his next yoga session. "Plus, there's a women's waterskiing team on the lake—I'm hoping they practice early so we can watch."

I blink at him. *Women's waterskiing team?* What the fuck is that? Like . . . gymnastics on water? I mean, I've heard of synchronized swimming, but synchronized skiing? Do they do backflips while getting dragged behind a boat?

"That's a thing?" I ask, genuinely baffled.

"Apparently," Elijah drawls. "Saw it on the camp itinerary."

"Camp itinerary?" Is it me, or did my eyes bug out of my skull? "Is that the sheet of paper hanging on the fireplace?"

How did this go from a relaxing retreat to one with required activities? With prizes for most participation? Are we earning badges now, like the Boy Scouts?

What's next? Arts and crafts time? Making friendship bracelets out of sea-glass beads, sourced from the beach and polished?

Elijah shrugs again, completely unfazed. "Nah, there's a whole list of stuff we can sign up for at the main cabin. Where Coach is staying. Waterskiing, canoe races, archery. You know, *camp* stuff."

"Camp stuff," I deadpan the words. "And here I thought we were supposed to *relax*."

"Relaxation through participation, man," Elijah says, sounding way too Zen for my liking. He obviously doesn't realize we're trapped in a web of competitive wilderness survival masquerading as *team building*.

"Dude. Are you high?" I ask him, hoping my voice won't carry across the lake.

High . . . igh . . . igh . . .

"No. I'm embracing the experience." He laughs, a little too laid back for my taste. "You should try it—maybe you'll surprise yourself."

I shake my head. "The only thing I'm going to enjoy is my bed while the rest of you are doing downward dog at dawn."

Which sounds fucking terrible.

Elijah shrugs again, still grinning. "Your loss. More for the rest of us."

"I'm sure I'll survive."

I watch as Elijah pulls out his phone, stares at it for a beat, then stuffs it into the back pocket of his athletic pants. He looks over at me with a nonplussed expression he's perfected. "Dex texted. A few of us are going downtown to a pub for a burger. Wanna come?"

I shake my head. "Nah, I'm gonna grab groceries. Think I'll pop an old movie into the ancient VCR back at the cabin and, you know—*embrace* the experience."

He chuckles, giving me a little salute. "You do you—but don't be jealous when the rest of us return home enlightened."

Chapter 2

Lucy

"Where did these giant men come from?"

The bar is packed with bodies, many of them broad shouldered. They're taking up more space than the average human, and I glance around, perplexed. It's like someone in town put out a Bat-Signal for giants, and they all decided to congregate here, crowding Lakeside Brew with their booming laughs and oversize appetites.

"I'm being serious. Where did these enormous men come from?" Annabelle asks again. She scans the room, perched on a barstool beside me, a glass of cheap wine in her hand. They don't serve wine at Lakeside Brew (it's mostly microbrews and IPAs), but Ben, the owner, lets her keep a bottle behind the counter. Why? Because this is Annabelle and rules bend for her the way trees bend for the wind.

Plus, Ben wants to bang her.

"I don't know." I spin on my stool, pretending I don't know who these guys are, to have a little fun with Annabelle. One of the guys is posturing three feet away, flexing his biceps as he talks. "Maybe they heard your cries for lumberjacks and came in droves."

Annabelle snorts. "The lumberjacks I hired look nothing like this."

Half of these behemoths are either pounding back beers or shouting across tables at each other, all testosterone and bravado. It's not exactly the usual crowd for a sleepy night in our sleepy lake town.

My best friend leans in. "Do you think they're a team or something? Or a beefcake contest?"

I laugh, shaking my head. "If it's a beefcake contest, I want a front-row seat."

"Preach." She raises her glass. "I do feel like these guys are like cockroaches—they're turning up everywhere." She clinks her wineglass against mine in solidarity. "I don't have time for testosterone-filled blowhards. Speaking of lumberjacks—I'm coordinating Fall Fest, and only *three* of my lumberjacks have shown up for practice."

"Know what I've been wondering?" I tap on the side of my drink. "Since when do they hire lumberjacks for the fall festival?"

Annabelle waves me off like I've completely missed the point. "Since it became trendy on the internet. We're going to have them chop wood in flannel shirts for a live demonstration." Her voice lowers dramatically. "Think: outdoorsy. Think: photo ops. Tourists eat that shit *up*."

She's not wrong.

We live in a popular lake town full of them; tourists appear with money and an appetite for anything giving them a real slice of quaint lake living. A little waterskiing show during the day, campfires at night—paired with an organic latte from the local café.

Suddenly they're posting about how they've *disconnected* and *reconnected* with nature, all while their gas-guzzling luxury SUVs sit parked a few feet away.

"Is this actually about tourists?" I roll my eyes. "Or is this an excuse for you to watch a bunch of buff guys chop wood?"

She sips her wine. "Can't two things both be true?"

"Yes, but—"

"Listen," Annabelle interrupts. "I paid those douchebags a deposit! Three out of eight showed up, Lucy! *Three.* I'm going to need more lumberjacks. Where does one even *find* more lumberjacks?"

"You still have time for them to show," I remind her. "The festival isn't until next weekend, and it's only Saturday."

Annabelle snorts. "I'm serious, Lucy. I need these logs split, or the country charm of Fall Fest will be ruined. I've got, like, an aesthetic to maintain."

"Clearly," I tell her, keeping a straight face, but inside I'm fighting the urge to laugh. Only Annabelle would stress about the *aesthetic* of wood chopping at a small-town festival. "What about pumpkins?"

After all, the festival is called *Fall* Fest.

"Way too soon for those," she says, waving me off. "It's only September."

The festival in Star Lake, Washington, is the town's biggest event of the year, and Annabelle's been planning it for months. I can't help but visualize her wrangling eight guys from Rent-a-Lumberjack like some kind of petting zoo.

Honestly, watching her figure this out will probably be more entertaining than the festival itself.

Maybe I'll sell tickets.

Annabelle sighs, then takes another long sip of her wine. "I swear, Lucy, if one more thing goes wrong with this festival, I'm going to lose it. Clarke Robinson was going to repaint the old sign and ended up needing stitches in his palm."

I'm dying to ask her how painting a sign could lead to stitches but don't want to trigger her.

"You're not going to lose it," I reassure her. "You're going to rally and pull off an amazing weekend because that's what you do. And then you'll act like it was simple and no big deal."

As the town's only wedding planner, Annabelle is the most organized and creative person I know. I'm struggling to plan our friend Kiersten's bachelorette party; I could never plan an entire event for an entire *town*.

The only thing I'm good at is yoga, which doesn't require creativity.

"Simple and no big deal? Stop flattering me." My bestie narrows her eyes at me, but I can see she's pleased with the praise. "You make me sound like some kind of hero." Annabelle tosses her hair.

I laugh. "Someone has to be the hero of the Fall Fest. And it sure as hell won't be *Clarke*."

"Freaking Clarke," Annabelle grumbles. "I swear to God. The worst part is, he's the only one I could get to volunteer! And can we not forget it's high season? I got stopped twice outside Loon Landing Café this morning by tourists asking for directions to the nearest Starbucks."

The nearest Starbucks is fifty-five miles away, if that gives you any idea about how remote we are.

She rests her chin in her hand, looking genuinely stressed. "I don't know what I'm going to do if the rest of those lumberjacks don't show up, Luce. I mean, three guys can't split all those logs by themselves. It'll take them all day!"

All the logs?

How many logs does she have if she needs all those men?

I nibble on my bottom lip. "Well, hmm. You could always fake it? Set up a bunch of already-split logs and let people pretend to chop them for fun." I grin, half joking. "Throw in a hashtag like #StarLakeStrong and you'll have people lining up for their turn with an axe."

If we don't mind all those severed limbs.

Annabelle stares at me for a moment, like she's actually considering it. "You know, that's not the worst idea."

"Uh. I was kidding. Say it with me: liability."

She shrugs, sipping her wine again. "It's better than people showing up to a lumberjack demo with no jacks and no demo. Besides, it's all about the *aesthetic*, right?"

So she keeps pointing out. "You really think people won't notice the logs are already chopped?"

"Have you *met* tourists? They'll take one look at those flannel-wearing hunks holding an axe and think they're witnessing some kind of historical reenactment." She leans back in her chair, looking wise and pleased with herself. "Trust me, they won't care."

I snort. "Well, in that case, maybe you should have the lumberjacks *pose* with the logs and skip the chopping altogether. They can hand out autographs after."

"I know you're joking, but don't think I wouldn't do it if I got desperate."

A loud laugh interrupts our musings, and we glance over at a group of buff dudes sitting several tables away.

They're loud, obnoxious—and trying to impress anyone within a fifty-foot radius. One of them is currently attempting to flip quarters into a beer glass, only for one to fly off the table and onto the floor. It spins before dropping with a metallic clank.

So immature.

"What are they, still in college?" I mutter, rolling my eyes. "Look how competitive they're acting. Like, jeez, they're flipping those things like there's a prize?"

Annabelle sips her wine. "Guys will do anything if it comes with a trophy at the end."

"True," I say, watching as another big guy attempts to get the quarter in the glass with a flick of his index finger. But it sails through the air and hits the person at the next table in the back.

"Honestly, I'd pay money to see *them* chop wood," I reluctantly admit.

Annabelle raises an eyebrow. "Would you actually?"

I smile despite myself. "Those big, sweaty muscles? Swinging axes in the sun? Uh—yes."

She grins. "Yeah, me too."

I laugh and take a sip of my drink. "I'm only human, after all."

And I haven't gotten laid in . . . Lord.

I have no idea how long—which isn't a good sign.

Annabelle and I turn to ogle the group again. "They're pretty to look at—I'll give them that. Even if they have the combined brainpower of a *light* bulb."

"Hey, we never said they had to be smart." I watch as one of the guys flexes his arms for no reason. "Just, you know—aesthetically pleasing," I tease, throwing her words back at her.

We laugh, watching for another minute before turning back to our drinks. They seem harmless, but it's like watching a pack of overgrown puppies try to act tough.

"Anyway." Annabelle sighs. "Enough about me. What's going on with you?"

My eyes dart to the men in the room, then back to my bestie.

"Well." I sip from my glass, savoring the cheap, delicious wine as it slides down my throat. "Those big dudes, mostly. I'm doing a few group sessions down by the harbor."

"Um. Can I come? And why didn't you say anything before?"

I laugh. "Of course you can."

She and I are both single and always ready to mingle, although to be fair, she and I are actually choosy about who we date.

And sleep with.

I'm not in a rush to start a family. In fact, I'm still on the fence about having kids of my own. But I would love to be in a relationship and all the things that go along with it.

Sex.

Sex.

And laughter, *obviously*.

Annabelle nudges me out of my daze. "Girl, you're about to live the dream. Teaching hot guys at sunrise? You'll be coach and eye candy, and I'm officially *jealous*."

Yeah right. Between the two of us, my friend has far better luck with men—mostly because she's bold and never lets an opportunity pass her by.

Oh, and she's currently hooking up with the mayor's son, Tim.

He looks exactly like a "Tim" and acts like one too—cocky, clean cut, and convinced he's the most interesting guy in the room. It's nothing serious—a casual fling to get over Mike—but she's getting some action out of it and the occasional free meal.

As much as my friend insists she'd love to swap places and escape her situationship, I think she secretly loves having sex with the mayor's son.

I, on the other hand, have the dating instincts of a gnat.

More than one person has told me I wouldn't recognize a man flirting with me, and honestly? They're right. I'm always the last one to realize when someone is romantically interested in me.

I smirk, swirling my glass before taking a sip. "We'll see how dreamy it is after tomorrow's first class. Something tells me they're going to spend more time falling over each other than doing yoga."

But I can't lie—I'm excited, and it will be fun to watch them fumbling around.

"Oh, please." She rolls her eyes. "You know they'll be coming to gawk at the pretty yoga teacher. I bet half of them don't know the difference between downward dog and a dog pile."

"A dog pile of *shit*?" I laugh, nodding. "I wouldn't be surprised if they don't take it seriously. I already feel like it'll be wrangling a herd of cats."

"Oddly enough that's what my mother says about *us*."

We dissolve into laughter, and I can't help but glance back at the players clustered around the bar, their boisterous energy filling the room. One of them, oblivious to his own size, attempts an awkward spin, nearly taking out a neighboring table.

"Tell me what else is going on," Annabelle begs. "Are you back on the dating apps?"

I hate that she's bringing this up, and groan. Ugh. "I tried the Kissmet app for all of twenty minutes before I realized every man on it was someone we already know."

Annabelle grins. "That, my friend, is what we call a cosmic joke."

"Right? It was like scrolling through my own personal nightmare. Or our yearbook. I'd swipe, and bam—Taylor from high school. Or the man who did my oil change. Then I saw the kid who works at the bank." I shudder at the thought. "After that, I deleted it. The universe is telling me to put the app on pause."

I can't escape.

I give my glass a swirl, eyeballing what's left of my wine. "I really am an idiot for not hooking up with tourists. They come, they go, no strings attached." My hand waves flippantly through the air.

Annabelle nods sagely. "True. Most of them are probably either married, old—or here for bachelor parties. It's slim pickings even on a good day."

"Exactly," I say. "You'd think living in a small town by the water would attract a *few* eligible men. But no. The only new faces we see are here for a weekend of questionable decisions before heading back to their real lives."

Don't get me wrong. Our little town is gorgeous. Glistening water in the summer and snowcapped mountains in the winter? It's like a postcard, if postcards came with an astronomical nightly price tag.

I probably wouldn't be living in this town if it weren't for my parents and the guesthouse above their detached garage where I live for free . . . one of the perks of having parents with prime real estate.

Despite the dwindling dating pool and the ever-present tourists, this town is home.

There's a sense of comfort in its familiarity, in the faces I see daily—even if those faces occasionally pop up on Kissmet with cringeworthy pickup lines.

Guh!

"Who knows?" I shrug, feigning nonchalance. "Maybe Mr. Right will magically appear in my yoga class tomorrow. Stranger things have happened."

Spoiler alert: Mr. Right does *not* appear in my yoga class the next morning.

Instead, I'm greeted by a crowd of eight massive guys who look like they've been dragged here by their fingernails. These aren't the bright-eyed, flirty singles I hoped for. And, judging by the glint of wedding rings on several fingers, at least half these hotties are off the market.

And Mr. Wrong? Doesn't look like he's showing up either.

Chapter 3

Harris

I am up at dawn despite swearing I would sleep the day away.

Fresh air will do that to a person, I suppose.

Inhaling a clean shot of pine, I stretch, then sit up with a yawn. Twist my body from side to side to get the knots out of my shoulders.

The cabin is quiet, save for the rhythmic creaking of the dock outside as waves lap lazily against the wooden posts. I pull on a sweatshirt and step out onto the porch, bare feet brushing the cool weathered boards. The lake is still, a mirror reflecting the soft hues of early morning.

It's the kind of serenity meant to relax you, but all I can think about is how much I need caffeine.

Back inside, I stare at the ancient coffee maker sitting on the counter. It looks more like a science experiment than a kitchen appliance, complete with levers, knobs, and a water reservoir. I try pressing buttons at random.

Nothing happens.

I fumble with the filter, spill some coffee grounds inside, and press the buttons again. Still nothing.

The quiet of the cabin is getting on my nerves.

"Fine. Be that way," I mutter, abandoning the piece-of-shit contraption. I grab my keys from the hook by the door and head outside, the gravel crunching under my boots as I make my way to my truck.

The drive into town isn't long—fifteen minutes, tops—but it's a winding road that hugs the lake on one side and the forest on the other. The scenery is postcard perfect, but I'm too focused on my mission to appreciate it.

A decent cup of coffee isn't a want at this point; *it's a necessity.*

I park outside a place called Loon Landing Café and stare up at an aged wooden sign swinging in the breeze.

Zero shops are open, except the café, and I watch as an older man in a flannel shirt steps out of the hardware store and begins sweeping the sidewalk in front of it.

The first thing I notice once I'm inside the café is the air; it smells like roasted beans and cinnamon, maybe? Bakery. Bread. My stomach grumbles as I eyeball the sweets inside the glass case, the young woman behind the counter greeting me with a smile almost as bright as the morning sun.

Yikes. *Chill, lady. Dial it down a notch, I'm still waking up . . .*

"Morning!" she chirps. "What can I get for ya?"

"Coffee." I smile. "Black."

She scrunches up her nose judgmentally. "Kind of boring, don't you think? How about something seasonal? With a splash of syrup?"

A small chalkboard near the register lists the daily specials in loopy handwriting: **Pumpkin Spice Latte, Maple Pecan Cold Brew, Apple Cider Chai.**

"Uh—no thanks."

"For here, or to go?"

"To go?"

My stomach growls again, louder this time, as my eyes wander back to the glass case. A stack of cinnamon rolls drizzled with icing sits front and center, mocking my weak resolve. I'm debating whether I should cave when the barista reappears, sliding a steaming to-go cup across the counter.

"Here you go—one boring black coffee." She winks, but it's playful, not annoying. "Anything else?"

I hesitate, glancing again at the cinnamon rolls. Damn it. "I'll take one of those too," I say, pointing.

"Good choice." She grabs one with a pair of tongs and slips it into a paper bag before handing it over. "Breakfast of champions."

Indeed it is.

The first bite of the cinnamon roll is fucking glorious—soft, sweet, the right amount of frosting and spice. I wash it down with a sip of coffee, and for the first time since arriving at this retreat, I feel like maybe this whole "disconnect from the world" thing might not be the worst idea.

I take another long sip of coffee, savoring the bitterness as I lean back in my chair. The place is getting busier now, the low hum of chatter filling the café.

I should go.

I stand, trying to hold both my coffee in one hand and my cinnamon roll in another, pulling the door open with the tip of my boot, managing to do so. Hold it open with my shoulder. The bell above my head jingles, and the cool breeze hits my face as I begin stepping out onto the sidewalk.

Ahh. Not bad. Not bad at all . . .

The sunshine is bright, almost *blinding* as it rises over the lake.

Distracted by the view, I remove the lid from my coffee cup to dunk the cinnamon roll inside, ready to sip my brew and lick frosting off the tips of my fingers when it happens.

Thud.

I walk straight into someone.

The impact sends steaming hot coffee sloshing over the rim of the cup, the liquid spilling across the front of my hoodie.

"Shit!" I hiss, the heat soaking through the fabric as I stumble back. I can feel it soak my skin.

"Oh God! I am so sorry!" a distressed voice exclaims, and I finally look up at the commotion I've caused.

A woman stands in front of me, wide-eyed with shock.

Her dark hair is pulled into a messy bun, and she's wearing a fitted pink jacket over matching pink leggings. Coffee streaks down the sleeve of her jacket as she crouches to grab the yoga mat that fell out of her hands when I crashed into her. Her cheeks are flushed, and she looks everywhere but at me. I bend to help her because that's what gentlemen do . . .

"Shit—sorry," I manage, though I'm still too flustered to string together anything coherent. Too tired. Still early. My coffee is officially a lost cause, dripping down the front of my gray sweatshirt and staining it.

"No, no, it's my fault," she protests, face inches from mine. "I wasn't paying attention."

"Neither was I," I admit, glancing around for a trash can. The coffee cup is still in my hand, but it's useless now, mostly empty and dripping like a leaky faucet. I stuff the remaining roll in my mouth and chew, buying myself time to think of something new to say.

Damn, she's cute.

I give her ring finger a quick glance: It's bare.

Things are starting to look up.

Maybe she'd be down to hang out, and by *hang out*, I mean have casual sex. I have time to kill, considering I'm not doing the whole retreat thing and have no activities planned.

As we both stand, she clears her throat, tucking the mat beneath her armpit, then brushes an invisible speck of dirt from the front of her pink jacket. She glances at me, her lips quirking like she knows I've been staring at her boobs, trying to figure out if she's flat chested or if the sports bra is holding them down.

Not that it matters. I'm an equal opportunity boob guy. Small tits, big tits—I love them all.

Her eyes narrow, but the corner of her mouth twitches. "Are you going to say something, or are you going to keep standing there, working out the square footage of what's inside my jacket?"

I blink, caught off guard. Laugh. "Sorry, my brain is running on fumes." Wasn't trying to be rude.

She arches a brow.

"I'm Harris—and I would shake your hand, but I got sticky fingers." I hold the door open so she can slip inside, then follow her, intending to buy her whatever she wants.

"Harris," she repeats, mulling the name over. "I can't say I've seen you around before. Are you in town for work or pleasure? Wait." She snaps her fingers. "Are you part of the group of men who took over half the rooms at the lodge?"

As if I would admit to being in town for a fucking *retreat.*

"I am here for work." *Forcibly, against my will,* ha ha. Can't deny it.

"You are?" Her brows shoot up farther into her hairline. "Oh my gosh. Are you a lumberjack?"

Am I a lumberjack? What the fuck is she talking about?

"'Cause my friend Annabelle is practically pulling her hair out waiting for y'all to get here," she goes on. "She wasn't sure you were coming."

I absolutely have no fucking clue what she's talking about, but she's so damn adorable I let her keep talking. Crossing my arms, I lean against a table next to the windows, playing along for the sheer entertainment value.

A lumberjack? Can't say I've ever been accused of being one of those, but it sounds fun, and it's been a mind-numbing twenty-four hours.

"Lumberjack?" I say. "What gave it away?"

This oughta be good.

She grins, enjoying this as much as I am. "Oh, you know. The broad shoulders, the mussed-up hair, the cuts and bruises on your hands. You give off 'I wrestle bears for fun' energy. It's so very lumberjacky."

I mull this over. "Interesting. I didn't realize I was giving off 'rugged outdoorsman.' Must be the coffee stains."

"Exactly," she says, her eyes sparkling. "No self-respecting lumberjack has a clean shirt. It's part of the aesthetic."

"Well," I say, leaning closer to her. "If I *were* a lumberjack, I'd say your friend Annabelle needs to work on her communication skills. I can't magically appear. She would have to give me an address."

And an axe.

She laughs, the sound light and musical, and it draws a grin out of me. "You're saying it's Annabelle's fault the lumberjack company is short staffed and only sent three of you?"

Only three of us? Dang. "How many had she ordered?"

"Eight!"

Well shit. Sounds like Annabelle better get her money back.

"All I'm saying is—I never got a call." It's the honest-to-God truth. "How does she expect us to roll logs, chop wood, and look rugged if she doesn't give us the proper tools—or, you know, the *address*? It's poor planning."

The woman shifts her yoga mat to her other arm. "I'll be sure to let her know you're already dissatisfied with management. Maybe she'll throw in some flannel shirts as a peace offering."

Flannel shirts? Me like. So warm. So cozy.

I nod solemnly. "It's the least she could do. Flannel is nonnegotiable. How am I supposed to live up to the lumberjack ideal without it?"

She narrows her eyes at me as if she's trying to decide if I'm being serious. "Flannel shirts and an axe. Got it. I'll pass that along to Annabelle. Anything else on your lumberjack manifesto?"

"Maybe beard oil." I stroke my jaw with mock seriousness. Beard oil sounds like something a lumberjack would use, eh? What else, what else . . . "Suspenders."

My new, nameless friend tilts her head. "You didn't come to town with any of these things?"

I shrug. "I'm the emergency fill-in lumberjack. I hopped on a plane as fast as I could to get here. It's not my fault I left most of my shit behind."

Goddamn, I'm good at improv. I should get paid for this!

Her mouth twitches as if she's fighting back a laugh. "An *emergency* fill-in lumberjack. Quite the backstory. You must be very dedicated to the craft."

I scoff. "*Dedicated* doesn't even begin to cover it." The words flow like I've been waiting to play a fake lumberjack for years. "I got the call from corporate in the middle of the night—'Harris, we need you. Star Lake is in crisis.' So I packed up what I could, threw on the closest thing to flannel, and here I am."

"Here you are," she deadpans, nodding solemnly.

"Annabelle made it sound like it was life or death," I ad-lib, getting further into character.

She laughs, finally letting her guard down a little. "Well, I hope you're ready for her wrath. She's pretty pissed off."

Wrath? I like that word.

"I'm the hero of this story. Annabelle should be thanking me for showing up at all."

"Oh, is that how it works?" she asks. "I thought you were doing a job. For money."

I snort, crushing the cardboard coffee cup in my mighty fist. RAH! "This is not just a job—it's a lifestyle."

"A lifestyle, huh? So you're saying you eat, sleep, and breathe lumberjackery?"

"Yes, exactly." I puff out my chest, fully committing to this role. "It's not for the faint of heart. Takes grit. Takes dedication. And, most importantly"—I lean in conspiratorially, lowering my voice—"it takes a *lot* of sex appeal."

"Wow." The woman finally loses it, her laughter spilling out in a way that's completely unguarded. Loud. "Just . . . *wow*. You are really something."

"Something great?" I raise my arm and aim, directing the crumpled coffee cup into the nearby trash can with a dramatic flick of my wrist. It goes in. Score! "Don't forget that part."

"Don't you worry, I won't."

"So." I get down to business. "When does Annabelle need me to start? Should I show up at dawn? Or does she prefer a midafternoon entrance?"

"You realize she's *actually* going to expect you to work," she tells me. "That's what you're being paid for: chopping wood, lifting heavy things for the tourists—you know the drill since it's the stuff you live and breathe." She rolls her eyes, and I'm somewhat insulted at her mockery.

"Lumberjacks thrive under pressure. We don't just carry logs, you know—we carry town festivals on our backs." I take a breath. "Passed down from generation to generation."

"Right. Sure." She's humoring me now, but I don't mind. Bumping into her has been the best part of my day so far. "And this sacred duty—does it include chopping wood in coordinated plaid outfits, or is that a bonus?"

"Only if you're advanced level," I reply, straight faced. "Coordination comes with years of experience. You earn the plaid you wear."

She's shaking her head now. "Well. I'll be glad to let Annabelle know I found one of her guys." Pause. "Do you have her number?"

I'm shaking my head now too. "No ma'am, I do not."

"Wanna give me your phone so I can give it to you?"

Give it to you. "I'd love for you to give it to me."

Her face scrunches up. "Don't be a pervert—it's too early."

"Sorry." It's a habit. After pulling my phone out of my pocket, I set it in her palm. "But fair warning, it's almost dead. No signal out here."

She snorts. "That happens in the mountains sometimes. And let me guess—you don't have a charger either?"

"Left it in my other flannel," I admit. "The one that matches my suspenders."

She doesn't respond. Rather, she focuses on punching her friend Annabelle's number into my cell. Her fingers move quickly over the screen, and I take the moment to study her—messy bun, slightly crooked smile. It's an easy kind of energy, making it hard not to smile back.

Or want to bone her.

"There." She hands my phone back. "All set. Now you have *no* excuses." Her eyes roam up and down my body. "You'd better not let her down, Lumberjack."

Let her down?

I'm a football player, not a goddamn lumberjack. The fact that she believes me has done *wonders* for my ego.

"Don't worry," I say, flashing her the teeth that cost me $60,000 out of pocket. "When I show up, I'll be the best goddamn emergency lumberjack this town has seen."

Her laughter follows her as she begins walking toward the counter. "We'll see about that."

"What's your name?"

She studies me a few seconds. "Lucy."

Lucy.

I play the name on a loop through my brain as I watch her order breakfast, chatting up the barista, and I find myself grinning like an idiot as I replay the last few minutes in my head. She orders a muffin—blueberry—and a steaming cup of tea. No coffee for her, apparently.

"What?" she asks.

"Nothing," I say, straightening up and attempting to look less like a guy who's been caught staring at her ass. "Only making sure you've got enough fuel for yoga."

She smirks, biting into the muffin. "Yoga's harder than chopping wood, I'll have you know. You might want to try it sometime."

Pass.

Hard. Pass.

"Just so you know, I can already touch my toes," I boast. "I choose not to."

She giggles softly, tossing the muffin wrapper into the trash as she clutches the tea. "Flexibility is the key to a long and healthy life."

"Flexibility is overrated," I counter, resisting the urge to flex my muscles. "Strength gets the job done."

Lucy sighs. "Good luck with that. I'll be sure to cheer you on at the Fall Fest if I see you."

Not gonna happen, but I nod anyway.

"I'll make it look easy," I shoot back with a grin. "The other dudes won't know what hit them."

"Well. I'll look forward to it." She steps toward the door, pausing to glance back over her shoulder. "See you around, Mr. Lumberjack."

Mr. Lumberjack.

I like the sound of that.

The little bell above the door tinkles, jingling softly, and before I can say another word, Lucy is gone.

Through the window, I watch her disappear down the sidewalk. It takes me a second to realize my grin has faded, replaced by a single nagging thought: *She didn't give me her number.*

It's not like I didn't give her the chance.

I mean, I *handed* her my phone—she had it in her palm! And she didn't use the opportunity! Granted, it was to type in Annabelle's number, but still. Most women I've met wouldn't need an invitation. Usually, they're slipping me their digits before I can even ask, batting their lashes, dropping not-so-subtle hints.

Not her.

She . . . *walked away.*

My ego stings a little. Okay, maybe more than a little. I'm used to women being all over me, and now I'm left here wondering why she didn't even *offer*.

No way was she not into me.

I could see it in her smile, the way she teased me. She's playing hard to get.

Yeah, that's it.

She wants me to chase her.

Maybe I will. After all, I've got her name now. And Annabelle's number.

More than enough to work with . . .

Chapter 4

Lucy

"I ran into one of your lumberjacks."

"Which one? Bill, Wally or Kyle?"

"Neither." I shake my head, hiding a smirk. "Harris. The new guy."

That gets her attention. Annabelle stops mid-keystroke and looks up, her forehead furrowing in confusion. "What new guy?"

"You know, tall, broad shoulders, coffee-stained sweatshirt? Kind of a Travis Kelce vibe but way better looking," I say, casually sipping my tea. "Apparently, he's your emergency fill-in lumberjack."

For a moment, she stares at me blankly. Then, slowly, a grin spreads across her face. "Wait—are you serious? I have four lumberjacks now?"

"Looks like it," I say, setting my cup down on her counter. "Though he didn't exactly come with an axe or flannel. Or tools. Seemed pretty unprepared, if you ask me."

Annabelle lets out a laugh, slumping back in her chair. "I don't care. I'll take whatever I can get! This is great news. Do you know how much easier this makes things? With three, we were barely scraping by. But with four, I have hope the others will show up too."

"Well," I say, leaning against the counter. "Don't get too excited. He talks a lot. And he's kind of cocky."

Annabelle waves a dismissive hand. "I'll knock him down a peg or two if I have to. As long as he's got two working arms and a pulse, I can put him to use."

He does. Nice ones. He's fit and cute and has a neck so thick she won't be able to locate his pulse.

"Oh, he's got working arms," I mutter, remembering how easily he leaned into the whole rugged-hero act. "And a talent for spinning bullshit. I couldn't tell if he was lying or not—you may need to keep an eye on him."

"Noted," she says, still grinning like she's won the lottery. "Honestly, I don't care if he's a drama queen or a beauty queen or a terrible logroller. I've been praying for these guys to show all week, and now one of them has."

"Then . . . if you're happy, I'm happy." I grab a slice of toast from her plate and take a bite. "At least you've got four now. Crisis mostly averted, yeah?"

Annabelle nods, letting out a long, dramatic sigh of relief. "For now. Four lumberjacks means I might *actually* sleep tonight instead of lying awake, stressing about that—and hayrides and cider stations."

Beside her on the table, her phone chimes. Annabelle glances at it, groaning as she picks it up. "And just when I thought I could relax . . ."

"What now?" I ask, then sip my tea.

She stares at the screen, thumb scrolling through a string of notifications. "My assistant, Blake, texted. Apparently, one of the guys is complaining about having to stack firewood. Says it's messing with his back."

I snort. "Do they realize he's been hired to lumberjack? In a festival? Stacking firewood and looking good while doing it is the job. For tourists."

"I get that. And you get that. But apparently, he's another pretty face with no work ethic." She sighs loudly, typing out a response. "He's decided he's more of a 'supervisory' type and less of the wood-chopping type."

These guys are unbelievable! "How the hell did you end up with a crew of diva lumberjacks?"

"Because. I have *the* shittiest luck." She takes a crunchy bite of toast. When crumbs scatter on the table and down the front of her sweater, she doesn't seem to care. "I swear to God, I'm never volunteering to do this again."

"How many times have I heard you say that? Last year you said it. The year before that you said it." I wave my hand. "You love this chaos, don't lie. You'd go crazy without a million things to do."

Or people to yell at.

My bestie is bossy.

She narrows her eyes but doesn't argue. Instead, she points her toast at me like it's a weapon. "Remind me the next time someone's trying to sucker me into organizing something, okay? Saying no will be my New Year's resolution."

"Then you only have to wait four more months." I laugh. "I'll make sure to remind you when you're coordinating Christmas carolers at the pavilion or trying to wrangle toddlers for the May Day celebration."

She glares at me. "I don't like you very much right now."

"Because I'm right?" I reply.

"Yes. I do not need the hard truth at the moment, okay?" Annabelle reaches for her coffee at the same time her phone dings yet again, forever blowing up.

"Hmm?" I ask, wanting to know all the drama.

She sets her cup down with a thud and glances at me. "It's the new dude, Harris. And praise be, he's asking when he needs to show up."

I blink back my surprise. "Really? That's great!"

"Oh, it gets better," she adds, holding up the phone. "He's also asking for your phone number."

My phone number?

My jaw drops, and I burst out laughing. "You have got to be *kid*ding."

"Nope." She shakes her head, her grin widening. "Apparently, he thinks the two of you are best friends now and says it would be helpful to have Lucy's number in case of any 'lumberjacky' emergencies." Annabelle looks at me and tilts her head. "What's a lumberjacky emergency."

I laugh some more. "Beats me."

"Sooo . . . should I give him your number?"

"Absolutely not," I say quickly, sitting up straighter. "If he wanted my number, he should have asked when he had the chance."

Annabelle smirks, leaning back in her chair as she twirls her phone in her hand. "Ooh, harsh. Playing hard to get, are we?"

I roll my eyes. "It's not playing hard to get. It's basic manners. If he wanted my number, he should've asked me directly. Not tried to weasel it out of my best friend."

"Fair," she says, glancing back at her phone. "I have to admit, though, I'm tempted to give it to him. See what he says."

"Don't you dare," I warn. "The last thing I need is some cocky out-of-towner blowing up my phone with fake emergencies."

"Are you done with dating apps and looking for the love of your life? These guys are all from out of town—we are running out of men to date. Eligible guys don't pass through town this often—all the good ones are taken."

True. But, "He never said he was single, and I am not *dating* an actor."

"He's not an actor. He's a lum—"

"Don't you dare say 'lumberjack.' I'm not dating one of those either! You are paying him to play Paul Bunyan."

"No." Annabelle rolls her eyes dramatically, setting her phone down on the table. "Be real, most likely he's a trainer at a gym and agreed to fill in for one of my no-shows."

Yeah. I can see that; he looked fit enough to be a personal trainer, *not* that I was scoping him out.

"Filling in as someone who pretends to chop wood for a living," I counter, crossing my arms. "That makes him an actor."

"You are grasping, my friend."

Maybe so. But I'm not comfortable giving a random guy my phone number until I've at least vetted him properly, the way I can do on an app by asking him questions. Especially a guy passing through town short term.

"Don't know what to tell you." I shrug as I sip my tea, which is now lukewarm. "I will say this, though—he was *really* cute."

"Cute? Now we're getting somewhere." Annabelle is tapping away at her laptop again. "Good-looking guys will bring women flocking to the show, which means more money for us."

True. "Speaking of money, how's it looking?" I ask, tilting my head. "With the budget, I mean."

Annabelle exhales, leaning back in her chair and stretching as if she's been sitting in that chair for days. "Not great. Fall Fest is supposed to make up for all the funding the community center lost this year, so it's on me to pull a miracle out of my ass. Since I'm volunteering my time for this while juggling a bride who can't decide between *ivory* and *cream*. Lindsey Vodgs is on the verge of buying two dresses."

I wince. "That sounds terrible."

"It's fine. I'm fine." She giggles, though we both know Annabelle uses the word *fine* the way other people use Bubble Wrap—to protect herself from having a meltdown. "Wedding planning pays most of my bills, but I also need to give back, you know?" Her sigh is loud. "Plus, I spent all my time at the community center as a kid—if we don't make enough money, we'll lose the winter programs."

I know how much this means to her. The programs she's talking about—free dinners, after-school events and babysitting, and sports—are a safety net for a lot of families in town.

Annabelle's been pushing herself to the brink to keep it all afloat.

"Okay," I say, determined to be supportive. "So the show needs to be a hit. We have to sell a ton of food. More sponsors? Maybe one of your lumberjacks will go viral for his wood-chopping skills."

Annabelle snorts. "We need one who looks like Thor."

"Thor? Now you're getting greedy," I tease, though I can't help but think of Harris—his broad shoulders, the scruffy jawline, the effortless way he looked like he belonged in a flannel shirt.

My mouth begins to water despite my objections to him having my contact information.

Annabelle narrows her gaze at me. "Why are you smiling like that? You have that weird look on your face."

"I have a weird look?"

"You *do*, actually."

I hold my hands up in mock surrender. "Listen. All I will say about it is, Harris will meet your Thor quota."

Her stares. "He looks like a superhero, and you won't let me give him your number? What is *wrong* with you? I'm offended on his behalf."

I shake my head. "He's just a guy. A guy who happens to have, you know—a chiseled jawline and great hair."

Windswept hair.

"*Just* a guy?" She slaps her desktop lightly, glaring at me. "No, Lucy. Larry from Lakeside Plumbing is *just* a guy. Harris sounds like the kind of guy we close our eyes and masturbate to."

Facts! He is.

"So?" Her words do not faze me. "I've learned my lesson about jumping too quickly into something that looks shiny on the surface."

Her teasing smile fades. "Yeah," she says, softer now. "You're not wrong about that. When you plan weddings for a living, you start to think you'll find the fairy tale too. Then *poof*, one day your boyfriend moves in uninvited with his beanbag chair, and the next he decides commitment is not his thing."

Michael—the guy who checked all the right boxes on paper and then casually tore Annabelle's heart to shreds. She doesn't talk about him much anymore, not unless he comes up accidentally.

"Freaking Mike." She forces a tight smile as she pokes at the edge of her laptop. "He who taught me a valuable lesson about red flags."

I sigh, knowing she's trying to brush it off; the truth lingers in the quiet space between us. "Listen. We all make mistakes, but those mistakes are lessons."

"I know that," she agrees. "But admit it—he was a waste of time. Three years down the drain for what? To get dumped because he needed 'room to breathe'? *Please.*"

I wince. "At least you got to keep the apartment?"

"And pay the rent *by myself*."

Yikes. "I'm sorry. You deserved better than that. Plus it's not like I've been killing it either."

Annabelle's gaze sharpens. "You mean Parker?"

"Shh! We're not saying his name anymore, remember?" I drag a hand down my face. "Why do you always bring his name up?" She's banging someone. Meanwhile, I haven't had sex in months—the least she can do is be more sympathetic!

Rude.

"Because Parker was a learning experience for all of us." Annabelle sits up in her desk chair, and I feel a lecture coming on. "Seriously, you were into him. And he—what?—disappears for a week to 'find himself' without telling you? For seven days, you thought he'd been abducted, remember? You made me help you check the local police reports like a lunatic, thinking you'd find his face on a missing-persons flyer."

I did do that. Turns out Parker was at a mountain lodge, finding inner peace with a bunch of strangers and organic smoothies.

Annabelle continues ranting. "Uh. Didn't he give you some bullshit line about 'silence speaking louder than words'?"

"Yes and it is by far the stupidest thing a man has said, in the history of men saying stupid shit to me." I plop down on a kitchen stool and continue to complain. "I can still hear his 'wisdom' echoing in my brain. I have nightmares. Silence speaks louder than words? You know what speaks louder? A damn text message saying you're not dead!"

I laugh, and my bestie joins me, our memories of men gone wrong equal parts ridiculous and infuriating.

To this day, I want to poke Parker Mitchell's eyes out.

"You dodged a bullet." Her hands hover over her keyboard again. "Imagine being married to a guy who takes off wherever the wind blows him, whenever he feels like it. Like, 'Hey, babe, can't do dishes today—I'm heading to the wilderness to become one with nature.'"

My face contorts as I shout "We *live* in nature!" I gesture wildly toward the window. "There's nothing but nature around here. We're in the mountains, Annabelle. By a lake! *Literally!*"

Annabelle shrugs, completely unfazed. "Still. You were so into him."

Head over heels, actually. And that's the part that stings the most—how much I let myself fall for someone who made me feel like a backup plan.

"I need you to stop reminding me."

"Let's be real," she continues, ignoring me. "He saved you from spending more time on someone who didn't really want to be there. The way Mike saved me from the same thing."

I glance up at her, meeting her gaze.

We both know what he put her through—three years of promises that added up to nothing. At least I only dated Parker for nine months.

"And at least we have each other," she adds with a small smile, reaching out her foot to nudge my leg. "You and me, babe."

I look down at my mug, tracing the rim with my finger. "It's not like I expect a fairy tale or anything, but I'd at least like someone who shows up. Is that too much to ask?"

"No, it's not," Annabelle says firmly, sitting up straighter. "And don't let Parker or *any* guy like him make you think it is. Mike's beanbag chair haunts my dreams."

"Beanbag chairs are a blight on humanity," I tease, trying to lighten the mood.

"They are," she says solemnly. "They're a metaphor for men who refuse to put in effort. Uncomfortable, shapeless—and *always* take up too much space."

I laugh, and she grins, her mood lifted.

I clink my cup against her mug for good measure, and for a second, I think we've successfully banished the ghosts of boyfriends past. I sit back and sip my tea, our laughter fading into something quieter. More pensive.

"Not to go on about it, but . . . I don't get it." I pause. "Why do we let these assholes in? How do we not see the signs?"

Annabelle's smile dims, and she tilts her head in thought. "Because we *want* to believe. That's all."

I glance up at her, surprised by the honesty in her voice. "You think it's that simple?"

"Of course. We want to believe the best in people, so we do," she continues. "We want to believe they mean what they say, that they'll be there for us. Sometimes it's not about ignoring the signs—it's about hoping we're wrong about them."

"Well, *that's* depressing."

"No, it's human." She's smiling again. "Look. Mike was charming as hell. He brought me flowers every Sunday, took me on road trips, cooked me dinner sometimes if he made it home first. I didn't see the signs because there weren't any. He was all in—until he wasn't."

That's true. When he left, it was a complete shock.

She clears her throat. "And Parker? You can't beat yourself up over him either. You liked him because he was different. A little weird, sure, but you thought he loved you, and so did I."

I nod, chewing on my lip. "I really did."

"That's why they were both bad breakups. They felt right but were so wrong."

"Yeah." I blow out a slow breath. "I think I'm done dating for a while. Me and my perfectly normal, drama-free existence. At least until the Fall Fest is over. You need all the help you can get."

Chapter 5

Harris

If you told me a few days ago that I'd be doing yoga every morning on a dock surrounded by people who actually know what they're doing, I would've laughed in your face.

But it's not about yoga.

And it's not about the view. I mean, *it is*—if by *view* you mean Lucy's ass in her tight-fitting leggings and cropped top. I'd be lying if I said it wasn't the only reason I dragged my sorry self out of bed at six a.m.

Sunlight spills over the lake, catching in her hair and glinting off the water like something out of a painting. And me?

I'm sprawled on this yoga mat on the expansive wooden dock, trying not to groan every time my hamstrings protest.

I've done two-a-day football practices. I've pushed through weight room circuits that left me seeing stars. Hell—I've been tackled by grown men charging full speed at me.

But none of that prepares you for downward dog.

Lucy's voice flows over the group of us—a mix of my football teammates and regulars from town—like the morning breeze, soft and soothing. Sexy, if I'm being honest . . . "Breathe into the stretch. Focus on your inhale . . . deep breath in . . . and exhale . . ."

Her words make the poses sound *easy*; as if my body wasn't on fucking fire right now and my joints weren't actively protesting against my life choices. Around me, everyone moves like they're made of elastic, flowing into their poses effortlessly.

It's like I stumbled into a synchronized-yoga cult by accident.

The fuck?

Here I am, trembling—losing my goddamn balance even though both my feet are firmly planted on the ground.

"Remember to breathe," Lucy softly says, her gaze briefly flicking my way as if sensing struggle. "In through your nose . . . out through your mouth."

I'm breathing, all right.

I'm winded.

She gives the class the command to shift into something called warrior two, and I'm positive this is where I die. My legs burn as I try to bend my front knee. My arms are stretched out to the sides, wobbling like I'm holding invisible dumbbells. Everyone else looks strong and poised, like statues. I look like I'm about to collapse into the lake.

Honestly, I wish I would.

It looks so refreshing . . .

Sneaking another glance at her perched serenely at the front of the dock, I can't help but think Lucy looks perfect.

Calm. Steady. Arms in a clean line, her gaze is focused on some invisible horizon.

Meanwhile, my arms are shaking like I'm bench-pressing a bus, and I can feel sweat dripping down my back, into my ass crack.

"Keep your breath steady," she instructs. "Feel the strength in your stance."

There's no strength here.

Only suffering.

My back leg twitches, and I stumble, waving my arms wildly to save myself from toppling sideways. I manage to stay upright—barely—but the mat lets out a loud squeak under my foot that echoes across the dock.

Lucy's gaze snaps to me, her lips twitching like she's trying not to laugh.

"Doing okay back there?" she calls out quietly, walking toward me like a teacher about to check my work. She stands next to me; her presence makes everything worse—not because she's intimidating, but because now I feel like I'm performing.

And doing a shitty job.

Stopping short of my mat, arms crossed, she stares down to where I'm doing what can only be described as an interpretive version of warrior two or whatever it's called.

"I'm fine," I lie, wobbling so hard that I look like my wheels are about to fly off. "This is part of my process."

"Your process?" Her brow lifts.

I nod solemnly, front leg starting to shake like I'm holding up the weight of the entire dock.

Water.

I need water . . .

"Yeah. I call it warrior one point five. It's an advanced technique, so you probably haven't heard of it."

"You're an advanced disaster," Elijah chimes in from his mat two spots over, grinning ear to ear. "Kick him out of class, Lucy!"

"She can't kick me out. I'm her favorite student," I shoot back, smirking up at her. Flirting.

Hot for teacher, ha ha.

I glance up in time to see her eyebrows lift, a slow, deliberate challenge in her expression.

Her favorite?

"Oh, really?" she says, her voice calm and controlled and professional—not flirty in the least. "If you're my favorite, then you're who I choose to demonstrate warrior three for the class."

The blood drains from my face. "Say what now?"

Next to me, Elijah hoots. "Yes! Show us!"

"Warrior three," Lucy repeats with a nod. She ignores Elijah and fixes her attention on me. "It's a balancing pose. You'll love it. Hands forward, one leg back. Like you're flying."

Flying? We've already established I can barely stand.

I glance at my buddies for backup, but they are absolutely no help. This was supposed to be relaxing. I was supposed to be ogling her ti—

"This is only a forty-minute class—hurry it along." She stands back waiting; now the entire dock is watching me like I'm about to perform solo in the Super Bowl.

"Are you always this bossy?"

"Yes." She chuckles. "Quit stalling."

"Fine," I grumble, straightening up and shaking out my arms like a boxer stepping into the ring. "Watch and learn, people."

I hinge forward, lifting my arms out in front of me. I'm sure I look elegant—graceful, even. *Like a damn swan.* Lift my back leg carefully, feeling the dock creak beneath me. The wood feels suspiciously wobbly all of a sudden, but I focus.

This is warrior three.

I am the warrior!

Until my front foot starts shaking, the weight pulling at my hamstring, and my arms are stretched so far they might dislocate. My back leg wobbles dangerously, and I'm basically a human seesaw.

"Would you like some help?" Instead of waiting for my reply, she gently nudges my back arm upward. "Your arms need to be in line. Not drooping like you're holding up bags of concrete."

"Is that what it looks like?" I glance over at Elijah for an answer.

Quinton—who is also on the dock but not doing yoga—has his phone out, angling it like he's preparing to film my impending disaster. Traitor.

Lucy ignores the other guys, shifting her focus to my front knee. "That's okay, you're here to learn. Try to center your weight." She presses a hand lightly to my back to adjust my posture, and I freeze.

I've forgotten how to breathe.

"You got this," Lucy says, but there's laughter in her voice now.

I don't. *I absolutely do not got this.*

My back foot swerves, throwing my whole center of gravity off, and in slow motion—like a movie car crash—I flail. "Whoa, whoa—"

It's no use. My arms windmill, my mat skids out from under me, and I stumble sideways with all the grace of a drunk giraffe. I try to recover, feet scrambling against the dock, but physics has other plans.

Splash!

I can't see the bottom, and the water is so fucking cold. Bone-chilling, breath-stealing cold.

For a second, all I hear is the dull roar of the lake in my ears as I sink beneath the surface. When I come up for air, gasping, all hell has broken loose on the dock. Elijah is doubled over, absolutely losing his shit.

Miles and Quinton are laughing so hard they look like they're crapping themselves, and—of course—they have their phones out, recording the moment for posterity.

I glare up at them, water streaming down my face.

"Did you take my picture, you asshole?" I sputter, lake water dripping from my hair and onto my face. "Delete those."

"Make me," Miles chokes out between laughs.

Lucy's at the front of the dock, hands on her hips, staring down in the water at me with wide eyes.

"If I didn't know better, I'd think y'all knew each other already." She laughs, trying to sound concerned, but doing a miserable job at it. "But are you okay? Did you hit the dock on your way in?"

"I'm peachy," I deadpan. "So refreshing. Highly recommend."

I needed that, actually.

"Glad to hear it," she says, her voice light and teasing as she steps to the edge of the dock. Her ponytail catches the breeze as she crouches down, her face coming into view above me. "Do you need a hand?"

I'm immediately suspicious. The grin is way too smug.

Cute, but smug.

"You're not going to let go of my hand and let me fall back in the water, are you?" I narrow my eyes, her expression one of innocence.

"Would I do that?"

"Yes," I say flatly. "I do believe you would."

She tilts her head, pretending to look hurt and jutting out her lower lip in a pout. "Where's the trust, Harris? You wound me."

Still.

Because I am an idiot, I extend my hand to her anyway, freezing and soaked to the bone, eyeing Lucy's outstretched palm. Could I easily walk back to the shore? Sure. Could one of my buddies, who outweighs her by a hundred pounds, heft me up? Totally.

I want her to do it.

Her delicate hand wraps around mine as I plant my feet against the dock, ready to pull myself up, gazing up into her pretty, angelic face.

"Pull hard," I instruct her, hoist mode activated.

She winks.

Tugs.

My eyes land on the smooth skin of her tan arms . . .

For one glorious moment, I'm halfway out of the water.

Victory is so close.

And then . . .

She lets go.

It happens in slow motion, my grip slipping as she lets my fingers fall through hers, and I fall backward again with another loud—

Splash.

My back hits the water with a flop, and I sink like a lead weight, flailing as I disappear under the surface.

Blub, blub, blub.

I'm shocked for the second time, bubbles rising out of my nostrils before I push up and out, gasping. Toss my hair back.

Glare.

She's doubled over now, too, her hands on her knees, laughing so hard she can barely breathe. It's not the polite laugh she held back during class—it's full-on, bellyaching laughter.

With the back of my hand, I splash her—and my friends, too, those dicks—spraying water as far as I can to give her a taste of her own medicine.

"The fuck?" I shout, wiping water out of my eyes so I can see. "You said I can trust you!"

"Did I?" she gulps between laughs, brushing at the corners of her eyes. "Today is not your day, I guess."

"You little liar!"

By now, the entire yoga class has gathered around, everyone amused and staring, including two women who look old enough to be my grandmother. They're positively delighted.

"Did you see that?" Elijah yells to the crowd. "She straight-up dropped him, dude!"

"I'm posting this to X," Miles adds, holding up his phone, which has unquestionably recorded the whole thing. "This is fucking fantastic."

I groan, flopping backward into the water so I'm floating, arms outstretched. Stare up at the blue sky.

"You're *such* assholes." I sulk. I want to look cool in front of chicks—not be caught with my dick in my hand.

"Oh, come on," her voice calls down to me as I float. "It was a joke. This is how I flirt."

I lift my head. "You're flirting with me?" 'Cause that would be awesome.

"Actually no—I'm fucking with you."

I roll, letting my feet reach the sandy bottom of the lake. "Wow."

The audacity.

Water drips from my clothes, which are weighed down, my hair plastered to my forehead. I give my head another shake, much like a dog would after a bath, and stray to the edge of the dock. Plant my hands against the wood, pushing down to lift myself out.

One, two—

My feet slip, hands scrabbling against the slick dock, and I crash back into the water with a splash that echoes across the lake.

Laughter erupts again, Elijah practically choking as he doubles over, and Lucy? She's holding her stomach, shoulders shaking, unable to hide her delight.

I surface, glaring. "I hope you're proud of yourself."

"Extremely." She wipes at her eyes, breathless from laughing. "You're making my entire morning."

"Well. I'm a swamp monster now," I announce to them all, accepting my fate. "Forever damp."

This time I'm successful, planting my hands more carefully on the dock and then hauling myself up in one determined motion. I flop onto my stomach first like a seal—real graceful—before rolling onto my back, clothes dripping, water pooling around me.

Kind of like I'm bleeding out.

"I am never coming here again," I grumble. "And you can't make me."

Lucy stands over me now, hands on her hips. "If you're this horrible in the water, how on earth are you going to perform in a logrolling competition? You can barely hoist yourself up!"

Oh shit.

"You ever seen a professional logroller?"

"No."

"Well, there's your problem—we come in all shapes and sizes." I get to my feet, pushing my soggy hair back. "My grandpa was a *legend*—three-time logrolling champion of the Midwest."

I am such an amazing storyteller!

Her lips twitch, and she's trying to look impressed. "Three-time champion?"

"Yep." I nod solemnly, tapping my chest. "It's in my blood."

"What's in your blood?" Elijah looks up from his phone, catching the tail end of the conversation. "What the hell are you talking about?"

"Nothing, you pipe down." I shoot him a glare before turning back to Lucy. "Traitor."

"The wilderness is making you crazy, dude, I swear," he mutters.

"Some people appreciate *talent*, Elijah," I fire back so he zips his yap. "Like my new friend Lucy here."

I smile down at her. She's so super talented, especially twisting and turning that lithe little body of hers.

She sure is gorgeous.

Lucy bites down on her bottom lip as I try to keep my eyes off her cleavage. "Is that what you're doing today? Rehearsing with Annabelle and the guys?"

Rehearsing?

The word hits me like a slap to the face. Then when I think I have no idea what she's talking about, it hits me: She's talking about lumberjack practice down at the marina.

I nod enthusiastically. "Absolutely. Big day."

She tilts her head, squinting up at me like she's sniffing bullshit. "What events do you rehearse?"

Miles snorts. "Yeah, Harris. What events do you rehearse? Tell us."

I shoot him a warning glare, mentally willing him to shut the fuck up. I need my friends to disappear, but they're hanging around, lingering like farts in the wind.

"You know . . ." I wave a hand vaguely, as though the details are too intricate to explain. "The usual stuff."

Lucy's brows arch higher. "The usual stuff? Like logrolling?"

My friends' brows all shoot into their hairlines simultaneously.

"Of course." I double down because why quit now? I am on a roll. A logroll, get it? Ha ha. "You think champions wake up one morning and say 'Hey, I'm gonna roll a log today'? No. It takes commitment. Practice. Skill. *Years* of grueling dedication."

Elijah wheezes next to me, completely unhelpful as he fake coughs the word *idiot*.

"Bruh," I grind through clenched teeth. "Go somewhere *else*."

He ignores me, still panting like he might actually choke. He loves this shit. He lives for drama, on and off the playing field.

But Lucy? She studies me, confusion beginning to mar her pretty features.

"You know," she says slowly. "I would *love* to stop by the marina later and watch you in action. If you don't mind."

My brain flatlines. "What?"

"I'm sure Annabelle wouldn't mind—the lumberjack thing was half my idea to begin with." She laughs. "We were out one night brainstorming, and one too many glasses of wine later . . . here you are."

Uh. "Can't wait."

"Well." She inhales a fresh breath of mountain air. "This was a fun morning, but I have to pick up these mats and get to an appointment."

With that, she begins collecting several borrowed mats, rolling them as if she's done it hundreds of times before. Looking as if she hasn't wrecked my entire afternoon.

"Need a hand?" I offer, though I'm not sure if I'm being polite or panicked, my friends watching every move I make. They're invested now.

"I've got it, but thanks." She flashes me a quick smile over her shoulder, all the mats now securely tucked under her arm. "See you at the marina, Lumberjack."

Lumberjack.

"See you," I choke out, careful not to turn my head, lest one of my buddies decides to—

The second her car door slams and the rest of the class is gone, my friends are on my ass like flies on shit.

"It's killing me to hear her call you a lumberjack."

"It's my favorite new nickname."

"Have you *actually* been hanging out at the marina?" Quinton asks, narrowing his eyes like he's interrogating a criminal. "Please tell us you're not actually logrolling. You're gonna get hurt."

"I'm not," I lie. I do not owe them answers. "I mostly watch."

Elijah bursts out laughing. "You are *such* a fucking idiot."

I snap, glaring at him. "Lumberjacking is my new kink."

"Kink?" Quinton folds his arms, grinning. "If you don't tell us what you're up to, we're going to start following you around—we will not rest until we know what you're up to."

Damn him!

I open my mouth, but nothing comes out, because there's no universe where the truth sounds normal.

"It's complicated," I start. "We ran into each other yesterday morning, and she assumed I was a lumberjack, and . . . I didn't correct her. So yeah, I may or may not dash down to the marina and check it out."

"Wait, wait, wait. So you *are* logrolling? I'm so fucking confused."

"I'm pretending to be a missing lumberjack." I avoid all eye contact and slide into my flip-flops, staring down at them like they're the two most interesting objects in the world.

Quinton throws his head back, sputtering. "A missing lumberjack? How do you become a lumberjack?"

"You are such a fucking idiot," Elijah says again.

"It just happened." I start the slow walk to the parking lot, and they trail along beside me. "We crashed into each other, started talking—and when she asked if I was a lumberjack, I thought it was so fucking funny that I—"

"Lied through your teeth?" Elijah cuts in, grinning so wide he might actually explode. "And now you're the star of the fall festival?"

He's saying it like it's a bad thing.

"I'm doing the Lord's work."

"Yeah. You remind us *so* much of Moses."

We reach my truck. I whip around to face them, hands raised like I'm about to deliver a motivational speech. "Listen. You guys are acting like this is impossible, but I thrive under pressure. You know this better than anyone. If anyone can learn how to roll a log in a few hours, it's me."

"So what's your plan? Google videos?"

"Great idea." We pile into my truck. "Hadn't thought of that."

"You're telling me," Elijah says, still laughing, "that you're going to master the art of logrolling on the internet."

"No, jackass—I'm going to watch and pay attention to the pros. How hard can it be?" I boast, shoving my key into the ignition, more confident than I was down by the lake. "You can learn *anything* by watching."

Quinton lets out a wheeze as he buckles his seat belt. "Yeah, like how to humiliate yourself faster."

"Or how to write your obituary," Elijah adds, still grinning in the back seat. "Because, buddy, that's where this is headed."

Oddly, I'm willing to take that chance.

What's the worst thing that can happen?

Chapter 6

Lucy

When I show up at the marina, I don't know what I'm expecting—maybe a group of rugged guys in plaid shirts, chopping wood with brooding intensity. You know, *actual* lumberjacks.

What I find instead is Harris.

Stacking logs.

In swim trunks?

The sharp thwack of an axe hitting wood echoes across the dock, and for the briefest moment I think I've wandered onto the set of a very low-budget reality competition show. Harris is at the center of it all, sweat glistening on his neck and arms as he hefts another log onto the growing pile beside him.

Three other buff-looking dudes are lounging nearby in varying levels of disinterest. One's scrolling through his phone, another is picking at his fingernails, and the last one looks half asleep with his feet propped up on a crate.

Poor Annabelle.

"Is there a plan here, or are you building a beaver dam?" I call out to Harris, stopping a few feet away from him with my arms crossed.

Harris straightens, leaning the axe handle against his shoulder. When he spots me, that cocky grin that's perma-plastered on his face gets wider.

"Hey, hottie," he says, genuinely pleased to see me. "You showed up. Couldn't wait to see the magic happen?"

He flexes for good measure, and my eyes drift down to his swim trunks, choosing not to ask the reason he's wearing them, focusing my attention on the logs he's stacking.

"If by *magic* you mean stacking firewood, then yeah—I'm totally blown away by your talent."

If he senses my sarcasm, he doesn't let on. "Not all heroes wear capes."

I laugh. "Is that what you call this?"

"We have a job to do, and I'm the team leader," he explains, leaning on his axe, gesturing toward the dudes who are sitting around *not* practicing.

"Team leader?" one of the other lumberjacks calls, not looking up from his phone. "You've been posing like a jackass influencer for twenty minutes."

Harris points the axe at him. "Respect the craft, Wallace."

"My name is Wally. I've corrected you at least ninety-two tim—"

"Enough bickering, dear God!" Annabelle comes stomping over from the shed—which has doubled as her office over the past few weeks—boots crunching on the gravel as she barrels toward us. "Listen, guys. We have less than one week to get our shit together, which means you all need to look *convincing*—"

"Already got that covered, boss," Harris interrupts, striking an exaggerated pose, one boot up on a log. He flexes his calf muscle, tan highlighted by the bright-blue wave pattern of his shorts. "Bam. Look at this definition."

Annabelle disregards his posturing. "Kyle, you're the chain saw demo." She pinches the bridge of her nose. "Wally, the two-man saw with Bill. Harris." She glances over at him, eyes homing in on the swim trunks. "You're scheduled for the main event: logrolling competition. I need all of you to try and not die."

Harris doesn't miss a beat. "I'll be fine. The crowd loves an underdog story."

One of the guys snorts. "An underdog story usually still involves someone who knows what they're doing."

"I know exactly what I'm doing," Harris says confidently, hoisting the axe on one shoulder like he's posing for a bodywash commercial.

Annabelle glances down at her clipboard. "How many times have you logrolled before?"

Harris shrugs. "I mean—how hard can it be?"

Wally grins. "I give you ten seconds before you biff it."

"I'll take the over on that," the other guy muses. "Fifteen before he eats it."

"Twenty!" I chime in on the roasting. "I have total faith in him."

"Jealousy doesn't suit you, *William*," Harris fires back at the burly man wearing a frown.

"My name is Bill, asshole. And you're as useful as a cardboard axe." He finally looks up. "We get it—you can swing an axe—but that doesn't mean you can chop wood."

"I'll do what it takes to keep the fans happy." Harris winks at me, and I immediately regret showing up to this circus.

Annabelle appears glassy eyed, as if she's stopped listening entirely. "Jeez, you guys! Stop!" She waves a hand in the air in defeat. "Do whatever you want. Just don't hurt yourself—or anyone else. Harris, *I swear*, if you *spin* that axe again, I'm pulling you from the event. I don't care how much the crowd loves a spectacle. It is not safe."

Harris rests the axe carefully against the log pile, then lifts his hands in surrender and steps away. "Okay, okay. No axe showmanship. But you're killing my creative flow, Annabelle."

Her glare could strip paint off a wall.

I can't help it—I laugh.

Harris hears me, of course, and whirls toward me with that smug expression plastered across his face. "See? Lucy believes in me."

"I don't think Lucy believes in you at all," Bill corrects, deadpan. "That was a pity laugh."

Harris points at him. "Keep talking and you're off my team."

"Team?" Bill scoffs. "Dude, for the second time today—we are not your team! We're coworkers."

"Enough!" Annabelle claps her hands sharply to cut them off. "Everyone back to work. I have actual things to organize that don't involve babysitting a bunch of overgrown boys."

She stalks off, muttering under her breath about *liability waivers*, leaving us standing in awkward silence.

I shift my feet.

Harris stretches as if he hadn't gotten scolded. "All right, you heard her. Back to work! Someone hand me another log." He wiggles his fingers.

"*Or*," Wally suggests. "You could stop showing off and actually learn how to roll one of those things. You know—since that's your job."

Wally's built like a truck—broad shoulders, tree-trunk arms, and a face that has seen one too many bar fights. His flannel shirt has the arms cut off; it's worn and faded, displaying the kind of forearms that could split wood without an axe. Sawdust clings to his jeans, and he's eyeing Harris like he's trying to figure out if he's joking or plain *useless*.

Kyle is a little lean for a lumberjack but no less imposing. He's perched with his booted feet planted wide, a hat pulled low over his sharp features. His beard is scruffy, peppered with premature gray, and when he looks up from his phone, his eyes are twinkling.

"All that fucker has done is *pose*," Bill drawls, flicking a wood shaving into the lake. "Didn't think this was a beauty contest."

"I'm versatile," Harris fires back, still grinning as he straightens up.

Bill snorts. "Versatile at what? Wasting time? Where the hell did they find you?"

Wally stands idly by, observing the chaos—the oldest of the group, with deep-set eyes and a voice that sounds like gravel. He's got thick arms and a scar cutting through one eyebrow and has a menacing glower. Unlike the other two, he doesn't bother cracking smiles or jokes.

He narrows his gaze on Harris and growls, "You think the log is gonna roll itself, pretty boy?"

Whoa.

I raise my eyebrows in response.

Harris lets out a low whistle, unbothered. "You're a black ray of sunshine, huh?" he quips. "Who pissed you off?"

Wally grunts, grabbing a log with one hand and chucking it onto the dock, where it lands with a thud. "This isn't summer camp, kid. Either pick up the pace or get out of the way."

Harris tilts his head, eyeing the guy up and down. "Jeez, dude. Do you practice that stare in the mirror, or does it come naturally?"

Wally doesn't blink. "You wanna waste time running your mouth, or you wanna learn how *not* to crack your skull open?"

Kyle mutters under his breath. "I kinda wanna see him crack his skull open."

I giggle, barely suppressing my grin. "Let's not encourage head trauma."

Harris holds up a hand, completely unfazed. "Relax, old man. I got this."

Wally wipes his hands on his jeans and folds his arms across his chest. "You ever actually been on a rolling log before, or were you hoping charm was gonna carry you across the lake?"

Harris puffs out his chest. Walks to the edge of the dock and gazes down into the water, where logs bob up and down from the wake. I watch as he bends over and drags one closer to the pier.

He plants one foot on the log.

The log responds *immediately* by shifting beneath him. Rolling. Wet. Harris wobbles, arms shooting out to the sides for balance, and I swear, the entire group collectively holds their breath.

"Careful now," the crabby guy grumbles. "Don't make me jump in and rescue you."

I can hardly bear to watch, peeking between my fingers.

"He looks real steady to me," Wally calls, voice heavy with sarcasm. "A true professional."

"Shut up, Wallace!" Harris snaps, doing his best to adjust his footing on a soaking wet log.

Everything about this is all wrong: his swim trunks, his boots. His attitude.

One foot on the log.

He steadies it, holding it still.

"The kid is about to baptize himself," Bill announces.

"Stop calling me kid, William," Harris grits out. From here, I can see him leaning too far to one side to remain stable. "I've got this."

"Five bucks says he's down in three seconds," Wally mutters.

"Two seconds," Bill corrects.

"One." I laugh.

As if on cue, Harris's feet slip out from under him, his arms flailing wildly before he hits the water with a spectacular splash.

The entire dock goes silent for a beat; the only sound is the rippling of water and the faint squawk of a seagull overhead.

Bill lets out a booming laugh. "Called it! Two seconds."

Wally doubles over, clutching his stomach. "*Ten out of ten* on the dismount! The boy cannot stay out of the water!"

Harris resurfaces with a sputter, blinking lake water out of his eyes. He pushes his soaked hair back with both hands before leveling the group with an unimpressed glare.

"You're sooo *hilarious*."

With a grunt, he hauls himself onto the dock, boots squishing as water pools around him. His drenched T-shirt clings to his chest, his swim trunks sag a little lower, and his pride?

Fully submerged somewhere at the bottom of the lake.

Bill claps a hand on Harris's soaked shoulder. "You're a natural, bro."

Harris glares at him. "Shut *up*, Bill." He plants his hands on his knees, water still dripping off him in steady streams. "Enjoy the show?"

I quirk a brow, crossing my arms. "You mean the show where you flailed before face-planting into the lake? Highlight of my day."

Wally snickers. "I'd pay to watch that again."

Hair soaked and plastered to his forehead, lake water dripping from his shoulders, his shirt clinging to every muscle like it was painted on. The swim trunks? A mistake on his part, but a gift to everyone else.

And by *everyone else* I mean *me*.

Much as I love roasting him, I can't ignore the very annoying fact that his body looks fantastic.

So good.

Which is so *unfair*.

Harris catches me staring and wipes a hand down his chest, drawing my eyes there. "Are you checking me out?"

"I—" I scramble for an excuse, coming up empty. "No! Your shirt is dripping wet. It's disgusting."

Really, Lucy? His dripping-wet shirt is disgusting? Liar, liar, pants on fire . . . lamest retort to ever retort—and embarrassingly transparent.

Harris hums—he does not believe me for a second. Then does the thing I did not want him to do: reaches for the hem of his tee.

"Don't—" I beg, knowing what's coming.

Too late.

We all watch as, in one smooth motion, he yanks the shirt over his head, then drops it onto the dock with a wet slap, leaving him in nothing but those damp shorts and work boots.

Water beads along the planes of his smooth chest, trailing down his abs—abs that, to my absolute dismay, look like they've been carved out of granite.

I swear the sun hits him just right, casting shadows onto his six-pack.

Where the hell did Annabelle find *this guy?*

Seriously.

He isn't giving lumberjack. He's giving . . .

Model.

The kind of guy who walks around shirtless and lets water spill down his bare body.

I swallow hard, resisting the urge to do something undignified—like drool.

The worst part? *Harris knows I think he's good looking.*

Then, as a test to my willpower, he runs a hand through his wet hair, shaking out the excess water in a move so effortless, so *calculated*, it nearly makes both my brain and my vagina short-circuit.

I *absolutely* refuse to be impressed.

"You know what you're missing?" I force the words to sound cool. Force my gaze to his face.

Harris tilts his head, intrigued. "Oh? Do tell."

I let the moment stretch. "A flannel shirt. Maybe a little plaid."

"Wow. So my raw, natural talent isn't good enough for you?"

I blink innocently. "What talent?"

Wally nearly chokes laughing. Bill claps him on the back.

Harris narrows his eyes at me, but amusement flickers there. He steps closer, shaking his head. "You *really* enjoy testing me, don't you?"

I flash him my most innocent smile. "What? I'm being honest."

"Don't count me out yet. The event is a long way off."

No, it's not. It's days from now, but he doesn't seem to be counting.

"And then you'll be gone."

"That's the plan." He smiles. "Why? You gonna miss me?"

I don't move. I should step back, put some distance between me and the walking hard body and his six-pack—but I don't. Instead, I hold his gaze, stubborn and steady.

Intense.

"Is that a yes—that you leave Monday?" I ask again, keeping the conversation on track.

He raises one eyebrow. "Unfortunately."

Does that mean he wouldn't mind staying?

Does that mean this back-and-forth between us isn't fun and games?

Not that it *matters*.

I clear my throat, pushing past the weird little flutter in my chest. "Well. I won't get attached, then."

Harris studies me while everyone looks on. "That sounds suspiciously like disappointment I hear in your voice."

I scoff. "You *wish*."

"Do I?"

I blink.

My brain stutters.

He's teasing—but *not just teasing*. There's something else there, something unspoken in the way he watches me, like he's trying to pull a reaction out of me. Like he's waiting to see if I'll flinch.

I won't.

I do what I do best—I deflect.

I scoff, rolling my shoulders back. "You're really digging deep for that ego boost, huh?"

Harris tilts his head, smirk flickering into something unreadable. "Trying to get an honest answer out of you, that's all."

"Honest answer?" I huff out a laugh. "How is this: I'll *miss* watching you wipe out anytime you go near the water."

"Is that why you stopped by today?"

I inhale sharply, my brain scrambling for an excuse. A good one. A logical one.

"I'm here because someone has to make sure you don't drown," I say, my voice even. "There are no lifeguards in this town."

Harris lets out a low whistle, placing a hand over his chest like I've wounded him. "Ouch. You really think a guy who looks like *this* is gonna drown?"

Then, because he's *Harris*, he gestures broadly at himself—shirtless, wet, and maddeningly smug.

And so damn *sexy*.

My pulse kicks up.

The air between us heavier than it was moments ago. He is still *dripping*—water sliding down the length of his arm, across the line of his shoulder, tracing over the muscles in the most distracting way.

"You know something, Lucy?" Harris drawls, voice smooth as sin. "There's nothing I'd rather be doing than showing you all the things I'm good at that have *nothing* to do with wood."

He grins.

I roll my eyes. "Wow. You're so subtle."

I won't pretend it's easy to think standing in front of this stupidly hot, frustratingly cocky man with his golden retriever confidence, his rough hands, his broad chest, and that damn smirk that says he *knows exactly* what he's doing to me.

Heat crawls up my neck. But still, I step closer to him, tipping my head enough to look into his pretty eyes with the long lashes. "You talk a big game, Harris. Hope your skills live up to the sales pitch."

Wally snorts. Bill coughs into his elbow, barely concealing his laughter. Even Annabelle—who has rejoined us—presses her fingers to her temple, her secondhand embarrassment for me palpable.

"Stop looking at me like that!" I snap, though the words lose their bite.

"Like what?"

"I don't know!"

"You're so fun to mess with," he adds, voice low and teasing. "But I'll save some teasing for later."

My stomach flips. "*Later?*" I repeat, half horrified, half tingling *all over*.

His smirk deepens. "We have days and days to dance around this."

"Days to dance around *what*?" I hear myself whisper, suddenly hyperaware of how close we still are.

Harris leans in. My brain goes into a tailspin. "To do whatever it is you want. With me."

Oh.

Oh *Jesus*.

My throat goes dry. My thoughts go *everywhere*.

"Like what?" I ask, and I *hate* how breathy my voice sounds.

His smirk widens, his gaze flickering over my face like he's memorizing every little reaction. "You'll figure it out."

I don't even get the chance to ask, because Harris chooses that moment to turn on the heel of his boot and walk away—leaving me standing there, absolutely ruined by a conversation I can't fully compute. Brain dumb.

Later that afternoon, as Annabelle and I gossip about him at Loon Landing Café, she leans across the table, transfixed.

"Days and days to do whatever you want?" She scoffs. "Told you to your face you could do *anything*?" She leans back against the chair. "Damn. That guy is *so* freaking hot."

I stab at my iced coffee with a straw, watching the ice spin. "I can't believe anyone would say that to my face. I was shook."

Annabelle gives me the most exasperated look I've ever seen. "Lucy, the man handed you an opportunity, and you fumbled it."

I groan again, avoiding her searing gaze. "I didn't *fumble* it—I strategically avoided a potential disaster."

She throws her hands up. "What disaster? A ridiculously hot guy flirting with you?"

"Yes!" I point at her like she's proving my own point. "Yes. Exactly that. Thank you for understanding."

Annabelle stares at me blankly. "That is *not* a disaster. That is a dream scenario."

I scowl, dropping my hand. "It's a *trap*, Annabelle."

Her eyes narrow. "Lucy, it's a shirtless, wet, gorgeous man flirting with you. Where is the downside?"

I groan, slumping forward onto the table. "It's a defense mechanism, okay? I can't help getting defensive with men."

Annabelle tilts her head, arms crossing. "Defensive? Or terrified?"

"I'm not terrified." I lift my head to glare at her. "He takes up way too much space. Physically, emotionally—whatever other *-ly* you can think of. He's like . . ." I wave a hand in the air, searching for the right word. "A golden retriever that hit the gym too hard."

Annabelle snorts. "A damn good-looking golden retriever."

"Not the point," I grumble, glaring at my coffee mug.

My best friend regards me, swirling her drink thoughtfully. "So what's the real issue here, Lucy?"

I blink at her. "The real issue?"

"Yeah." She gives me a look like she can see straight through my nonsense. "You're flustered because he's hot? Or because he got under your skin?"

"Neither," I snap, a little too quickly.

Annabelle's smirk widens. "Uh-huh. Sure."

"It's true!" I insist, ignoring the warmth creeping up my neck. "He's *obnoxious.* Completely full of himself. And—and he thinks he can get whatever he wants with a grin and a wink."

"Can't he?"

I freeze, my brain short-circuiting at the memory of Harris standing too close, grinning that *stupid* grin, and the way my heart did something absolutely traitorous in response.

Annabelle knows *exactly* where my mind goes. "Oh my God. He can."

"He cannot!" I snap at her.

She bursts into laughter, way too pleased with herself. "Lucy, I love you—but you're such a liar. In fact, I'm going to do you a favor here and send him your number."

"Don't. You. *Dare.*"

"Why not? You're too stubborn about this. We both know you didn't show up at the marina to see me—you barely saw me standing there."

Facts. I hadn't said hello. I was too busy staring at Harris and flirting with him.

"Please don't give him my number. Don't you dar—"

But Annabelle is already typing, thumbs flying across her screen like some kind of texting ninja.

"Annabelle!" I lunge halfway across the table to yank the phone out of her grasp, but she's too quick for me, wrenching it out of reach, cackling like the traitor she is.

"This is for your own good!" she singsongs, waving the phone tauntingly in the air. "What's the worst thing that could happen?"

"So many things," I snap, straightening in my seat like I'm about to present a PowerPoint on all the ways this could go horribly wrong. "For starters, what if he's messing with me? What if he's some kind of pathological flirt who says that to every girl he meets?"

"Okay, drama queen." Annabelle rolls her eyes. "You're smart, you're funny, you're gorgeous. Why wouldn't he be into you?"

I open my mouth to argue—because arguing is what I *do*—but the words die on my tongue. I blink at her. "You say that like dating is easy."

"It *is* easy." She sips her drink, annoyingly casual. "Confidence, Lucy. Fake it till you make it."

"Confidence *isn't* my problem." I slouch in the booth. "Men like Harris are my problem. He's too much."

"Too much *what*?"

"Too much charm. Too much *every*thing." I wave a hand vaguely in the air. "He's the kind of guy who could talk his way out of a speeding ticket *and* get the cop's numb—"

My phone buzzes, cutting me off mid-sentence. Annabelle arches an eyebrow, eyes like a hawk zeroing in on its prey.

"Gee. Who could that be?" She feigns innocence as if she didn't know who was messaging me.

I glance at the screen, heart stumbling. Then I groan. "I seriously hate you."

"You love me."

"No, I really don't."

Annabelle is undeterred from torturing me. "Then why are you smiling?"

Am I?

My fingers go to my face, and I touch my mouth.

Shit.

I *am* smiling.

Chapter 7

Harris:
Miss me yet?

Lucy:
I would have to know who this is first before I can answer that question.

Harris:
You know who this is, don't be coy.

Lucy:
Give me one hint . . .

Harris:
Hot but WET

Lucy:
Wow. You are so full of yourself.

Harris:
I'm full of myself for telling you I'm wet?

Lucy:
No, because you called yourself hot.

Harris:
I'm only hot because I'm in the sauna.

Lucy:
Oh. Whoops.

Harris:
But I'm also hot.

Lucy:
LOL

Harris:
Did that make you laugh?

Lucy:
Wow, you really think you're irresistible, don't you?

Harris:
Do you agree?

Lucy:
I'll let you believe whatever helps you sleep at night.

Harris:
Oh, I sleep fine.

Lucy:
I am not taking that bait.

Harris:
What bait?

Lucy:
The bait where you say you're in bed. Then I ask "What are you wearing?" Then you say "nothing." Then you try to lure me into a sex exchange.

Harris:
Actually, Little Miss Know It All, I'm now post-sauna and wearing the flannel pajama bottoms with Santa faces that my mom gave me for Christmas last year. Oh. With a hoodie that says "Terry Crews for President"

Lucy:
I have no idea what to say to that.

Harris:
Sounds like you don't think Terry should be President . . .

Lucy:
LOL stop it.

Harris:
You're laughing. I take that as a win.

Lucy:
Fine. I'll let you have this round.

Harris:
Finally, some honesty.

Lucy:
Don't let it go to your head.

Harris:
Too late.

Harris:
So. What are you wearing?

Lucy:
DANG IT! What did I say about that question? It leads to no good!

Harris:
RELAX. All I meant was, are you in comfy pajamas or are you one of those people who sleeps naked like a psychopath?

Lucy:
Definitely not naked. Sweatpants and a college sweatshirt, but at some point I'll put on shorts.

Harris:
What I'm hearing is that you probably sleep with a ceiling fan on?

Lucy:
I can confirm.

Lucy:
Also, why are you in bed so early???

Harris:
I have a yoga class at the ass crack of dawn. And as a rule, I generally wake up early. 4:30 when I'm not on vacation.

Lucy:
I draw the line at any o'clock before 5

Harris:
Cold plunge, cup of coffee.
Sometimes I run. What about you?

Lucy:
Wake up at 5:30ish, depending.
I started yoga at dawn for your friends, but word got out. Typically my first classes aren't until 8.

Harris:
How many classes a day do you have?

Lucy:
Four or five, depending on the day. I mix in private sessions too.

Harris:
Private sessions, huh?

Lucy:
Don't even THINK about it. The answer is no.

Harris:
LOL, wow. Not even at a premium, eh?

Lucy:
You couldn't afford me.

Harris:
Oh, so now I'm broke?

Lucy:
No, they're really expensive rates.

Harris:
You sure they're not excuses to avoid spending more time with me?

Lucy:
Or MAYBE I'm playing hard to get.

Harris:
Oh, so you admit it—you want me to chase you.

Lucy:
I didn't say that.

Harris:
You kind of did . . .

Lucy:
Maybe I'm curious.

Harris:
Curious about what?

Lucy:
About what you'd even plan if I did let you take me out.

Harris:
Oh, that's easy. I'd take you hiking.

Lucy:
Hiking?

Harris:
Or not.

Lucy:
I mean, it's not my first choice . . . even though we're both "athletic."

Harris:
Uh. Why is "athletic" in quotes?

Lucy:
I'm saying, that because someone LOOKS like they're good at sports, doesn't mean that they are. You know? Some guys go to the gym and are in shape. That doesn't necessarily mean they can play soccer or have stamina.

Harris:
Ummmm are you telling me I'm not athletic?

Lucy:
I don't want you dying on a hike. Yes, you have muscles, but does that mean you can walk for 2 hours without giving yourself a heart attack? I don't know.

Harris:
Wow. You really know how to bruise a guy's ego.

Lucy:
It's not my fault you're sensitive.

Harris:
Sensitive? I'm trying to figure out why you think I'd die on a hike!!

Lucy:
I didn't say die. I said you might have a heart attack. Big difference.

Harris:
Oh, that's SO much better.

Lucy:
Looks can be deceiving. I don't know your endurance level.

Harris:
My endurance level?

Lucy:
You know, how long you can last.

Lucy:
On a hike. I MEANT ON A HIKE!

Harris:
Sure you did.

Lucy:
Don't make this weird.

Harris:
Too late. It's already weird. And you sure are cute when you're flustered.

Lucy:
How do you know I'm flustered.

Harris:
I'm not talking about right now—I'm talking about the times I've seen you in person. It's cute that I get you all riled up.

Lucy:
For the record, I'm not THAT worried about your endurance.

Harris:
Oh? Should I take that as a vote of confidence?

Lucy:
Let's say I'd be willing to test it. Strictly for science.

Harris:
Science, huh? But seriously, Lucy, tell me something. Why do you think we butt heads every time we talk?

Lucy:
Hmm, let's see . . . maybe it's because you like pushing my buttons.

Harris:
Guilty. But you push back as hard. I like that about you.

Lucy:
I guess I'm not used to someone keeping up with me. Most people get frustrated and give up.

Harris:
By people, do you mean men??

Lucy:
Perhaps. And since we're being honest—are you single??? For all I know, you have a wife hidden away somewhere.

Harris:
Wow. Going straight for the deep stuff, huh?

Lucy:
Just making conversation.

Harris:
I am single. No wife, no girlfriend, no secret family hidden away. You can breathe easy.

Lucy:
Good to know. For the record, I'm also single. No hidden husbands or boyfriends.

Harris:
I would hope not. That might complicate things.

Lucy:
So, why is someone like you single?

Harris:
It's complicated.

Lucy:
Complicated how?

Harris:
I don't have the best track record with relationships.

Lucy:
Care to elaborate?

Harris:
Let's see . . . my last relationship ended because she thought I was too focused on my job and not enough on her. Before that, it was my college girlfriend, who was pissed when I moved to another state for work and moved in with some buddies instead of her. I can't win.

Lucy:
That sounds rough.

Harris:
It's not all bad. It means I haven't found the right person yet. What about you?

Lucy:
Yes, I'm so single it's a joke at this point.

Harris:
When was your last relationship?

Lucy:
Gosh, months ago. I've been focusing on myself, which is what we should all be doing, yeah? After my last relationship, I needed some time to figure out what I wanted.

Harris:
What happened?

Lucy:
He was . . . ugh, how do I put this? Super zen. He left for a week without telling me! He was soul searching and ultimately it got to be too much. The uncertainty.

Harris:
Wow. That sounds . . . chaotic.

Lucy:
It was. Don't get me wrong, he wasn't a bad person. He was too free-spirited for me.

Harris:
And you need stability.

Lucy:
Exactly. Stability, communication. You know, the basics. I realized it's not about finding the perfect person, it's about finding someone who matches your energy. It's hard, isn't it? Balancing what you want with what someone else needs.

Harris:
Right. Like how do you find someone who fits into your life

without feeling like you're giving up a part of yourself?

Lucy:
Also, it's about finding someone who complements you. Someone who doesn't just fit into your life but makes it BETTER.

Harris:
You sound like you've thought about this a lot.

Lucy:
I suppose I have. All I want is a man who challenges me, makes me laugh, and doesn't run off to "find himself" without warning.

Harris:
Well, I can promise I'm not running off anywhere.

Lucy:
I mean, you will by the time you leave. Where do you live, anyway?

Harris:
Arizona. Originally from Pennsylvania.

Lucy:
Arizona? That's far.

Harris:
Not really. That's what flights are for.

Lucy:
So now you're telling me you'd fly all the way to Washington to see me?

Harris:
Maybe. If you're worth it.

Lucy:
Bold of you to assume I'd let you.

Harris:
Bold of you to assume I wouldn't make it worth your while.

Lucy:
So, Pennsylvania to Arizona. Big change.

Harris:
It was. Grew up in the cold, now I live in the heat. You get used to it. What about you? Always been local?

Lucy:
Pretty much. Born and raised here. I've thought about leaving, but it's hard to imagine living anywhere else. There's something about the

mountains, the forests, the rain. Never had a reason to move.

Lucy:
What's something I'd see if I ever visited Arizona?

Harris:
The desert mountains. There's nothing like them when the sun sets and rises behind them and you see the outline of cactuses. And the stars at night? Unbelievable.

Harris:
Not as pretty as you though, obviously.

Lucy:
Laying it on thick, are we?

Harris:
Not at all.

Lucy:
Okay Mr. Honesty, what's something you're attracted to?

Harris:
Physically?

Lucy:
Yes, physically.

Harris:
A great smile. Eyes that make you forget what you were saying. And I've got a thing for nice legs.

Lucy:
Nice legs? Really?

Harris:
Legs. Boobs. Ass. Don't know, hard to choose. Brown hair, freckles.

Lucy:
Ha ha, now you're describing me.

Harris:
Guilty.

Harris:
So what about you? Your turn.

Lucy:
Strong arms. The kind that look like they could pick me up without breaking a sweat.

Harris:
Oh, so you mean MY arms. I'll scribble that in my diary.

Lucy:
I also love a nice ass, so we have that in common.

Harris:
Remind me to do more squats.

Lucy:
I don't think you need to. Your ass is fine.

Harris:
Aww, you say the sweetest things when you're not being prickly!

Lucy:
LOL That's how I flirt. What else are you attracted to?

Harris:
Confidence, the kind that sneaks up on you. Like, at first, you don't notice it then suddenly it's all you can think about. A woman who's sure of herself. Not insecure. Can't date someone who doesn't trust me, either.

Harris:
A great laugh. The kind that's loud and a little out of control. You know, the kind that makes other people start laughing too.

Lucy:
That's ODDLY specific.

Harris:
It's true. What about you? What's something oddly specific that you're into?

Lucy:
A good voice. Not necessarily deep, but maybe? The kind of voice that could give you an orgasm hearing it over the phone.

Harris:
Jeez, you keep describing ME.

Lucy:
You do have a deep voice, I will give you that. It's not terrible.

Harris:
I'll take it. What else?

Lucy:
Strong hands.

Harris:
Oh? And what would you want those strong hands to do?

Lucy:
I meant for practical things, like carrying groceries or opening jars.

Harris:
Ugh, THE MOST BORING USE FOR HANDS.

Lucy:
LOL. I can't stop picturing you in Santa pajamas and a Terry Crews hoodie.

Harris:
Well. If you want to come over for a first-hand look, I'll go unlock the door.

Lucy:
Why don't you send me a selfie, instead?

Harris:
Incoming. Try not to fall in love with me.

Lucy:
Oh my God. You weren't kidding about the pajamas.

Harris:
Told you. Both festive AND functional.

Lucy:
Functional? How?

Harris:
They're warm. And they make a statement.

Lucy:
The statement being "I'm ridiculous"

Harris:
No, the statement being "I know how to rock Christmas spirit year-round" so get on my level.

Lucy:
I take it that's your favorite holiday?

Harris:
Yeah, hands down.

Lucy:
What do you like about it?

Harris:
Uh, EVERYTHING! Lights, trees, lights, being home, seeing my family. I have twin sisters and between them have seven nieces and nephews. It's fuckin awesome. You?

Lucy:
Well, I'm an only child, so no nieces and nephews, though I do love the holiday. Ice skating on the lake, bonfires on the lake, tree lighting ceremony . . . My parents leave the day after Christmas for a cruise. It sucks being alone but I've gotten used to it.

Harris:
I've done cruises over the holidays.
Not Christmas, but New Year's.
Total blast.

Lucy:
Yeah, my parents love it.

Harris:
But not you?

Lucy:
No, no, I do. I'd rather be home, though, where it's cold and snowy. I love sitting on the couch and watching cheesy movies. But that's me every night of the year, ha ha.

Harris:
This cabin I'm in has an old VCR. I'll probably put a tape in tomorrow night. You're welcome to join me.

Lucy:
What would the dress code for this be?

Harris:
Clothes optional.

Harris:
KIDDING! Pajamas, obviously . . .

Lucy:
Would you be feeding me?

Harris:
I'd be nibbling on your toes. Does that count?

Lucy:
No!

Harris:
Darn. I was excited for a second . . .

Lucy:
Fine. What time?

Harris:
Are you serious?

Lucy:
Don't make me change my mind.

Harris:
No, no! I'm pleasantly surprised.

Lucy:
I figured someone has to see these pajamas in person. Plus, I need to make sure you're not lying about the VCR.

Harris:
Oh, it's very real.

Lucy:
Be advised: If I see one spider, I'm leaving.

Harris:
Noted. I'll make it spider-free.
Anything else I should prepare?

Lucy:
Popcorn. Pizza. Hot chocolate.

Harris:
Anything for my first official
pajama party guest.

Lucy:
This is a party now?

Harris:
You can wear a bag if you want to.

Chapter 8

Harris

I spend the day nervously planning for my date with Lucy.

Planning.

Working out.

The day starts with me bailing on yoga. No way am I going to keep my cool twisted into baby poses with my mind spinning about Lucy coming over tonight.

So I plan some more.

By *planning*, I mean I race around the small town for hot chocolate and popcorn like a chicken with my head cut off. And even though I've only been here a few days, I clean the cabin to ensure there are no spiders in sight.

Yeah.

Productive stuff, I know.

Then, as if I'm not already losing my damn mind, I decide to join the team for one of those bonding activities in the lodge. You know, the kind where someone says, "This will bring us closer together," but really it highlights how much we all secretly want to strangle each other.

Today's activity? Would You Rather.

"Would you rather share a hotel room with Coach for an entire season or have him move into your house for a month?"

That gets everyone groaning.

"Do we actually have to talk to him in either scenario?" Elijah asks. "'Cause if so, I'm picking hotel room. At least I can leave during the day and I'm not a prisoner in my own damn house."

"You think you'd survive him snoring all night?" a lineman named Smith shoots back. "I've heard he sounds like a chain saw."

"Never mind, you're right." Elijah frowns. "My fucking house has six bedrooms."

"Better than him seeing my place," I say. "Can you imagine? Christ, he'd criticize everything about it. 'Bennett, why do you have a pool table in your living room? Is this what you call discipline? What's up with all your laundry?' No, sir, that's what I call my housekeeper having the day off."

Everyone laughs except Coach, who grunts out his displeasure at being roasted. He has no sense of humor.

Then Miles, bless his twisted mind, offers up: "Would you rather accidentally text your ex 'I miss you' or post a shirtless selfie on social media with the caption 'Who wants some of this?'"

They fall silent before Elijah mutters, "I think I'd move to another country if either of those things happened. Monica would post the screenshot on social media, and I'd never hear the end of it."

Preach.

Being in the public eye isn't for the faint of heart. We have to be careful who we're sleeping with—and who we date. Fame is a double-edged sword.

By the time it's my turn, the room is in full chaos. I go with something tame: "Would you rather have Coach read your private texts out loud to the team or have him write your dating profile?"

"Dude, that's evil," Smith says, shaking his head.

"Text messages," Quinton says immediately. "I can live with public humiliation in group settings. What I can't live with is Coach trying to convince women I'm a 'hard worker' who's 'dedicated to my craft.'" He uses air quotes.

"Right? He'd probably list *early riser* as one of my top qualities," Elijah adds, rolling his eyes.

That brings on a whole new wave of arguments, but I can't stop laughing. For the first time all day, I'm not stressing about Lucy or obsessing over what could go wrong tonight.

But now the game's over, the cabin's ready, and my nerves are creeping back in.

Me. *Nervous?*

What the fuck.

So unlike me.

I glance at my phone and see her latest text.

Lucy:

Be there in less than 10.

Less than ten minutes? Holy shit.

I bolt to the bathroom to check my reflection, and lean forward, baring my teeth. I ate some popcorn already—yeah, yeah, I cheated—and sure enough, there's a sliver of kernel stuck between two of my teeth.

"Damn it," I gripe, grabbing a toothpick, and chisel away at it.

Once my teeth are kernel-free, I step back to examine the rest of me. Santa pajama pants? Check. Terry Crews hoodie? Check. Hair? Not terrible. I swipe a hand through it anyway, just in case.

I glance around the bathroom, making sure there's nothing embarrassing in plain sight. Toothpaste cap? On. Razor? Put away. The last thing I need is for her to walk in and see my stuff looking like a crime scene.

My phone buzzes again.

Lucy:

Pulling up now.

Double shit. That was fast.

I practically sprint to the living room, double-checking the popcorn, the hot chocolate setup, and the vintage movies stacked neatly on the coffee table. *Home Alone*, *The Great Outdoors*, *Coming to America*, and *Jerry Maguire*—it's a solid lineup.

The crunch of gravel outside makes my heart do this weird double thump.

She's here.

I pull open the door before she even has a chance to knock. And there she is—wearing a crewneck sweatshirt and sweatpants, her hair pulled into a messy bun. She looks good enough to eat, and when I catch a whiff of her, I suddenly want to have a taste.

Down, boy.

"Hey," I say, forcing my voice to sound casual. "Come on in."

"Wow." Lucy steps inside, glancing around the cabin. "This is cozy. I've never actually been in one of these cottages."

"Really? Never?" I ask, closing the door behind her. "You've been missing out. Want a quick tour?"

She raises an eyebrow, a playful smile tugging at her lips. "Isn't it, like, one room?"

"Technically, it's two," I say, holding up the peace sign. "The living area and kitchen. But there's also a bathroom and a small bedroom. Don't underestimate the grandeur of this place. I'm digging it so far."

"That's because it's decorated so damn cute." Her gaze sweeps over the space, landing on the walls. "Look at this wallpaper—it's fantastic."

I glance at the wallpaper, a pattern that looks like it came straight out of the '70s: pine cones and berries. A round wooden mirror hangs over a tiny table in the small space comprising the entrance. "*Fantastic* is one way to describe it."

She laughs, running a hand over the back of the couch. "No, really, it's cute."

I lead her toward the tiny kitchen, which takes all of three steps to get to. "This is where the magic happens. By *magic*, I mean popcorn and hot chocolate."

She leans against the counter, arms crossed. "Is that why you have a pot on the stove and marshmallows at the ready? You were really prepared for this, huh?"

"Always," I say, smirking. I don't disclose the fact that the only thing I've been thinking about today is her arrival. "The kitchen's tiny, but efficient. And the fridge doesn't smell weird, which is a win."

"High standards," she teases.

I motion toward a small door in the corner, then walk over and push it open so she can peer inside. "Voilà! Here we have the bathroom. Complete with a mirror, a toilet, and zero spiders. As promised."

"You weren't kidding about the rustic charm. Cute and cozy."

"It's home for the week." I lean against the doorframe. "Does the trick."

We head back to the living room and sink onto the couch; Lucy pulls her legs up under her and attempts to get comfortable.

"Welp. I'm officially in love with this place." Her fingers stroke the throw blanket there. "Fun fact: Annabelle's aunt and uncle own the lodge, and oddly, she and I never spent the night in any of the rooms. Or these cabins. But maybe I should suggest it for a staycation—this is too, too cute."

"You're welcome to hang out here as long as you like."

She tilts her head, studying me. Ignores my suggestion with a shake of her head, smile fading as she glances at the coffee table. "All right, let's see if your movie selection lives up to the hype." She pulls out *Coming to America* and holds it up. "Let's start with this one. It's a classic."

"Good choice," I say, leaning back as she sets up the tape.

As the opening credits roll and she settles back onto the couch, I can't help but glance at her out of the corner of my eye. Her messy bun is slightly lopsided, her hoodie sleeves are pushed up to her elbows, and she looks completely at ease.

And that's when my brain begins with the *There's a girl in your house, dude.* A female. And she smells good. Like vanilla and something faintly floral. How do girls do that? Smell like a delicious candle but also: sunshine?

I shift slightly, trying not to overthink it, but my brain's having none of that. *She's sitting close enough that if you moved a few inches, your knee would touch hers.*

Do it.

Touch your knee to her knee.

I shake my head and force my focus back on the screen. Eddie Murphy is talking, jokes are being made, and I'm trying my best to keep up.

But then she laughs—a soft, genuine laugh that pulls me right back out of the movie and straight into the fact that a sexy woman is beside me, all snuggled up, giggling at the TV.

One I have been horny for since the second I saw her.

"I can feel you looking at me," she says, turning her head slightly but not fully looking at me.

My stomach drops, and I blink like a deer caught in headlights. "What? No. I wasn't—"

"You totally were," she cuts me off, meeting my gaze, lips twitching into a small smirk. "You're a terrible liar."

I grin. "You would think that would be a selling point."

"Oh, yeah," Lucy says. "Every woman's *dream*: a man who can't lie to save his life. Every now and again I appreciate being told I look gorgeous even when I know I look wretched."

"You're in luck, because I'm honest to a fault. And an open book. Practically a saint."

I lay it on thick, grinning as I deliver the line. It pays off when a bubble of laughter rises in her throat, and she giggles again—this time at me, not the movie.

"A saint, huh?" she says, tilting her head to the side as her eyes narrow in mock suspicion. "Tell me more."

"I've never stolen anything," I say, pausing for dramatic effect. "Unless you count the fancy crayons I snagged from the grocery store when I was six. In my defense, I was racked with guilt by the time we hit the parking lot, and took them back."

She laughs, shaking her head. "So, what you're telling me is, your life of crime started and ended with a crayon theft?"

"Exactly. Clean slate ever since," I reply, grinning. "I'm practically a model citizen."

She picks up a piece of popcorn and tosses it at me, her smirk growing. "What's the craziest thing you've ever done in public?"

Let me count the ways:

1. Play football in front of thousands of people.
2. Give press conferences on live television.
3. Sprayed a bottle of champagne that cost $25,000 in a club during a New Year's Eve celebration.
4. Had the king of England try on my Super Bowl ring, also on national television.
5. Ran naked through downtown Phoenix at three in the morning.

The list of crazy, fucked-up shit goes on and on.

"Uh. Let me think." Hmm, what can I tell her without giving away details about my actual life? "I had sex in public when I was in college. Does that count?"

It was behind a fraternity house, and it was with a girl I was dating at the time, and I'm fairly certain the girl was trying to accidentally on purpose get pregnant.

Lucy rolls her eyes, unimpressed. "*That's* your craziest? Sex outside? Come on—tell me something wild. Something stupid. Something that could get you *arrested* if the wrong person was watching."

I smirk, leaning in slightly. "Arrested? Can't say that I have been close to being arrested."

She shrugs, tossing another piece of popcorn into her mouth. "I'm saying, everyone's got a story."

"All right, all right." I go through the Rolodex in my brain and come up with something that might impress her. "There was this other time in college—we were at this big bonfire party, and someone dared me to climb up the scaffolding they were using to build the homecoming float."

Her eyebrows shoot up. "And you did it?"

"Of *course* I did it." I snort, offended by the suggestion that I didn't. "Made it all the way to the top before campus security showed up. I had to jump down and sprint into the woods to avoid getting caught."

She shakes her head, her smile widening. "So, what you're telling me is, you were an adrenaline junkie?"

"I prefer the term '*adventurous*,'" I say with a grin. "What about you? Any skeletons in your closet?"

She bites her lip, her smile turning mischievous. "Hmm. Well. When I was a teenager, I had this thing for stealing real estate signs out of people's yards."

"Real estate signs? Like the for sale ones?"

"Yep," she says, popping the *p* with pride. "My friends and I thought it was *hilarious* to 'rescue' them from yards and stick them in our friends' yards—you know, so anyone that drove by would think the house was for sale."

"How many are we talking here?"

"Eh." She waves a hand. "A dozen? In my friend Cara's trunk."

I let out a low whistle. "So . . . you had a stockpile of real estate signs?"

"Oh no," she says, her grin widening. "We were driving down a one-way street and got busted by our friend's neighbor. He called the cops because he thought we were out vandalizing—the cops showed up at my house, and that was the beginning and end of my crime spree."

"The cops actually came to your house over for sale signs?"

"Yup, totally." Lucy tosses a piece of popcorn into her mouth. "I answered the door, and there they were—two officers to chew my teenage ass out. My mom was so seriously pissed. I mean—everyone in town knows everyone."

I am hanging on her every word. "What happened? Did they arrest you?"

"No. I was seventeen and had barely gotten my license." She says it with a smile, as if fondly recalling the memories. "We had to return the signs and apologize to the man who called the police on us. Do you have any idea how awkward it is to knock on someone's door to apologize for a crime that hadn't yet been committed?"

"Young and dumb?"

"Exactly."

The room falls quiet as I think of something more to say; the sounds of the movie fill the space between us. I glance at her, the corner of my mouth quirking up as an idea strikes.

"Want me to rub your feet?"

She narrows her eyes at me, suspicious. "You're offering a foot rub. Voluntarily."

I nod solemnly. "I'm an excellent multitasker. I can watch the movie and pamper you at the same time."

She snorts. "Pamper me?"

I hold up my palms so she can see them. "I have big, strong, capable hands. It would be a shame not to share them with the world."

She laughs, tossing a piece of popcorn at me.

I wiggle my fingers at her. "Come on, hand 'em over."

She bites her lip, clearly debating. Then, with an exaggerated sigh, she props her feet up in my lap. "Fine. But just so you know—if this is some elaborate scheme to tickle me, I will end you."

Chapter 9

Lucy

Oh God, his hands are magic.

Actual.

Magic.

The second his thumbs press into the arch of my foot, my head tips back like I've ascended to another plane of existence. It's embarrassing how good this feels. I can't stop the soft groan that slips out.

The moment the sound escapes, my eyes snap open in horror. Did I—?

Harris smirks without even looking up. That slow, knowing, infuriating smirk. "Good?" he asks, his voice dripping with smug satisfaction.

"Sure," I say quickly, trying to sound indifferent, but it comes out more like a squeak.

"Want me to stop?"

"No!" The word flies out of me like a reflex. I wince. Way too eager. Way too loud.

His smirk deepens, and I hate him. And by *hate*, I mean I want to crawl into his lap and—oh no. Nope. Stop that. Brain, behave.

"Didn't think so," he murmurs, his thumbs finding a new spot on my arch that nearly has me sliding off the couch in bliss.

I grip the armrest like it's a lifeline.

OhmyGod.

Oh. My. God.

"Relax," he says, glancing up at me with those warm, teasing eyes.

"I am relaxed," I lie, my voice trembling like a bad alibi as another shiver runs up my spine.

He raises an eyebrow like he knows I'm full of it. "If you say so."

Then his hands shift, his fingers kneading beneath my toes, and I swear the earth tilts off its axis.

"Mm-hmm," I hum, my head falling back against the couch as my whole body melts into a puddle. My brain is screaming at me to get it together, but my body? Oh no, my body is fully committed to this. This is heaven.

"You good?" His voice is laced with a cocky edge, like he knows exactly what he's doing to me—and he does.

He absolutely does.

"Fine," I whisper, though it's clear I'm anything but fine.

"Fine?" His thumb drags slowly along the ball of my foot, and a strangled whimper escapes me.

"Great!" I gasp, trying to sound composed and failing miserably.

"Amazing. Now can you stop talking for one second?" He chuckles, and the sound is low and rich, vibrating straight through me.

My eyes flutter shut. For a second, I let myself get lost in the rhythm of his touch—firm, deliberate, and way too intimate for something that's supposed to be platonic. Each press of his fingers sends warmth spiraling through my body, pooling in places I definitely shouldn't be thinking about right now.

Focus. This is a foot rub. A totally normal, innocent—oh my God, What is he doing with his thumb?

A soft, involuntary sigh slips out before I can stop it.

"Enjoying yourself?" His voice cuts through the haze, and my eyes pop open to find him grinning at me like the insufferable jerk he is.

"Shut up," I snap, sitting up straighter and pulling the blanket over my lap like it'll somehow hide my embarrassment—or the ridiculous heat crawling up my neck.

He laughs, leaning back like he's got all the time in the world, his hands still casually massaging my foot.

Damn him. Damn his stupid hands.

Strong. Calloused.

Big.

Oh no. My brain is wandering to places it should not go. Places like—stop it! This was supposed to be a relaxing movie night. Not whatever this is turning into.

And yet, as his fingers work their magic again, I can't seem to move.

In fact, I might never leave.

But then his thumb does *something*—a slow, circular pressure under the ball of my foot—and I swear to God, my soul leaves my body for a moment. My head falls back against the couch, and this time, I can't hold back the groan.

"Oh, wow," Harris says, mischievously. "I didn't realize I was *that* good."

I slap at his arm blindly, heat flooding my face. "Stop teasing me."

He catches my wrist easily, his grip warm and steady. "Teasing? I call it flirting."

I start to protest again, but the words die in my throat when his fingers glide up to my calf, kneading the muscle there with the same infuriating expertise.

Oh no. Nope.

This is risky territory.

"Harris," I warn, though it comes out far weaker than I intended.

"Hmm?" He looks up at me, all wide-eyed innocence, like he's not fully aware of what he's doing.

"You're . . ." My brain is scrambling for words, but all coherent thought has left the building. "You're making it worse."

"Worse?" His grin turns downright devilish. "You mean better?"

"No! I mean—" I gasp as his hands move higher, his thumbs digging into the back of my knee.

This is fine. Totally fine. Except it's absolutely *not* fine because now all I can think about is his hands on my thighs.

"If you want me to stop, you can say so," he says casually, like he's commenting on the weather and not driving me to the brink of insanity. "I can stop at any time."

"I—" The word catches in my throat because, let's be honest, I don't want him to stop.

Instead of answering, I pull the blanket up higher, covering my face completely. Maybe if I hide, this whole situation will reset itself. Maybe he'll forget I exist and leave me to die of mortification in peace.

But of course he doesn't. Instead, I hear his soft chuckle, followed by his hands returning to my foot, kneading away like this is another normal evening.

"Still good?" he teases, his voice warm and low.

"So good," I moan despite myself. "I admit it—you're ridiculously good at this. Happy now?"

Harris chuckles, low and smug. "I knew you'd come around."

I don't even have the energy to glare at him anymore. Every muscle in my body is dissolving under his touch, and honestly? I don't care. Let him have this victory. Let him think he's a foot-massage god.

He kind of is.

"This is dangerous, you know," I say, my voice softer now, more playful. "You're setting the bar way too high. What if I get addicted to this and demand a foot rub every time I see you?"

He glances up, his lips curling into that maddeningly cocky grin. "I don't mind. As long as you keep making those noises."

My cheeks flush, but this time, instead of shying away, I lean into it.

"Oh, so you like my noises?" I tease, arching an eyebrow at him.

"Maybe." His hands slide up to my calf, his thumbs pressing firmly into the muscle. "Depends. Got any other good ones?"

A laugh escapes me, light and unguarded, and I let my head fall back against the couch, the tension finally melting away.

"Those hands are magic." I finally say the words out loud that I've been thinking since his thumbs pressed into the pads of my feet, my teeth biting down on my lower lip. "I'd pay for this."

Harris's grin turns wicked, his thumbs still kneading my calf with maddening precision. "Oh, you'd pay for it, huh?"

"Absolutely," I say, my voice teasing, but there's a slightly breathless edge to it that I can't quite hide. "You've got talent, Bennett. Don't waste it on lumberjacking."

He chuckles, the sound low and smooth, as his fingers glide down, tracing slow, deliberate circles over my ankle. "I think I like the idea of you owing me more than a paycheck."

The way he says it—quiet and suggestive—sends a shiver skittering down my spine. My head tilts back again, and I let out a soft, contented sigh, the words slipping out before I can stop them. "Careful. I might start thinking this is foreplay."

His hands pause for a heartbeat; then he laughs—a deep, rumbling laugh that makes my stomach flip.

"Who says it's not?" he murmurs, his voice lower now, his hands moving again, slower this time, more deliberate.

I snap my head forward, meeting his eyes, and the look he gives me is so warm and full of amusement, I can't tell if he's actually joking or testing the waters.

My heart skips, and I decide to test him back. "Well, if it is . . ." I lean forward slightly, a playful smile tugging at my lips. "You're doing a damn good job."

His grin widens, but there's something sharper in his expression now, something that makes my breath catch. He shifts closer, his knee brushing mine, and his hands slide back up my leg, stopping below my knee.

"Good to know," he says softly, his thumbs pressing into my knee in a way that's both innocent and completely not at the same time.

The air between us is thick.

Heavy with unspoken words.

His hands still, resting on my leg, his fingers warm against my skin, and when I glance up at him, his eyes are locked on mine.

His hands linger, his fingers curling slightly, the heat of his touch radiating through me. I can feel the weight of his gaze, steady and unwavering.

"Tell me to stop," he murmurs, his voice low and thick, a quiet invitation rather than a demand.

I don't say a word.

I won't tell him to stop, because I do not want him to, even if I can't say the words out loud.

My body betrays me, leaning slightly closer as if drawn to him by some invisible force.

His hands move, gliding up slowly, teasingly, until his palms rest above my knee. The pressure is firm but careful, his thumbs brushing lazy circles over my skin. It's intimate, dangerously so, and I don't want it to end.

"You're quiet," he says, a faint smirk tugging at his lips. "That's not like you."

"I'm thinking," I reply, my voice barely above a whisper.

"About?" His hands shift again, sliding a fraction higher, and I suck in a sharp breath.

"About how unfair this is."

His brow arches, the smirk deepening. "Unfair?"

"Mm-hmm." My lips curve into a slow smile as I lift my chin, meeting his gaze head-on. "You get to be the one in control, and I'm melting into the couch."

Like butter.

Harris's chuckle is quiet, warm, but there's a flicker of something darker in his eyes now. "You like it."

He's not wrong.

Not even a little.

His hands inch higher, fingers skimming along the curve of my thigh, and every coherent thought I've ever had flies out the window.

The tension between us crackles like a live wire, and I swear the air in the room feels heavier, charged.

"This okay?" he asks, his voice softer now, his touch still but present, his gaze searching mine.

Better than okay. I nod, throat too dry to speak.

My body responds as I shift a little closer, the space between us shrinking by the second.

The corner of his mouth lifts in a crooked grin, but there's no teasing in his expression now—a quiet intensity that makes my heart race. His hands slide up again, slow and deliberate, until they rest on my upper thighs.

I tilt my head, my lips parting, and the faintest, most teasing smile tugs at my mouth. "So. Are you gonna kiss me, or are you gonna keep pretending this is all about a massage?"

His laughter is soft, a low rumble that makes my stomach flip, but his hands don't move. "Maybe I'm waiting for you to ask."

His challenge sends a spark shooting through me, and suddenly, I don't feel like teasing anymore.

"Consider this me asking."

Chapter 10

Harris

I don't think she realizes what she's doing to me.

The way she's sitting there, her legs still draped over mine, her voice soft but steady as she says, "Consider this me asking."

For a second, I don't move. I stare at her, trying to wrap my head around the fact that *she* said it—that Lucy has the balls to ask me to kiss her.

Most women act coy. Or play hard to get. Or are so overtly sexy to make it clear that sex is what they want.

They usually don't come out and say the words.

Lucy watches me, lips curved into a smile, like she knows she's thrown me completely off my game.

Like she's daring me to make the next move.

God help me, I'm not strong enough to resist her.

I let my hands slide a little farther up her thighs, feeling the warmth of her skin under my palms, and lean in slowly, my eyes locked on hers. Her breath catches—the smallest sound, barely audible—sending a jolt straight through me.

"You sure about this?" I murmur, my voice low, rougher than I mean it to be.

Her smile widens a fraction, and she tilts her chin up another inch. “I wouldn’t have asked if I wasn’t.”

There it is again—that quiet confidence that drives me absolutely insane. It’s like she knows she’s got me wrapped around her finger, like she’s been waiting for this moment as much as I have.

I don’t give her a chance to take back the words.

I close the distance between us in one smooth motion, my lips brushing against hers, soft and slow at first. Testing. Playful. But the second she sighs into the kiss, her hands sliding up to grip the front of my shirt, something inside me snaps.

I tilt my head, deepening the kiss, my hands tightening on her thighs as I pull her closer. She tastes like trouble—sweet and sharp and addictive as hell—and I know I’m done for.

Her fingers curl into my shirt, pulling me closer still, and suddenly, it’s not enough. The space between us, the slow and careful pace—I want more. I want *her*.

But then she lets out this quiet little sound against my mouth—half laugh, half moan—and it’s like she’s grounding me all over again.

Reminding me who I’m dealing with.

Lucy.

Badass.

The boss.

She is in charge, and I love it.

“You have no idea what you’re doing to me,” I say, my voice barely above a whisper.

Her laugh is soft, breathless, and entirely too smug. “I think I have some idea.”

I shake my head, grinning despite myself, because of course she’d say that. Of course she’d be completely unfazed while I’m over here trying not to lose my damn mind.

“You’re wicked,” I murmur, my thumb brushing absently over the curve of her thigh.

“Only to you,” she quips, and I can’t help but laugh.

Her words hang in the air, playful and sharp, but there's something else there too—something that makes my chest tighten. Before I can think too much about it, she leans in, capturing my mouth again, *and just like that*, I'm done thinking altogether.

This kiss is different—bolder, hungrier. Her hands slide up, tangling in my hair, and a soft sound escapes her that has my grip tightening on her thighs.

She shifts closer, knees pressing against my sides, and suddenly, I'm sinking back into the couch, her weight following me down.

"Wait a second—" I manage, but the words are lost as her lips move to my jaw, trailing heat down to the corner of my mouth, then back again.

She pulls back to smirk at me, her cheeks flushed, her breath shallow. "What?" she asks, her tone equal parts sweet and teasing. "You said I'm wicked. Let me pretend that I am."

I don't get a chance to respond because her hands are on my shoulders now, pushing me gently until my back hits the cushions. She moves with me, her legs straddling my hips as she settles on top, and the shift in control is so seamless, so deliberate, it leaves me reeling.

"Jesus, Luce," I murmur, my hands instinctively finding her waist, anchoring her in place.

"Luce," she repeats. "Some of my best friends call me that."

"Does that mean we're friends?" I ask, my thumbs brushing soft, lazy circles over her waist. There's a teasing edge to my voice, but my heart is pounding harder than I'd like to admit.

She leans in closer, her lips quirking into a half smile. "Friends?" she repeats, her voice light, almost mocking. "I don't kiss my friends like this."

Before I can reply, she dips her head, her mouth finding mine again, and any semblance of control I thought I had vanishes. Her kiss is deliberate, commanding, like she's making sure I know exactly who's in charge here. Her weight on me, her hair falling around us like a curtain—it's too much and not enough all at once.

"You're enjoying this."

"Guilty," she says, unrepentant, her fingers tracing idle patterns over my shirt. Her gaze flickers down, lingering on my lips before snapping back up to my eyes. "But so are you."

"Obviously."

I'm a goner. She knows it.

But instead of saying anything, I let my hand slide up to the back of her neck, pulling her back down to me, and for a moment, there's nothing but the sound of our breaths mingling, the warmth of her body against mine.

I don't know how far this is going to go, and honestly?

I don't care.

Instinctively, my hands slide from her waist to the hem of her sweatshirt. My fingers pause there, hesitating, but when she shifts slightly, pressing herself closer to me, it's all the encouragement I need.

I slip my hands under the fabric, the warmth of her skin against my palms sending a jolt straight through me as they move higher, tracing the line of her ribs, and the sound she makes has me ready to lose my damn mind.

My hands shift, fingers skimming over her bra, the thin fabric doing nothing to dull the aching in my pants.

My dick is so fucking hard.

Her breath catches again, and this time, she breaks the kiss, leaning back slightly, her head tilting to look down at me, her cheeks flushed, her lips swollen.

My lips feel swollen too.

She moves again, more deliberate this time, and I can't stop the low groan that escapes me. The sound seems to spur her on, her body pressing harder against mine as her lips find my neck, her teeth grazing the sensitive skin under my jaw.

"Fuck," I mutter, my hands sliding lower, gripping her hips as I guide her movements.

The fabric of my jeans feels like sandpaper against me, but I don't care. Not when she's making those soft, breathless noises that go straight to my head, and lower.

Her hands are everywhere—my chest, my shoulders, my hair—like she can't get enough of me, like she's as desperate for this as I am. She tilts her hips, grinding against me, and my head falls back against the couch, my breath coming in short, uneven bursts.

"Lucy," I manage, my voice hoarse, but I don't even know what I'm trying to say.

Her name is the only thing that makes sense, the only thing that grounds me as she moves against me, slow and purposeful, the heat between us building with every passing second.

Her hands slide down, gripping my shoulders as she rocks her hips again, her movements gaining a little more urgency. I can feel her through the thin fabric of her leggings, the pressure sending sparks of pleasure shooting through me, and it takes everything I have not to lose it right there.

Her head falls forward, her lips brushing against my ear as she whispers, "*You feel so fucking amazing.*"

The words hit me like a freight train, my hands dragging her closer, pressing her more firmly against me.

"You're killing me," I breathe, my voice rough, and she lets out a soft laugh, the sound muffled against my neck.

"That's the point." Her breath is warm against my skin, and then she's moving again, her rhythm matching the frantic pounding of my pulse.

Every roll of her hips, every brush of her hands, every breathless sound she makes—it's consuming and overwhelming, and I'm completely, hopelessly lost.

"I feel sixteen," she says. "The last time I dry humped someone was in high school."

"Same." I was having sex at an early age but indulged in the occasional dry-fucking session.

Her laugh is quiet but throaty, like she's savoring every second of this. She shifts, the pressure perfect; my hands grip her tighter, my fingers digging into her waist as I try—and fail—to keep my composure.

"I can't believe we're doing this," she murmurs, lips grazing the shell of my ear, her voice sending a shiver straight down my spine.

"Believe it," I manage, though my words are strained, almost lost under the sound of my own breathing. "I'm going to f-fucking c-come in my pants."

"I would be so flattered if you did," she says, lips brushing against my neck. "I can feel how hard you are."

Like a rock.

I laugh, low and rough, my hands sliding up her back, pulling her even closer still . . .

"I'm gonna lose it," I admit, my voice rough, and she laughs again, soft and breathless, her lips brushing against mine in a kiss that's all heat and desperation.

"Me too," she whispers.

Her hands tangle in my hair, tugging. Sending a bolt of heat through me.

I curse under my breath, meeting her gaze.

Her eyes are bright, wild, and full of something that feels like freedom—like she's ready to jump and take me with her.

That's it. That's all it takes.

Fuck.

Fuck, fuck . . .

"Oh shit," I groan, the words catching in my throat as the hot rush of release hits me, thick and undeniable. My body jerks, and I pull back, mortified. Heat floods my face, and I press my palms to my eyes like I can somehow erase what just happened.

I keep my hands over my face, not daring to look at her, but I can feel her eyes on me, feel the tension hanging heavy in the air.

She pauses, her eyes widening for a moment before her lips quirk into a teasing smile. "Did you just—?"

"Come in my pants? Yeah," I clarify, running a hand through my hair, mortified. "Not my finest moment, I know."

Her laugh is soft, warm, not mocking in the slightest. "You're adorable," she says, brushing her fingers over my cheek. "So relatable."

Adorable.

So relatable . . .

Every man's dream come true.

I groan, burying my face in her shoulder, half laughing at myself. "You're being way too nice about this."

She tilts my chin up, her smile softening. "You think I'm done with you? Not even close." Her tone is teasing, but there's heat in her gaze that sends a fresh jolt through me despite everything. "But maybe we take this slow for now."

I groan, leaning back and covering my face with my hands. "I think I broke the record for most embarrassing moment."

She laughs softly, pulling my hands away. "Come on. That can't be the most embarrassing thing that's happened to you. Besides"—her gaze drops to my lips, and she bites her own—"I'd say it's a compliment."

I narrow my eyes at her teasing grin. "You're enjoying this way too much."

"Maybe a smidge." Lucy traces my jaw with the tip of her finger. "And can I say: You're ridiculously hot when you're flustered."

"Hot as in good looking and sexy, or hot as in sweaty and gross?"

"Sexy." She hesitates. "And a little sweaty."

That's all I need to hear.

Hefting myself up off the couch, I tug my shirt down self-consciously over my semi-boner, hoping she doesn't notice—or worse, that she absolutely does.

My face burns either way.

"On that note, I need a minute to clean up."

Her eyes sparkle with mischief as she leans, one hand draped lazily over the back of the couch. She's watching me like a cat who's cornered a mouse, completely unbothered.

"Don't take too long. I might miss you." She pauses to tap her chin. *"Might."*

"Seriously," I call over my shoulder. "You're insufferable."

"You like it," she replies, her voice singsongy and full of amusement.

In the bathroom, I shut the door and let out a long breath. Turning to the mirror, I catch sight of my reflection—flushed, disheveled, and still way too keyed up for my own good.

"Get it together," I mutter to myself, running a hand through my hair.

I splash water on my face, the coolness shocking me out of the lustful haze she's left me in. Glancing at my reflection again, I shake my head.

Red cheeks. Messy hair. Dilated pupils.

"She's going to be the death of me," I mumble to no one. "And quit acting like you've never felt a woman's tits before."

So embarrassing.

If I come in my pants from five minutes of dry humping, how long would I last inside her?

Don't even want to think about it . . .

I would never hear the end of it.

I pull down my pajama bottoms and stare inside. Push them all the way down my hips, the sticky mess gobbed to my underwear and leg as I yank them off. Ball them up and toss them to the corner of the bathroom.

The thought of leaving them there crosses my mind; I groan and pick them up, throw them into the basket instead. No point in risking a follow-up roasting session if she finds them later.

In the hamper they go, banished to the depths of laundry purgatory . . . take a washcloth and wipe up the residue stuck to my inner thighs.

I need clean bottoms. I can't waltz out there with my nads hanging out. After snatching a pair of pants from the hook behind the door, I pull them on.

Taking a deep breath, I open the door. Lucy is still on the couch, sprawled out with her legs tucked beneath her, scrolling on her phone.

Her head lifts when she hears me, and the second her eyes land on my bottoms, her lips curl into a sly grin.

"Huge fan of the gray sweatpants."

I grunt. "They're keeping me decent."

Lucy's eyes rake over me from head to toe, landing on my middle section. My dick. It's not a casual once-over either—it's deliberate and sets every nerve in my body on edge.

I should head to my room, put on some damn pants, and pretend this never happened.

That's the logical choice.

But logic left my brain the second she gave me that look.

I take a step forward, and her brows lift slightly in curiosity. Before I can second-guess myself, I'm kneeling in front of her on the plush carpet, hands spreading her thighs apart.

She gasps.

Doesn't pull away, beautiful blue eyes widening as my palms gently slide over her flesh.

"What are you . . . ?" she whispers as she watches, transfixed, lips parting, her phone slipping from her hand and landing on the couch cushion beside her with a soft thud.

"Your turn," I say, my voice low, teasing, as I look up at her through my lashes.

For a moment, the room is silent except for the sound of our breathing, the air between us charged with something I can't put into words. My hands stay where they are, waiting, giving her the choice to decide what happens next.

Chapter 11

Lucy

Is he about to do what I think he's going to do?

'Cause that would be awesome.

I haven't had a guy go down on me in forever—can't remember the last time.

The thought sends a rush of heat through me, breath catching in my throat as his hands slide a little higher, his thumbs brushing over the inseam of my leggings. He's watching me so intently, his dark eyes searching mine like he's waiting for permission.

I should say something—maybe crack a joke to break the tension—but the words stick in my throat.

Instead, my hands tighten on the couch cushions, my heart pounding so loud I'm surprised he can't hear it.

"Lucy," he says, the needy sound of his voice sending a shiver down my spine.

"Mmm?" I manage to reply, my voice shaky despite my best efforts to sound composed.

"I'm about to eat you out so hard you're going to forget every guy who came before me," he murmurs, his voice rough, full of confidence, and utterly devastating.

Oh.

Oh . . .

That's all I can manage.

His hands slide up my legs, steady and deliberate, pausing at the waistband of my leggings. He raises an eyebrow, giving me one last moment to stop him, but I don't move—I can't.

I nod, a quick, jerky movement that's all the permission he needs.

His fingers hook into the fabric, and with a practiced ease, he starts to tug them down, his touch grazing my skin as he goes. The sensation sends a ripple of goose bumps up my arms, and I bite my lip, my heart thundering in my chest.

Yes . . .

I want this so bad.

I'm giddy with excitement.

So glad I shaved my legs this morning.

I release a shaky breath, leaning back into the cushions as he works the leggings off completely, then tosses them to the floor.

The room feels warmer, smaller, like it's closing in on us, but in the best possible way. His hands slide back up my legs, lingering, exploring, like he's mapping out every inch of me.

I watch, mesmerized, as he reaches the waistband of my baby blue lace panties, his fingers slipping beneath the fabric with a confidence that sends a shiver through me.

"You're shaking," he murmurs, his voice low and steady, though there's a hint of amusement in his tone. "I take that as a good sign."

"I'm not shaking," I manage, fingers tightening on the couch cushions as his hands move, sliding the fabric aside. "You're staring."

He glances up, a slow, crooked smile spreading across his face. "Can you blame me?" Harris replies, his tone teasing but laced with something deeper. "You have the most beautiful pussy."

Beautiful pussy . . .

I bite my lip, unsure of what to say—if there's anything to say at all. He doesn't seem to be waiting for a response. His focus shifts back to what he's doing, his movements purposeful and unbearably slow.

I swallow hard, my fingers loosening their grip on the cushions as I try to breathe and focus on the way his touch feels, on the way he's looking at me like he's a starving man and I'm his next meal.

"Perfect," he whispers. Grins. "You're not going to be able to walk."

Oh . . .

A shaky laugh escapes me, but it's cut short as his lips brush against my inner thigh.

It's soft at first—deliberate—like he's savoring every moment. My head tips back, and I release a gasp, hands slipping from the cushions to thread through his hair.

Harris's movements are slow and unhurried, as if he has all the time in the world to drive me absolutely insane.

He licks the sensitive skin on my inner thigh. Kisses it.

His mouth presses a series of soft, maddeningly gentle kisses up my thigh, each one sending a fresh wave of heat coursing through me. When his lips finally touch where I want him most, I can't help the broken sound that escapes my throat, fingers still running through his hair.

He doesn't stop, doesn't pause to tease.

I lift my head to look at him, hands clutching at his hair.

"Oh my God," I gasp, my voice trembling as my body tightens in response to him.

"Look at me," he demands, voice low and commanding, the vibrations of it sending shivers through me.

My gaze drops to meet his, and the sight of him between my legs, his dark eyes burning with desire.

He sucks.

Sucks more, as if his life depends on it. As if it's his job.

I watch, eyes glassing over. Face flushed.

Legs spread.

I am wanton, and it feels incredible.

"Yes . . ."

The pressure inside me coils tighter and tighter until it finally snaps, and I shatter completely, my body trembling. He doesn't stop, drawing out every last ounce of my release, his hands firm and grounding on my skin.

Aftershocks ripple through me, leaving me utterly spent and weightless.

He doesn't move right away, his lips brushing kisses against my inner thigh.

"You're so sexy." Harris slides his hands gently up my thighs, caressing them—going from teasing and confident to soft and reverent.

"I'm so limp right now." I nervously giggle.

"I'm not."

Not sure what to say to that.

I stare at the ceiling, blinking rapidly, trying to appear nonchalant while my brain scrambles to process the situation. Is this a date?

I shift slightly, feeling the absence of my panties like a glaring neon sign over my head. Where *are* they?

The floor?

The couch?

Oh God, what if they're on the coffee table? I act casual, leaning around Harris's broad shoulder to get a glimpse of the living room, my eyes darting over the couch, the floor, anywhere my underwear could have landed in my frantic scramble to get undressed.

But there's nothing. No sign of them.

"Looking for these?"

He's holding my underwear with his index finger, swinging them ever so slightly, a devilish smirk on his face.

"Yep," I say, nodding furiously. "Thanks. I'll—" I lunge, but he pulls them out of reach, his grin turning downright sinful.

"Please. Allow me."

I swallow as I watch Harris deliberately slide my underwear up my legs, the soft fabric brushing against my calves, knees, *thighs*. His hands are warm and firm, his touch just this side of too slow, and the way he looks up at me through his lashes makes my breath stutter.

"There we go," he murmurs, his thumbs grazing the skin at the tops of my thighs before he tugs the waistband back into place, his hands lingering just a moment too long.

My entire body is on fire, and he knows it.

Harris rises to his feet, that devastating grin still firmly in place. "Now," he says, his thumb tracing a lazy line along my hip, "we need to finish our movie. And we've barely touched the food."

Oh.

Right.

The movie and snacks.

Clearly—since he's putting my clothes back on—he's not planning to strip me *completely* naked and have his way with me on the couch. Oddly, I'm somewhat disappointed—is that weird?

"Yeah, totally. The movie. Pizza." My voice comes out awkward and a little too chipper as I snatch my bottoms from the floor and pull them up my hips. I'm not about to sit here in only my thong.

Harris leans back, stretching out like he owns the place—and grabs the remote from the armrest. "You want to start over from the beginning or pick up where we left off?"

"Uh . . ." I glance at the screen, where the characters are bickering as they enter a restaurant for dinner. "Where we left off is fine."

He is so close.

Smells so damn good, *and now I know what his mouth feels like . . .*

I shift slightly, tucking my legs beneath me in a poor attempt to create space between us. But Harris notices, of course. His arm dips lower, his fingers brushing my shoulder. It's barely a touch, but it sends a ripple of heat down my spine.

Wow. Who knew the smallest touch could create this much chaos?

"I don't do this kind of thing," I admit quietly, the words slipping out before I can stop them.

"What kind of thing?" His brow furrows slightly.

I gesture vaguely between us. "Fooling around with people who take my classes."

He chuckles, the sound low and warm. "We met before I was in your class, remember?"

I roll my eyes. "I meant guys I don't know how to *handle*."

He's amused. Grins. "I'll let you handle me any way you want while I'm in town."

My heart sinks—an involuntary, unwelcome reaction that surprises me. I shouldn't care. *This is casual.* Temporary. I'm not foolish enough to think it could be more.

He studies my profile while I chew. "Lucy," he says, his voice coaxing. "What's going on in that head of yours?"

Nothing.

Everything.

I glance at him, his expression open and curious, and for a second, I consider brushing him off. But something about the way he's looking at me—earnestly, as if he actually gives a shit—makes me pause.

I go for honesty.

"I'm . . ." I clear my throat, searching for the right words. "Trying to figure out how this works."

"This?" He raises an eyebrow.

"This *fling*."

"Fling," he deadpans, lips twitching. "You're so cute. Who said this had to be a fling?"

He's teasing me. I can see it in the way his eyes are crinkling at the corners.

"Um—the fact that you live in *Arizona*?"

He laughs softly, the sound low and rumbling, and for some reason, it makes my stomach flip. "Fair point," he admits, leaning forward to rest his elbows on his knees. "But that doesn't mean this has to be meaningless."

I narrow my eyes at him skeptically. "You're telling me you think a few days of . . . *whatever this is* means something to you?"

He is so full of shit!

Harris's head tilts as he considers my question. "I'm saying it could. If we want it to."

I'm thrown off by his candor.

He says it like it's the easiest thing in the world, like the logistics don't matter. Like I'm not here and he's not there and it wouldn't be a massive pain in the ass to *try*.

"Harris," I start, trying to inject some logic into this before we get swept up in a discussion about it. "I repeat: You live in Arizona. We barely know each other. This has *temporary* written all over it."

"And?" He shrugs, like it's no big deal. "Why does temporary have to mean it's not worth it?"

I blink, pizza halfway to my mouth.

I stare at him, my mouth opening and closing as I try to come up with a rebuttal.

The truth?

I don't have one.

Chapter 12

Harris

Is there any realm of possibility where you want to spend the night with me?

I'm in the bathroom again, taking a piss, practicing the line because Lucy isn't a normal woman—she's complicated. Not easily swayed. And cool as fuck.

I have to wonder: If she knew who I was—one of the douchey football players that's invaded the town—would she be tripping all over herself to get in my pants?

Probably not.

Lucy's not the type. She's too sharp for that, too good at calling out bullshit. She's the kind of woman who wouldn't let a guy like me coast by on charm alone—not without putting up one hell of a fight.

And honestly? That's part of her appeal.

I flush, wash my hands, and catch my reflection in the mirror.

"Jesus Christ," I mutter, leaning in closer. "What the hell is going on here?"

My hair's a mess, sticking up in every direction from where I've raked my fingers through it a hundred times tonight. There's a spot of marinara sauce on the collar of my T-shirt from the pizza, and my jawline's beginning to show signs of a five-o'clock shadow.

Basically, I look like a guy who stress-cleaned his entire cottage for a woman and played a bonding game with his teammates.

"What am I fucking doing?" I slap the countertop for emphasis.

Leaning forward, I brace my hands on the sink, staring myself down. "You've got this, Bennett. She likes you—probably. Or she hates you. Either way, you're not going to find out by hiding in the damn bathroom."

What the hell am I saying? Why am I talking to myself?

"Get it together, Bennett," I growl at myself, jabbing a finger at my reflection. "You're a professional athlete. You've been tackled by grown men weighing three hundred pounds. You've faced down players who wanted to *kill* you. And now you're hiding in the bathroom because you're too chicken to ask a woman to spend the night?"

My reflection doesn't answer, which is so rude.

I swipe at my face with a towel and square my shoulders.

"All right. You're doing this. You've got this. Don't be weird. Ask her to stay the night. No pressure, no expectations—a casual, totally cool suggestion from one adult to another. You've got this."

I give myself a thumbs-up.

"And for the love of God," I add, pointing one last time. "Stop talking to yourself like a lunatic. She can probably hear you."

With that final pep talk, I push the door open.

Lucy is curled up on the couch like she owns the place. Her hoodie is pulled up around her shoulders snugly, her legs tucked under her, and she's scrolling mindlessly through her phone with the kind of focus that tells me she hasn't sensed me standing here yet.

No big deal.

"Hey." I step into the living room. "Did you miss me?"

She glances up. "Oh, hey you. Did you leave the room? I didn't notice."

Her eyes are twinkling.

My shoulders relax.

The clock on the wall ticks loudly, despite the television being on, each second dragging by.

"Ouch. Brutal." I flop down on the couch next to her, keeping a careful amount of space between us—though it kills me not to lean in closer. "And here I thought we were bonding."

"We were." She sets her phone down on the armrest, tilting her head. "You ruined it by leaving for an entire ten minutes."

Oh shit—so she is aware how long I was fucking around in the bathroom.

Awkward.

"What were you doing in there for so long anyway? Talking to yourself? Staring at your reflection?"

She's teasing, but my ears burn regardless.

"What? Pfft. *No.* Who talks to themselves in the mirror?"

"Uh-huh." Her smile widens. "Sure you weren't."

I groan, scrubbing a hand over my face. "Fine. Maybe I was—hypothetically—mentally preparing for something. Is that a crime?"

"Depends." She leans forward, resting her chin on her hand. "What were you mentally preparing for?"

Her eyes are too sharp, too curious, and it throws me off balance. I glance at the TV for a second, pretending to be engrossed in the movie.

I take a breath and say it. "I was gonna suggest you stay over. If you want."

Lucy blinks, caught off guard. "Stay over?"

"Well, if you're not too traumatized, there's always the chance for an encore." I clear my throat, scratching the back of my neck. "You could stay. Tonight."

Her eyebrows shoot up, her phone lowering slightly. "What?"

"You heard me." I meet her gaze, praying I don't look as nervous as I feel. "You don't have to, obviously. But if you're comfortable—and if you want to—I'd like it if you stayed."

The words hang there, and for a split second, I swear I see her cheeks flush.

Her mouth opens. Closes.

For once, Lucy—the woman who *always* has a comeback—is speechless.

I realize, in that moment, that I'm completely screwed. And that's when the nerves creep in.

"Or, you know—forget I said anything," I add quickly, trying to sound casual as my heart pounds like a damn jackhammer. "It's totally fine if you need to go. I thought—"

Then I do what I do best: *double down.*

"I mean, I can think of a lot worse ways to spend a night." I sound like a douchebag. "You. Me. No interruptions."

She arches an eyebrow, unimpressed. "Interruptions like *sleep*?"

Exactly.

"I'm not sure if I'm allowed to fraternize with the lumberjack hired help—Annabelle has no idea I'm here. She may want you in bed early so you can be at the lake, practicing."

"Fuck practicing. I'm a professional. She has no faith whatsoever in my logrolling abilities." I pause. "The good news is, now she also has me chopping wood."

My date considers this new information. "Are they giving out participation trophies, too, or is the pile of logs supposed to be your reward?"

I narrow my eyes. "Awards? Don't get me excited—I love those." Especially the shiny trophy they give you after a Super Bowl win. I stretch out, draping my arm casually over the back of the couch. "The way I see it, chopping wood is an art form. One swing for a split down the middle. Takes patience," I boast. *"Precision."*

Her eyebrows lift. "Patience? Precision? Wow."

I fake a wounded look, pressing a hand to my chest. "You think I don't have it in me?"

I keep reminding myself that we haven't met before this week and she doesn't know what I do for a living.

Which suits me fine.

Nothing has been more entertaining than pretending to be a fucking lumberjack, of all things.

"Oh, I think you've got a lot in you." Her voice is smooth, a touch teasing, and the way she leans forward slightly makes my heart thump louder than it should. "But patience? That's not the first thing I'd associate with you."

"What do you see when you look at me?" *Curious minds want to know.*

She studies me for a few quiet moments before saying "I see someone who can't take himself seriously for more than two seconds."

She wounds me.

For real.

It's like she doesn't know me at all! If only she knew what it took to win a Bowl game. Or get drafted.

So rude . . .

My butthole stings, if I'm being honest.

"Wrong," I announce, punctuating the word with a buzzer sound. "I can be serious. *Dead* serious." I straighten, giving her my best stone-cold look.

I lean forward, resting my elbows on my knees, letting my grin soften. "All right, since you think I'm all jokes and no depth, ask me something. Anything. I'll prove you wrong."

Lucy tilts her head, that playful sparkle in her eye still there, but I can tell she's curious now. "Anything?"

"Anything," I confirm, laying down the challenge with a shrug. "Make it count."

She bites her lip, thinking—*God help me, that bottom lip*—and asks, "What's the most serious thing you've ever done?"

I pause, caught off guard. I didn't think she'd go straight for the deep end. My first instinct is to brush it off with a joke, but for some reason, I don't.

I lean into the question, running a hand over my jaw, my voice dropping a little as I say, "The most serious thing I've ever done? That's easy. When I was a kid, I took care of my mom after my dad walked out."

Her smirk vanishes. She blinks at me, surprised. *"What?"*

"Yeah." I shrug, trying to keep it casual, even though the memory still stings. "My dad bailed when I was eight. Left my mom with three kids, a mortgage, and not much else. She worked her ass off—two jobs, sometimes three. Barely had time to breathe, let alone deal with me and my sisters. So I stepped up. Made sure my sisters got to school, did their homework, didn't burn the house down. You know, the usual stuff."

"Right. The usual stuff." Lucy stares at me, her playful demeanor completely replaced by something. "That's a lot of responsibility for an eight-year-old."

No shit.

I also had to get myself to and from football practice and sign myself up for camps because Mom would forget to do it. And when we didn't have the money, I was the kid who begged the coaches to let me practice with the team anyway.

Whatever. It made me the man I am today—and made me appreciate what I've earned.

Nothing was more satisfying than retiring my mother the day I signed my contract with Arizona.

Nothing.

"Yeah. It was a lot." I shrug again, memories coming at me all at once. "You do what you've gotta do, right? It wasn't all bad. I learned how to cook—well, mostly how not to set spaghetti on fire. And I figured out laundry, though that was always a mess. Turns out you're not supposed to mix dark colors and light. Who knew?"

She lets out a soft laugh, but her eyes don't leave mine. They're softer now, more serious. "I never would have guessed."

"It's not exactly first-date material, is it?" I scoff. "'Hi, I'm Harris. My dad is a deadbeat, and I know how to fold a fitted sheet.' Such a panty dropper, right?"

"Actually? Yes." She leans forward, mirroring me, her elbows on her knees. "You're full of surprises."

"You have no idea." The words come out quieter than I intend, but I don't bother covering it up. For once, I don't feel like putting on a show. "Don't let this ruin your image of me as a goofy, carefree lumberjack. I've got a reputation to protect."

Her nod is slow. Lucy settles back onto the couch again, and I watch her raise a glass to her lip and take a sip. "I don't think it ruins anything. If anything, it adds a bit of complexity."

"Complexity," I repeat, raising an eyebrow. "Is that a good thing or a bad thing?"

"Don't know," she teases, but her eyes—those eyes—say otherwise. "Haven't decided yet."

I lean closer, dropping my voice low. "Well, I don't have a ton of time to convince you." Pause. "What about you?" I ask. "What's the most serious thing you've done?"

"Most serious thing I've done?" she repeats, tipping her head back against the couch.

A faint smile plays at her lips that doesn't quite reach her eyes as she considers my question in kind, like she's trying to come up with something that sounds as impressively complicated as my answer, but nothing comes.

"Honestly?" She shrugs. "I don't know. I've never done anything big or crazy. Never left my town, never packed up and started over somewhere new."

I blink. "Seriously? You've never lived anywhere else?"

She shakes her head. "Nope. Born and raised right here. Went to school here, got my first job here, and somehow I'm still here."

"Wow." It slips out before I can stop it, but I mean it. "I don't know if I could do that. I mean, staying in one place that long? Doesn't that feel—I don't know—limiting?"

"Sometimes," she admits quietly. "But it's home. My family's here. My friends. Everything I know."

I study her for a moment, trying to reconcile the fearless, quick-witted woman in front of me with someone who's never stepped outside the bubble of her hometown. "So you've never even thought about leaving? Not even once?"

She hesitates, fingers brushing the edge of her glass. "I've thought about it," she says softly. "But thinking about it and actually doing it are two very different things. And I don't think I'd even know where to start."

I nod slowly, letting her words sink in. There's something raw and real about the way she says it, and I can tell she's not looking for pity or judgment.

She's being honest, and that's what I asked for.

"For what it's worth," I say, leaning forward, "you strike me as someone who could figure it out if you wanted to. You're smart, resourceful, and let's face it, a little intimidating when you want to be. I don't think there's much you couldn't handle."

She blinks at me, surprised. "You think I'm intimidating?"

"Obviously. Beautiful, confident women always are."

Lucy looks taken aback by that comment too. "Beautiful and confident?" She repeats the words like she's rolling them around in her mouth, testing how they taste. "You really lay it on thick, don't you?"

"Hey, I call it like I see it. Plus, it's not laying it on thick if it's true."

"Thank you," she whispers. "I feel like such a dipshit not having done anything . . . I don't know. Adventurous."

"Everyone has their version of adventure. It doesn't have to be skydiving or jet-setting across the world. Sometimes it's just about stepping outside your comfort zone."

Lucy lets out an unladylike snort, fingers fiddling with the edge of her hoodie sleeve. "You sound like a motivational speaker."

"I try." I grin.

"I have a confession to make," she blurts out. "I am so small town that I live above my parents' detached garage." Lucy cringes. "Is that bad?"

My head tilts back when I laugh.

"Wait," I say, still chuckling. "Above the garage? Like a real-life, fully functioning apartment or are we talking a futon and mini-fridge kind of situation?"

Lucy presses her lips together. "Somewhere in between. There's a bed, a kitchenette, and the world's tiniest bathroom. It's cozy, okay?"

"Cozy," I repeat, leaning forward with a grin. "Is that the word we're using?"

"Don't make fun of me!" She swats my arm, her cheeks flushing. "I like it there. It's private, and it's not like I need a lot of space."

I lift my hands in surrender. "I'm not judging. Honestly, it sounds kind of great. No annoying neighbors—plus, you can probably guilt your parents into delivering food right to your door."

"I never said no annoying neighbors—sometimes my parents drive me nuts, especially my dad, who's nosier than my mom." She grins, the tension melting from her shoulders. "Mom brings me leftovers all the time. I think she feels bad for me."

"Why would she feel bad?" I ask, genuinely curious.

"Because I never left? Everyone else went off to school, doing big, exciting things—college, careers, traveling—and I'm still here, living over a garage and teaching yoga classes."

I watch her carefully, noting the way her gaze drops to her lap, like she's bracing herself for me to say something stupid or patronizing.

I don't.

Instead, I lean back against the couch, arms stretching across the backrest.

"You ever think maybe they're the ones missing out?" I ask, my voice calm, steady. "I mean, yeah, traveling and careers are cool and all, but there's something to be said for staying close to the people you love. Being home."

"Home," she repeats softly, testing the word.

I nod. "Am I allowed to visit this above-the-garage apartment of yours, or is it strictly a no-lumberjack zone?"

"I'll think about it." Lucy laughs. "What about you? What's your living situation? Give me a visual."

Do I tell her the truth: that my living situation is a McMansion perched in the hills? Or do I dial it down to something less . . . obnoxious? Something that doesn't scream *I have way, way too much money and no clue what to do with it*?

"Shit." The word slips out before I can stop it, and Lucy eagle-eyes me curiously.

"That bad, huh?" she teases, tucking her legs under herself like she's settling in for a bedtime story. "Come on, don't hold out on me. I gave you my above-the-garage confession—what's yours?"

I rub the back of my neck, stalling. "It's not bad. Just not small-town relatable."

"Pfft." Her brows lift in challenge. "Try me."

There's no way to explain this without sounding like a total tool, so I blurt out: "All right: a sprawling modern house. Too many rooms for one person. A kitchen I barely use with ridiculously expensive appliances. A pool I didn't want taking up the entire backyard but somehow ended up with."

Her eyes narrow, like she's trying to gauge if I'm screwing with her or not. "A *pool*?"

"Yep. And not just any pool. It's heated. With an infinity edge."

Her jaw drops, but instead of the awe I was bracing for, she busts out laughing. Full-on, head-tilted-back, bellyaching laughter.

"Oh my God," she gasps. "For a second, I thought you were serious. You live in a mansion with an infinity pool? That's hilarious."

I am stunned into silence by her mirth.

"That is a good one, Harris," she continues. "Seriously, you should've led with something even more ridiculous. Like telling me you have a private bowling alley or a helicopter pad."

Well, I personally don't—but several of my good friends do. One of the guys who attends her yoga class, as a matter of fact.

"Right," I manage, trying not to let my ego deflate entirely. "*Totally* joking."

Ha ha.

She wipes at a tear in the corner of her eye. "Infinity pool. You are too much."

I force a laugh, deciding it's better if she thinks I'm kidding. Now is not the time to argue—*that would make things awkward*—and besides: I'm pretending to be an actor pretending to be a lumberjack, hired help for Lake Loon Days or whatever the hell the jingle jamboree is called.

Lucy leans back into the couch, still chuckling to herself, completely oblivious to the reality she laughed right over.

Maybe it's for the best.

Because the second she finds out the truth about me, it could very well come back and bite me in the ass and change the way she views me.

Chapter 13

Lucy

Plot twist: I did not spend the night with Harris.

I did not pass go as much as I may have wanted to.

Baby steps, Lucy.

I don't care that he's only in town for a few days.

I.

Do.

Not.

Want.

A.

Fling.

It has been decided. I simply do not have the stomach for casual sex.

At least . . . I don't think I do?

Sighing, I do my best to refocus, the men on the beach surprisingly agile for such an early morning—and considering they're so large.

Harris was a no-show, but his new friends showed up.

"Breathe deeply, gentlemen," I call out, adjusting my tone to sound both authoritative and *calm*, like the yoga instructor I am. "Feel the sand under your feet, the stretch in your muscles. Focus on the now."

The guys grumble a little, but they follow my lead, leaning into their stretches with a surprising amount of effort for a group of men who probably think yoga is glorified napping.

"I don't want to feel the sand under my feet," one of the guys mutters. "I want to be in bed."

I rack my brain, struggling to remember their names.

Eli? Miles? WHY CAN'T I REMEMBER WHO IS WHO ANYMORE?

"I'm not hating the view, though," the other one (I think his name is Quinn? Quinton?) whispers, not-so-subtly glancing my way.

I roll my eyes. "You better be talking about the lake and not my ass."

There. That sounded commanding, didn't it?

Professionalism, Lucy. You're a yoga instructor, not a flirt instructor.

"I love a sunrise over the water." Someone giggles—actually giggles.

I roll my eyes, facing forward, then twisting my torso. "Eyes on your mats, boys. Pay. Attention." Jeez, they're as bad as a group of unruly elementary school kids. "This isn't a spectator sport."

A few of them laugh, but it doesn't bother me. I've had worse students. *Much* worse. I taught a bachelorette party once, and they came hungover, loudly laughing and falling over one another, shouting. Giggling.

The sun climbs higher, warming the sand beneath us, and for a moment, I forget about lumbersexual Harris and his infuriating appeal.

Why can't I take my mind off him?

This is so unlike me.

I concentrate on the rhythm of the class, the sound of waves lapping against the shore, the groans of men struggling not to fall on their faces the way Harris did in the one and only class he's taken with me.

One by one, they start to drop out of their poses, collapsing into the sand like soldiers after a battle.

Elijah flops onto his back dramatically and grumbles, "I thought yoga was supposed to be peaceful."

Who on earth told him that? Ha.

"Peaceful when you're doing it right," I shoot back, earning a low chuckle from Quinton, who's been doing surprisingly well. He seems to be taking it seriously.

"Or. Maybe you're making it hard for us on purpose," Dex teases, brushing the sand off his forearms. His grin is full of trouble, and I get the sense that he loves to goof around and give his friends a hard time.

"On purpose?" I scoff. "Why would I do that?" I flip my hair over my shoulder and motion to the area around me with my hands. "This is a safe space."

"So you keep saying. Dude, I'm not feeling safe," Miles adds, pointing at his legs. "My hamstrings are *cooked*."

"I'm flattered." I laugh. "I also noticed you skipped half the stretches."

This is a him problem, not a me problem. He who skips stretching pays for it in the end. As an athlete he should know to stretch. It's as if he thought yoga would be *easier* the third time around.

Miles scratches the back of his neck, caught. "Fine. You got me. But in my defense, I'm not bendy. Flexible but not bendy, if you catch my drift."

Oh brother.

Dex snorts, ass planted in the sand. "He was built to tackle, not touch his toes."

"Excuses, excuses," I say. "You don't get to blame skipping stretches on already being in incredible shape. I had an older woman with two left feet in class last week who managed to stay in downward dog without collapsing."

"That sounds suspiciously like a challenge," Quinton says, grinning as he feigns a weak stretch.

"Nope." My chin hitches up. "Merely pointing out a fact."

Miles studies me before leaning back on his hands, digging his heels into the ground. "So what's your story, Luce? Is this your full-time gig?"

I laugh. "Yup, pretty much yoga. Which largely consists of wrangling hungover tourists when they think it's a good idea to book a sunrise class."

Dex raises an eyebrow. "So what you're saying is that we're better behaved than some of your other students?"

"Shockingly, yes," I reply, chuckling. "You'd be surprised how rowdy people can get when they're recovering from margaritas."

Miles gestures toward the shoreline. "But you like doing this, right? I mean, you're not teaching because you got tired of corporate life or something?"

"I love it," I say. "There's something peaceful about being outside, hearing the waves . . . even when my students are stubborn guys who complain more than they stretch."

Quinton chuckles. "I feel seen."

I smile, squinting at them through the sunlight. "What about you guys? What do you do in your spare time?"

Dex shakes his head. "Uh, sometimes we play football together. Sometimes we work out. Other times we, uh—condition."

Miles raises his hand. "I took a ballet class once."

I bet. These guys don't look like slouches, and the fact that so many of them have been showing up for this early-morning session proves how dedicated they are to their health.

Harris not included.

Not that I lump him in with these guys; he's in Star Lake strictly for lumberjacking and whatever postworkout muffins I want to bribe him with. But I know for a fact he works out, considering *I* was the reason he was bending and twisting last night. Late last night . . . and had I not had this class scheduled—I'd be home, in bed, asleep, too.

Definitely maybe dreaming about his *stupid* grin . . .

"Do you guys have anything planned for the rest of the day?" I ask, shaking the thought of Harris loose before it takes over, and stand, dusting off my knees. "Knitting, perhaps?"

Quinton cracks his knuckles, stretching lazily. "Ha ha, pretty much." He doesn't elaborate.

Dex yawns as if he's just waking up. "Maybe I'll build a sandcastle later. And there's a pool at the lodge. I might take a nap later."

"Sounds like a solid itinerary." I smile. "Do you mind my asking . . . if you have families?" I ask, genuinely curious about what their lives are like. "Kids, girlfriends, stuff like that?"

Dex grins, sand and dirt covering his arms as he props himself on his elbows. "Yeah, I have a girlfriend. Margot—she's cool about these trips and shit. She knows the deal."

The deal. I wonder what he means by that but do not pry. "How long have you two been together?"

"Since December," he replies with a lazy smile. "She's basically a saint for putting up with me."

Miles laughs. "That's putting it lightly. Margot should get a trophy."

"Ha ha, very funny, dickhead." Dex throws his towel at him and scrambles to stand. "Shit, that reminds me—we have a date to FaceTime this morning, so I have to hustle."

The remaining guys begin standing, too, brushing nature off their legs and limbs and collecting their things.

"What about you, Lucy?" Elijah wants to know. "You married or somethin'?"

I shake my head the same way I always do when someone asks this question—it's a question I get a lot, actually. "Nope. No boyfriend. No husband—just me." I shrug. "Hey. You don't have to look shocked. People survive without being in a relationship with someone."

Elijah grins. "Yeah, but it's surprising someone hasn't snatched you up."

I roll my eyes. "Or maybe I'm too busy being awesome."

Miles has the nerve to snicker, twirling his black water bottle. "That, or you're dodging idiots like us."

Idiots like them? Hardly. A girl would consider herself lucky to be involved with any one of these guys—I mean, granted, they're a tad pervy but not terrible. Stable jobs, up at dawn? Most of them seem like a good catch.

A soft breeze rustles through my hair, and I close my eyes, letting it cool my flushed cheeks. I open them to the sound of laughter carrying over the boats gently bumping against a nearby pier, and the sound of water lapping against the rocks.

The morning sun glints off the hood of the guys' truck, and the scent of pine and earth lingers in the air, fresh and clean. Miles slings a towel over his shoulder, no doubt making a wisecrack that has them all doubling over as he tosses their gear into the bed of the truck. Elijah loudly calls shotgun, leaping onto the step with the kind of energy that only comes from a post-yoga high.

I stretch my arms overhead, the warm ache in my muscles a reminder of how long we stayed on the beach, breathing in the fresh air.

In.

Out.

In.

Out . . .

The rhythm of it calms me, but my mind refuses to stay still. I tilt my head back, letting the sun kiss my skin, and flirt with the idea of dating someone who lives in another state entirely—not that anyone is asking me to.

Not yet, anyway.

But that's how it always starts, isn't it?

Someone you can't stop thinking about, conversations that last long past midnight, and suddenly you're trying to convince yourself that distance is just a number.

Harris lives so far away. Arizona. Seriously? It's such a far cry from where I am now, and it's not the physical miles that weigh me down—it's everything those miles represent. Time zones. Missed calls. Moments I'll never be a part of.

Could I do it?

Could I be the girl who spends her Friday nights curled up with her phone instead of with him? Could I handle waking up to texts instead of lazy morning kisses? And what if those texts start feeling like a substitute for something I really want but can't have?

I sigh, rolling my shoulders as seagulls call overhead.

It's not like Harris has promised me anything, but the way he looks at me . . . it's enough to make me wonder if he's thinking about it too.

"We've had orgasms but haven't had sex sex. Yet. Relax," I mutter under my breath, half laughing at myself.

We've only just met.

But meeting him doesn't feel new. It feels familiar in a way that shouldn't be possible. Like he skipped the awkward introductions and walked straight into the places that make me vulnerable.

Maybe that's why I can't stop thinking about him.

"Girl, get out of your head. The first step would be inviting him over."

Inviting him over.

To your parents' house.

Above their garage.

I groan, lifting a hand above my head and tilting to one side, fingers pointed to the sky.

The stretch loosens the tension in my back, but it doesn't do much for the knot twisting inside me. Inviting Harris into that space—into my life as it is now—feels like asking him to see everything I usually try to gloss over. The hand-me-down furniture, the patchy Wi-Fi, the constant sound of my dad hammering away in the workshop below.

I mean, can you imagine?

The horror.

I tilt my head back, watching the clouds drift lazily across the sky. There's a simplicity to their movement that makes me wish I could think less and feel more. Let the uncertainty sit where it is without constantly trying to solve it.

But that's not how I'm wired.

Instead, I picture Harris standing in my tiny studio space, ducking slightly to avoid hitting his head on the low ceiling. I laugh, imagining it. Exhale slowly and drop my arm, the breeze catching strands of my hair and brushing them across my face.

Maybe the question isn't whether or not I could make long distance work, but whether or not I'm ready to let him see every messy, imperfect piece of me—and stay for the night.

Just do it . . .

"Do it."

Don't be scared.

Before I can continue overthinking it, I grab my phone out of my belt bag and stare at his number, tapping on it.

Chapter 14

Harris

Turns out, I'm as terrible at chopping wood as I am at logrolling.

You'd think being a linebacker would help, but no.

My form sucks, my swings are off, and I'm pretty sure the last piece of wood I'm attempting to split is made of concrete.

"I have no idea what to do with you." Annabelle moans, pinching the bridge of her nose like she's on the verge of firing me. "You have the muscles, but that's all you're bringing to the table. I don't get it!"

I wipe the sweat from my brow, glaring at the log. "I'm better when I'm hitting things that *move*."

Annabelle lets out a short laugh, tossing a water bottle at me. "Unless you plan on tackling the logs, I'm afraid you're out of luck."

I twist the cap off and take a long drink, letting the cold water drown some of my frustration. Across the training field, the other guys are chopping wood like they were born holding an axe, sweat glistening on their backs as chunks of wood fly in clean splits.

As if they're actually professionals.

Fucking irritating as hell.

She watches me watching them and sighs loudly. "I hate to break it to you, but the festival crowd does not want a wrestling match in the middle of the lumberjack stage, so you're gonna have to figure this out." Her hands go to her hips. "Try again."

I groan internally, picking up the axe. Annabelle glares like Coach, and the pressure feels heavier than it should. I take a breath, grip the handle tighter, and bring it down.

Miss.

"Shit." Annabelle snorts, and I scowl at her over my shoulder. "Don't laugh at me. I'm working on it."

"I'm laughing *with* you," she lies. "Come on, Harris. At this rate, you're going to be the comedic relief of the festival."

Fantastic.

Exactly what I want.

To be remembered as the lumberjack who couldn't split wood to save his life.

My phone vibrates in my back pocket, and I almost ignore it, but something about the timing makes me pause. I pull it out and glance at the screen.

Lucy:

So. I've been thinking . . .

I blink at the message, the axe suddenly forgotten in my hand.

About me, obviously, I type back, smirking as I wait for her response. She's going to be so irritated.

When it comes, I can't help but chuckle.

I'm about to respond when Annabelle claps her hands behind me, snapping me back to reality. "Hi. Remember me? I hate to remind you that we have a show to do in a mere matter of days—so unless that text is someone giving you step-by-step instructions on how to chop wood, I suggest you focus."

Jeez. What a hard-ass.

I tuck my phone back into my pocket, my thoughts still half on Lucy. "One more try."

I raise the axe again, trying to shake off the mental image of Lucy smirking at me through the screen, teasing me the way she always does. This time, I focus on the damn log and swing with everything I've got.

Crack. The axe buries itself halfway through the wood, but it doesn't split cleanly. It sits there, mocking me like the universe wants to test my patience.

"Better," Annabelle says, her tone somewhere between encouragement and pity. "We might make a lumberjack out of you yet."

I doubt that.

I wipe the sweat from my forehead, laughing under my breath. "Or I'll be the cautionary tale for future recruits."

She taps the clipboard in her hand, smirking. "Either way, you'll be remembered."

Little does she know this will probably be all over the evening news, once people realize who it is making an ass of himself.

The guys around me are still going strong, splitting logs like pros, while I contemplate whether to throw my axe into the lake.

"Wally is a fucking show-off." I can't stand that dumbass.

Huffing, I swing the axe again. This time, it grazes the log and sends a sharp vibration up my arms. I grit my teeth as Wally splits another log effortlessly and grins over at me like he's the king of the goddamn town festival.

"I *hate* that guy," I grumble to Annabelle as I shoot him a glare, tempted to tackle him as a reminder to him who the *real* athlete is—then remember no one knows I am who I am.

These dudes do not follow football, or they would be fawning all over me, period.

That oughta give me some satisfaction, but it doesn't.

Annabelle laughs, grinning as she marks something on her clipboard. "You know, if you hate him this much, maybe you should beat him in the axe-throwing competition. Show him who's boss."

I smirk at the thought but quickly shake it off. "If today's any indication, I'd probably end up killing someone in the crowd by accident."

Annabelle waves me off. "Nah, you'll figure it out. You're *built* for this, Harris. Just a little rusty."

Rusty. That's putting it kindly.

I pick up the axe again, ignoring the ache in my arms and the growing frustration settling in my chest. Normally, I'd thrive in an environment like this—competition, adrenaline, all eyes on me. But right now, the only person I want to impress is the one blowing up my phone with texts.

Speaking of . . .

My phone buzzes. I pull it out and skim the new message from Lucy, the corner of my mouth lifting.

Lucy:
So this might seem random, but . . .

Lucy:
I was wondering if you want
to come to my place. Tonight,
specifically.

I can barely believe my eyes!

Her invite settles deep in my chest, igniting something primal—something that makes me want to drop this axe right here and sprint to my car. My fingers hover over the keyboard, thoughts racing as fast as my pulse.

"Get this," I tell Annabelle, knowing they're friends and excited to have gossip to share. "Lucy invited me back to her place tonight."

My boss's brows shoot straight up into her hairline. "For real?"

I nod. "Yup."

Cocky now, I swing the axe, suddenly mastering the skill of wood chopping, blade connecting *perfectly* with the log, splitting it clean in half. I let out a triumphant "WHOOP!" of victory, standing taller. "Hell yeah!"

"Thank God." Annabelle says with a chuckle, jotting something down on her clipboard before palming her phone and reading the screen. "If you'd missed again, I was going to have you stacking logs."

She of little faith.

"Not today, Satan." I toss the axe to the ground like I'm ready to retire undefeated. "I have a date tonight."

"Maybe she's your lucky charm," she teases, leaning her clipboard against her hip. "I knew the two of you were texting but didn't realize you were at the point where you were hanging out."

"She was at my place last night," I inform Annabelle with a satisfied grin. "We watched a movie."

And fooled around.

Then I begged her to stay, and she turned me down, so I jerked off after cleaning up and climbing into bed.

"Let me get this straight—Lucy was at your place last night—and now she's invited you to hers? What world am I living in right now?"

"Why are you saying it like that? In that tone?"

Annabelle shrugs. "There's no tone. I'm just shocked! This is so unlike her." She pauses to study my face. "Are you bringing her wine, flowers—or just showing up?"

"Probably wine?" Did I answer correctly? I feel like this is what she's looking for—but I've had the invite to Lucy's for all of five minutes, so Annabelle can climb down off my nut sack about hostess gifts. "Yes?"

"Yes." She taps her pen to her lips. "And make sure it's a *good* bottle. Nothing with a screw cap, unless you want her thinking you picked it up from the gas station."

"Noted—no screw cap." I chuckle. "You should be my dating coach."

She gives me a sly grin. "Trust me, you don't need a coach."

Aww. I'm flattered.

"Every so often I could use the help," I say, grabbing my water bottle. "My friends are assholes."

I take a long swig, thinking about Lucy's place and all the possibilities that await. The idea of being in her space makes my pulse kick up another notch.

Annabelle gives me a playful nudge. "My only advice—as your dating coach—is don't mess this up, dude. Lucy is one of the good ones."

I roll my eyes at her warning, putting the cap back on my water jug. "Duh."

"I'm not kidding. She doesn't invite anyone to her place," she points out. "She's particular."

My brows go up. "Is that a code word for *high maintenance* and *picky*?"

Annabelle lifts her shoulders up and down. "Bit of both, probably."

Fair enough. "High maintenance and picky don't scare me."

Bring it on.

The next ten minutes go by in a blur of sweat, sawdust, and a growing anticipation in my gut. By the time I'm done stacking the last log, Annabelle's already given me a once-over, like she's silently calculating how much of a mess I look.

"You can't show up to her place smelling like tree sap," she warns, scrunching up her nose. "Go shower. Maybe shave that scruff a bit. It's borderline caveman right now."

"This is my signature scruff."

She raises an eyebrow. "Your signature scruff has wood chips in it."

I pluck a stray chip from my beard and flick it to the ground. "Adds to the rugged charm."

"Does it, though?"

Guess not.

"Oh! And before you go dreaming about romance, let me remind you that you need to be here Saturday morning at seven o'clock sharp for the show."

I groan. "Seven in the morning?"

"Yes," she replies with zero sympathy. "We're doing final prep before the main event starts at noon. Don't be late, or I'll have you hauling logs solo. Wear flannel, jeans, and those boots you wore the other day—they make you look like an actual lumberjack and not someone pretending to be one."

"Flannel and boots." I nod enthusiastically. "Got it."

She taps her pen against her clipboard. "Oh, and leave Lucy's place in time to get some sleep. I need you rested and in one piece."

I salute her. "Anything else, boss?"

"Tell all your friends, if you have any. We still have some VIP tickets, and I would love to get those sold." She inhales a breath. "In hindsight, having front-row seats next to the water may not have been a draw—but it's as close as you can get to the action. We even have a dunk tank."

"Let me guess," I say. "You're putting me in the dunk tank if I'm late."

She grins. "You're going in the dunk tank regardless."

Half an hour later I'm storing the axe and saying goodbye to the other guys (the actual lumberjacks), waving over my shoulder as I slide into the driver's seat of my truck. With the windows down and the wind blowing through my already mussed-up hair, I let the anticipation settle back into my chest.

The weight is heavy—the *good* kind of pressure before a big game. Adrenaline-like pressure . . .

The kind that makes you want to perform your best.

Back at the cabin I hit the shower. Scrub away the wood chips and dust within an inch of my life. Dry off. Throw on a plain black T-shirt and jeans. Slide on some sandals. Swipe the wine bottle off the counter, and I'm out the door.

The drive to Lucy's parents' house takes no time at all, and the scenery alone makes it feel like stepping into a damn postcard. Towering trees line the long driveway, their branches casting shadows across the gravel as the evening sun dips lower into the horizon. The house itself is a sprawling lakefront property, all windows and warm wood accents—it's the kind of place that makes you pause and appreciate how lucky some people are to grow up here, surrounded by nature.

Lucy's apartment sits above the detached garage near the side of the main house, accessible by a wooden staircase wrapped in ivy and chipped paint.

I park my truck on the gravel lot next to a shiny black SUV and take a moment to breathe, the lake's reflection shimmering in the distance, sending ripples of calm through me.

One deep inhale, exhale.

Then I grab the wine.

The steps creak beneath my weight as I make my way up, the evening breeze carrying the faint scent of pine and freshly cut grass. When I reach the top landing, I see the small porch is decorated with potted plants and wind chimes that sway lazily in the breeze.

Her door—a simple navy blue with a brass knocker—feels inviting and personal, and after two soft taps with my knuckles, I wait. My heartbeat kicks up, thumping a little faster than it should for someone who was acting cocky an hour ago.

Then the door opens.

Lucy stands there, barefoot, wearing an oversize cream-colored sweater that falls past her shorts. Her legs are bare, smooth, and slightly tan from afternoons spent outside. Her hair is down, a little messy but in that way that feels effortless. She smells like vanilla and something floral, freshly showered and ready to settle in for the night.

"Hey, you," she says softly, her lips curving into that familiar smile that always throws me off balance.

"Hey," I manage, holding out the wine. "Hope you're into red."

She takes the bottle, her fingers brushing mine. "Cabernet," she murmurs, inspecting the label. "You really know how to impress a girl."

Behind me, crickets chirp as the sun dips lower, the orange glow fading into dusk.

I already want to kiss her, but hold myself back to savor the anticipation.

As I step over her threshold—almost needing to duck because of my height—movement flickers in my peripheral vision. Glancing toward the main house, I see her.

A woman peeking out from behind the curtain of a side window, fingers parting the fabric enough for me to catch her watching. Lucy's mom?

Must be.

She freezes. For a moment, we're locked in an awkward, silent standoff.

She stares. I stare back.

Neither of us flinches, like it's some sort of showdown. Then—before I can react—the curtain snaps shut so fast, I half expect the rod to come crashing down.

"I think your mom sees me," I whisper, turning back toward Lucy.

She rolls her eyes, but her laughter bubbles up anyway. "I swear, if she doesn't send me a text about you within the next minute, I'd be shocked."

"Should I wave and get it over with?"

"Don't you dare!" Lucy grabs my wrist, laughing so hard her grip is weak. I give her a playful wink and pretend to raise my hand toward the window like I'm seconds from introducing myself. She swats me with a giggle. "Stop!"

"I'm kidding!" I say, chuckling. "Sort of."

I have zero issues making nice with her parents. People love me. I've charmed cranky grandmas, tough coaches, and even my one snotty neighbor who thinks I'm "too young to live in such a big house by myself."

Her words, not mine.

Winning over Lucy's mom? *Easy.*

"Get in here before my dad sticks his face against the glass."

Her dad? Dads love me too!

Lucy closes the door behind me once I'm all the way inside, and my eyes scan the space.

It's a loft-style apartment with exposed wooden beams running across the high ceiling, rustic and cozy but expensive looking, like something out of an interior design magazine. The walls are painted a soft cream, with accents of warm, earthy tones. One wall is entirely brick, which is fucking cool; the open layout makes the place feel bigger than it is.

The kitchen, to the left, has butcher-block countertops and modern brass fixtures. There's a large farmhouse sink that looks way too pristine to have ever been used for dishes. Shelves lined with glass jars full of spices. A copper-colored mixer. I inhale. The smell of cinnamon lingers in the air, mixing with the faint scent of fresh pine wafting in from the open window.

To my right, the living room flows seamlessly from the kitchen, with an overstuffed leather couch positioned in front of a small gas-burning fireplace. On the floor, against the wall? A tall stack of books that looks precariously close to tipping over. Fairy lights are strung along the exposed beams overhead, casting a soft, ambient glow that makes the space feel even cozier.

The pièce de résistance? The view. Large windows line the far wall, framing the lake outside like a living painting. The surface of the water glitters under the fading sunlight, and beyond it, a line of trees sways gently in the evening breeze. Somewhere out there is my little rental cabin.

"Nice fucking place," I say, genuinely impressed.

Lucy snorts, setting the wine bottle on the kitchen counter. "I'll take that as a compliment."

"It is. This view is incredible," I assure her, stepping closer to run my fingers over the back of the leather couch. "You decorate yourself?"

She nods, a hint of pride in her smile as she pours a glass of wine. "Eh. My mom helped me pick out a few things, but I did most of it."

"I'm sure she loves having you close by."

Lucy laughs, the kind of laugh that hints there's a whole backstory I'm about to hear. "That's putting it mildly. Anytime I come home with groceries, she's standing in the driveway asking 'Who are those avocados for? You never ate those as a child. Are you having people over? Why are there so many bags?' Like, *Mom,* they're for me. I'm not feeding a secret boyfriend."

No secret boyfriend? "That's good news."

She laughs again, the sound filling the loft and making it feel even warmer. "We'll see how long it takes for my dad to text asking questions about you. I don't think he's home yet."

"Let him ask away." I raise my glass. "I'm an open book."

"Careful," she teases. "You might become the new family favorite. They're dying for me to get hitched."

Yeah, mine too. Kind of. I mean—my mom would love grandkids. She realizes I'm at the height of my career and still young, but brings babies into every single conversation.

Thank God for my sisters' kids 'cause I'd never hear the end of it.

I follow Lucy to the living room, and we settle on the leather couch; it creaks softly as we sink into its comfort. She tucks her legs beneath her, facing me with her glass resting on her knee. Lucy raises her hand, and I notice a remote; three seconds later, soft music starts playing.

"Tell me something," Lucy says, swirling her wine. "What's the most embarrassing thing you've ever done in front of someone's parents?"

I chuckle, leaning back. "Oh, you're starting with the tough questions, huh?"

"What?" She grins. "You're the one who said you were an open book."

I take a long sip of wine, thinking. "All right. There was this one time in high school. I was meeting a girl's parents for dinner, and the dog wasn't supposed to be let out because it would run away. But at one point I went to the garage for a soda and the dog ran out and ran away. They spent the entire night looking for him, and it didn't come back until the next afternoon."

She gawks at me.

"I wasn't invited back." I laugh at the memory. "Man, her dad was pissed."

Lucy shakes her head, covering her mouth to stifle her laughter. "That's terrible! Did you help look for it?"

"Of course I did," I say, grinning. "But let's be real, I wasn't exactly their MVP. The dad kept muttering under his breath about me being a dumb jock."

Lucy tilts her head, giggling. "And you never saw the girl again?"

"Oh, I saw her." I smirk. "Just not at her house." Shelby Bauer and I had lots and lots of secret sex after her dad kicked me out of their house for letting their dog loose, mostly in the bed of the pickup truck I drove in high school. "I was a teenager with raging hormones and a grudge against her dad," I confess. Seemed like the perfect combination.

"Please tell me you never got caught."

"Not by her parents," I admit. "But once, we did get interrupted by a park ranger banging on the tailgate with a flashlight."

Lucy gasps, covering her face with her hands from the secondhand embarrassment. "You're kidding."

"Nope. We panicked and pretended we were stargazing."

She bursts out laughing. "Stargazing?"

"I said we were studying constellations," I say, unable to stop my own laughter. "Shelby went with it, pointing at the sky like she knew what she was talking about."

Lucy shakes her head, still giggling. "Did it work?"

"Barely. The cop rolled his eyes and said, 'Next time, study at home.'"

"Oh God, I can't even imagine." She nudges my leg with her knee. "I would have been horrified."

"You asked for embarrassing stories."

She smirks, setting her glass on the coffee table. "Yup, that's a good one. But now I'm afraid to take you anywhere with a view of the stars."

"Relax," I tease, inching closer. "These days, I stargaze the responsible way."

"And what's the responsible way?"

"With wine, a couch, and good company," I murmur, brushing a strand of hair behind her ear, admiring the view of her.

Her eyes flutter to my lips. "You seem to have it all figured out."

"Only because you're making it easy," I say.

"That was so cheesy," she whispers.

"Did it work?"

She nods.

Our lips meet, soft and warm, the faint taste of wine mixing between us.

Her hand slides up to my shoulder, fingers curling into my shirt as she pulls me closer. The teasing falls away, replaced by something deeper—something I've been wanting to do since the moment I saw her smile at the door.

Chapter 15

Lucy

He tastes so good.

The best kind of dessert . . .

The kind of dessert with a hint of red wine lingering on his lips. I could easily lose myself in the warmth of his mouth, the feel of his hand sliding up my back, pulling me closer like he can't help himself.

My fingers tangle in his hair, and for a moment, the world outside disappears—no parents watching, no worries about what will happen tomorrow. Just us, the hum of the crickets outside, and the steady rhythm of his breathing against mine.

When we finally break apart, I'm breathless. My lips tingle, and my pulse races like I sprinted a mile. He rests his forehead against mine, both of us catching our breath, and then his fingers brush against my jaw, a soft, almost lazy caress that makes my heart skip.

"Wow," he murmurs, his voice low. "That was sexy."

"So sexy," I whisper back, smiling. I feel lightheaded, like I've had more than one glass of wine, but it's not the alcohol making me feel this way—it's *him*.

Tingles!

Shivers!

Guh! *All the things!*

He leans back, his arm draped around my shoulders, and takes a sip of wine. His gaze flickers to mine, full of warmth and mischief. "Okay, I told you my most embarrassing story. Your turn."

I groan, burying my face in my hands. "No. You got the good wine, so you don't get the good dirt."

"That's not how this works," he teases, gently pulling my hands away from my face. "Come on, what's the worst date you've ever been on?"

I sigh, knowing I have to tell him. Turnabout is fair play. "Fine. But don't laugh."

"I make no such promises."

I swat his arm, but I'm laughing despite myself. "Okay. It was sophomore year of college, and this guy—who shall remain nameless—took me on a date to an all-you-can-eat wings place."

He raises an eyebrow. "That doesn't sound too bad."

"Oh, it gets worse. Trust me." I take a sip of wine, bracing myself. "So, he ordered the spiciest wings they had on the menu because he wanted to impress me. Ten minutes in, he's sweating bullets, bright red, and *crying*. Like, full-on tears streaming down his face."

Harris bursts out laughing. "No way."

"Way," I say, grinning. "To make it even worse, he kept trying to play it off like he was fine. But then he choked, knocked over his drink, and the waitress had to bring him a glass of milk and a wet towel."

Harris laughs so hard, he nearly spills his wine. "Did you help him, or did you let him suffer?"

"Oh, I stood up to give him the Heimlich maneuver, but at that point he was done dying," I say solemnly. "Every time I asked if he wanted me to call it a night, he insisted he was fine. He even tried to kiss me after—with hot sauce still on his lips."

Harris winces, shaking his head. "Please tell me you didn't kiss him."

"Indeed I did. I felt bad!"

"And?"

"And . . ." I cover my face briefly before letting out a groan. "His lips were basically fire. I'm not being the least bit dramatic—my mouth was actually burning. *Third-degree* burn."

The second our lips touched, I felt the literal heat. At first, the spicy wing sauce was manageable . . . until it wasn't. My tongue started burning, and my eyes started watering, and that was the beginning of the end for that horrific date.

"That wasn't even the worst of it," I continue. "He tried to make jokes about it so I wouldn't go home. *Oh, the heat is the chemistry between us.*"

So cringey.

"That story makes mine sound lame." Harris pouts. "A dog running away? Basic."

We both laugh at that, the sound echoing softly through my cozy little loft. I take another sip of wine, warmth settling in my chest as I lean my head against the back of the couch and glance over at him.

"All right. Tell me this: What's the shortest date you've ever been on?" I ask.

He groans, running a hand through his hair. "Oh, man. You're digging deep now."

I smile, waiting patiently.

"Okay," he says, exhaling dramatically. "There was this girl I met in college. We agreed to grab coffee. Seemed simple enough, right?"

"Right," I say, grinning. "How do you mess up coffee?"

"Let me explain," he says, laughing. "We sit down, and within the first five minutes, she starts asking me about my credit score."

I choke on my sip of wine. "No. Way."

"Swear to God. She wanted to know if I was financially responsible before she even knew my middle name."

"Oh my God." I press a hand to my mouth to stifle my laughter. "What did you say?"

Harris laughs. "My credit score. It was super low at the time—embarrassingly low. But like, I'd rented furniture for a shared apartment and stopped paying the bills and went apeshit buying electronics and could never afford the minimum monthlies." Oh. *Yikes.* "When our coffee came I made up an excuse about needing to help my roommate move furniture."

"The furniture you weren't paying for?" I tease.

"Exactly." He nudges me with his toe. "Shortest date ever and never spoke to her again."

"You ghosted her?"

"I mean—technically, I didn't ghost her." He holds up a finger in protest. "I politely ignored her texts forever."

A giggle escapes my throat. "That counts!"

His head tilts to the side, and he considers this. "Does it?"

"One thousand percent."

"The good news is, I've matured since then and haven't done anything as stupid since." He pauses. "Fine, that's not necessarily true—I've done a ton of stupid shit."

I lean back against the couch. "Okay, give me your top three."

"Okay," he says, holding up three fingers. "Number three—one time, I accidentally texted my ex-girlfriend instead of the girl I was dating. I didn't realize it until she replied with 'Wrong girl, you prick.'"

"Oh my God." I gasp, unable to fathom. "What's number two?"

"Number two . . . hmm." He hesitates. "I tried to jump off a roof into a pool at a party and missed. Landed in the shallow end and sprained my ankle."

Jesus! I clutch my queasy stomach. "Please tell me you were sober."

Harris shakes his head. "Negative, Ghost Rider, and I'm glad I was drunk because I didn't feel a thing."

"Shit. That drunk?"

He looks sheepish. "Yeah. It wasn't great. I've never seen my mom so pissed off in my entire life. I was playing football in college, right? So it was a whole thing, spraining my ankle."

I can only imagine. "I'm afraid to find out what number one is . . ."

"You should be afraid. The dumbest thing I've ever done: I thought it would be romantic to surprise my high school girlfriend by climbing through her bedroom window. You know—like in the movies?"

"Stop it, you did not!" I laugh. "What happened? Did you fall?"

"No—worse. Her mom was sitting at the end of her bed. When she saw me, she started screaming for the dad. It was a fucking disaster."

"Wow. You sound like you were . . . seriously something else growing up."

Harris laughs, rubbing his face like he's still embarrassed by the memory. "Oh, I was definitely something else. Thought I was smooth as hell, but really, I was such a douchebag. But I've learned my lesson. No more grand romantic gestures involving windows."

"Aww, I wouldn't say that—the gesture sounds super sweet. No one has done anything as remotely romantic as that for me." I barely get flowers from my dates, let alone have them scale a building to see me.

We sit in comfortable silence for a moment, the soft hum of the lake breeze drifting through the open window. I sip my wine, watching him out of the corner of my eye as he leans back, looking completely at ease.

"I appreciate you saying that." He watches me for a moment, his smile soft. "Your turn. What's the dumbest thing *you've* ever done for a guy?"

"I don't know." I scoff. "Let him live with me?"

He goes quiet. "When was *this*?"

Parker. I should never have brought him up because now Harris wants details. I can see it on his face.

I take another sip of wine, trying to play it off like it's no big deal. "It was a long time ago."

Harris shifts slightly, setting his glass down on the table. "College?"

"Uh, no. Like last year." I laugh softly because that is definitely *not* a long time ago—I only wish it was. "I hate talking about it. He was not the guy for me."

Harris doesn't say anything right away, but I can feel the weight of his attention, like he's reading between the lines of what I'm not saying.

"And?" he finally asks, his voice curious.

"And." I sigh. "That's it. I loved how nothing rattled him—until I realized nothing *motivated* him either."

Harris rests his elbow on the back of the couch, his body angled toward me. "So he was *too* laid back?"

I nod, swirling the wine in my glass. "Yeah. I was working long hours trying to grow the yoga business—and he'd be at our apartment meditating or talking about how 'everything works out when the universe decides.' Um, no, the universe isn't going to pay the rent on the apartment we shared, dude."

The more I think about it, the more annoyed I get. My nostrils flare as I remember how Parker always had a spiritual excuse for not taking responsibility. If he didn't get a job, it was because he wasn't meant to yet. If I asked him to help clean the apartment, he would say, *You're too attached to material things, Lucy.* Fuck you, pal! Sorry for wanting a clean floor!

Lazy asshole.

How stupid was I to tolerate his shit for so long?

Ugh!

Harris studies me as if he's trying to decide whether to say something or let me stew. Then he reaches over and takes my hand in his. "For what it's worth, you deserve someone who's all in. Someone who doesn't need you to carry the whole weight."

"That's . . ." My breath catches. "What Annabelle always says."

"She's smart."

"She is," I whisper, my fingers tightening around his for a moment before I pull back, exhaling the last of Parker from my system. "What about you?" I switch gears. "What was your last relationship like?"

Harris shifts slightly, running a hand through his hair. "Messy."

I tilt my head. "Messy how?"

He lets out a soft laugh with no humor behind it. "She was using me."

My stomach twists. "Using you for *what*?" His body? His looks?

"My giant axe." Harris winks at me but again—no humor.

I laugh, but there's a hollowness to it because I know he's deflecting. "Come on, don't do that. Be serious."

He sighs, rubbing the back of his neck. "Status. Attention. Dating an athlete was a flex for her. I thought she was in it for me, but turns out, I was an accessory."

I frown. *Is he talking about college here?* "That's awful."

"It wasn't great," he admits, looking down at his hands. "She'd post pictures of us online like we were the perfect couple, but when it came to real stuff—supporting each other, being there—she checked out. And I was too blind to see it."

My heart aches for him, but I know that kind of blindness all too well. "What was the breaking point?"

He exhales, shaking his head. "After a bad game, I got benched for a couple of weeks. I was in a rough spot, and instead of sticking around, she started hanging out with some guy on the rival team. I walked in on them making out at a party."

"Damn." I set my glass aside, shifting closer to him. "You didn't deserve that."

"No." His jaw tightens. "But it taught me a lesson. People who are only around when things are good? They're not worth it."

I bite my lip, the heaviness between us settling like a shared wound. "How long were you together?"

"A year," he says, shaking his head again. "Too long, considering how it ended."

I nod, thinking about Parker and how long I put up with his excuses. "I get it. I let my ex hang around too long, hoping he'd change."

Harris looks at me, a softness in his eyes. "Sometimes we want to believe in people more than they deserve."

I swallow, that simple truth hitting me square in the chest. "Yeah."

He brushes a strand of hair behind my ear, his touch lingering. "But you're here now. You let him go."

"And you let her go."

We sit like that for a moment, the weight of it lifting slightly, replaced by something warmer—something that feels like a fresh start. Then his lips curve into a small smile.

"For the record," he says, his voice lower now, "I think you deserve someone who's in it for *you.* Not for what you can give them or how they look standing next to you."

My throat tightens, but I manage a soft smile. "Same goes for you."

"You're so fucking cute," Harris murmurs, leaning toward me, his lips a breath away from mine.

I feel the heat rise in my cheeks, but it's nothing compared to the warmth blooming low in my stomach. "Thanks."

He waits for me to say more . . .

Grins when I don't.

"You're a sassy thing."

I am.

No denying that.

"You can lower your walls, Lucy. I'm not going to disappoint you."

My heart stutters, and for a second, I can't speak. The way he says it—like he means every word and he's willing to prove it—makes my defenses flicker.

"I know," I whisper, my voice softer than I intended.

"Do you?" His hand gently cups my cheek, and I lean into his touch, closing my eyes for a moment to soak in the warmth. When I open them, he's watching me closely, gaze so intense it feels like he can see straight through me.

I shake my head. "No." *But I'm going to throw caution to the wind and take you at your word.* "What if you get more than you bargained for from me?"

He grins, but there's nothing cocky about it. "Do I look like I can't handle more than I bargained for?"

I bite my bottom lip, trying to keep the squeamish flutters out of my stomach.

Impossible. Harris is irresistible. "How was practice today?"

His massive shoulders shrug as he slides closer to me still. "Let me put it this way: If Annabelle wasn't desperate, I'd be out on my ass and out of a gig."

"That bad?" Aren't men born with a wood-chopping gene?

"*That* bad." The thing is, he doesn't seem the least bit bothered.

"At least you're not embarrassed."

He leans toward me, voice dropping, making my pulse race. "What's the point of being good at everything when you can be bad and have a little fun?"

I swallow hard, my voice barely above a whisper. "You make it sound like being bad is your goal."

"I'm not much of a masochist. I like winning too much to not at least give it effort."

For a moment, neither of us says anything, and I wonder if he's thinking the same thing I am: that maybe this conversation isn't about lumberjacking. Maybe he's talking about sex. Or relationships. Or . . .

Or . . .

"What do you usually do on the weekends?" Harris switches gears again, diving into a new topic.

I tilt my head to the side, thinking about what a typical weekend looks like. Boring. "Um. I work. I hang out in town. Hike."

Harris raises an eyebrow, a slow grin spreading across his face. "Hiking, eh? Let me guess—you've got one of those cute backpacks with a water bottle on the side and snacks perfectly packed."

I laugh, nudging his shoulder. "What's wrong with being prepared?"

"Nothing." His eyes flicker with amusement. "I can't see you roughing it in the woods."

"That's because I hate roughing it in the woods—the only time I want to see a tent is if it's pitched in someone else's backyard for a party."

He chuckles, the sound rumbling low in his chest. "Good to know. So if I ever invite you camping, I should probably throw in a promise of a luxury cabin."

"With Wi-Fi, please," I joke. "And maybe a hot tub."

Harris whistles. "High maintenance."

I raise a brow. "I prefer 'knows her worth.'"

"I'll give you credit—you don't seem like the type to fake being outdoorsy to impress someone."

"Why fake it when I can be impressive in other ways?" I shoot back, and his smile falters for a second, as if the weight of my words hit harder than I intended.

"Oh, you've got my attention," he murmurs, eyes locked on mine. "What other ways are we talking?"

My heart thumps in response, but I keep my cool. "Wouldn't you like to know?"

"Yeah." He leans close enough to make the air between us crackle. "I *really* would."

I swallow, my pulse racing. Maybe this conversation wasn't supposed to go down this road—but I'm not exactly mad about it. "Are you flirting with me?"

Harris grins. "I thought it was obvious."

I giggle at how easy it is for him to say whatever is on his mind. "There's nothing subtle about you."

"Would you *want* me to be?" He raises a brow, tone teasing.

I shake my head, biting my lip. "No."

He shifts, knee brushing against mine. "Good. I'm not great at playing hard to get."

Chapter 16

Harris

I'm not great at playing hard to get.

That makes her face go blank—as if she's desperately trying to school her expression.

Fine. I'll dial it back.

It's easy to forget sometimes that Lucy doesn't come from a world where teasing is armor and flirting is second nature. My world is one of locker-room banter, deflections, and always having something sharp to say when things get too real.

Hers is quieter. Thoughtful.

She's careful.

Maybe that's why I can't seem to stop pushing her. I want to know what she's hiding behind those walls. What she's afraid to let out.

I lean back, resting my arm on the couch, giving her space to breathe. "You okay over there?" I tap my finger against her hand.

Her gaze flicks to mine, and she hesitates. "I'm fine."

But I can tell she's not. The words come out too quickly, like she's trying to convince herself.

I let the silence settle between us, waiting her out. If there's one thing football has taught me, it's patience. You don't always have to charge headfirst—sometimes, the play is to stay still and let the other team make the first move.

She exhales softly, her shoulders sinking into the cushions like she's surrendering. "It's just . . . I'm not used to this."

I tilt my head. "Used to what?"

"Men being so direct."

"I prefer being direct to playing games." Head games are for pussies and are a waste of fucking time. I'd rather be honest, even if it blows up in my face. "I don't see the point of making someone guess how I feel."

"Honestly, you make me nervous."

"I do?"

"Yes."

"Good," I say, my voice softening as I scoot a bit closer. "Because you make me nervous too."

Her eyes widen. "You?"

I cross a hand over my chest. "Scout's honor."

She seems to consider this information, unsure whether or not to believe me. "Why?"

"Because you're not like the people I usually meet. You don't let me get away with anything." I pause, smirking. "And you have this way of making me feel like I have to earn your attention."

Her lips twitch like she's fighting back a grin. "You *do* have to earn it."

"Yeah, I figured." I sigh dramatically, running a hand through my hair. "The things I do for you."

"Oh, please." She playfully rolls her eyes. "As if it's a hardship."

"It is!" I press a hand to my chest like she's wounded me. "I'm out here busting my ass trying to impress you!"

"How have you been trying to impress me?" She laughs.

I lean back into the couch cushions, weighing my options. Should I tell her the truth, that I'm not actually a lumberjack part-time? I mean, the truth will come out eventually, and when it does, she's going to be pissed at me regardless.

"Oh, *you know*—chopping wood, flexing muscles, pretending to be outdoorsy and rugged . . ."

Her laugh is immediate and loud, and it makes me grin, even though my brain is screaming at me that this is a terrible idea.

"You're not outdoorsy and rugged?" She reaches over to squeeze my biceps, which I immediately flex for good measure out of habit. "Could have fooled me."

I shift on the couch. "I have a confession to make."

Lucy goes still. Sucks in a breath. "Oh my God—don't tell me you're married."

I shake my head. "Nope, not married."

"In a relationship?"

Another shake.

"Gay?"

"Nope."

Lucy rubs her chin. "Give me a hint."

"Let's say . . . I didn't just meet the dudes at yoga. We came together 'cause . . . they're teammates."

"Teammates of what?"

I shake my head again, biting back a grin. "Guess."

Lucy narrows her eyes, studying me to solve the puzzle. I cannot believe she hasn't sussed this out yet, but I'm not going to judge her for believing my story from the jump.

"I hate guessing games. I'm no good at them." Her brows draw together. "Teammates, teammates . . ." she muses, wheels in her brain turning. "You're not married, not in a relationship, not gay, and they're your teammates. Of what, Harris? What am I missing?"

I rub the back of my neck, my grin fading a little. "I'm a professional football player."

For a second, Lucy just stares at me. Not a word. Not even a blink. Like she's been frozen in place.

Then her eyes go wide, her mouth falling open. "Wait—what? You?"

"Yeah."

"And Miles and Dex and Elijah—"

"Yep."

"Miles and Dex and Elijah are *football* players?"

Uh-huh. "All of us."

Her jaw drops even lower, and I'm convinced she's about to burst out laughing. Instead, she just blinks at me as if I've told her I'm actually an alien from another planet.

"You're a football player?" She shakes her head, eyes darting around the room like she's trying to piece together the last few days of knowing me. "You told me you were a lumberjack."

"False," I correct her. "You assumed I was because of my size. I told you I was here for work, and I am, but not to roll logs."

"But . . ." Lucy rubs her temples. "Why would you let me believe you were a *lumberjack* this whole time? Now I feel like a dumbass!"

I scratch the back of my neck, already bracing myself. "Honestly? I thought it was funny."

Her mouth falls open. "*Funny?* You've been out here chopping wood for a mock survival competition as a *joke*? What the hell is wrong with you?"

Lucy smacks me on the arm.

"Hold up now," I say, raising a finger. "In my defense, I thought I'd be good at chopping wood."

She bursts out laughing at my stupidity. "You thought you'd be good at it?"

"I figured it couldn't be *that* hard!" I grin. "You swing the axe, the log splits. End of story."

Lucy leans forward, still giggling. "And you didn't think maybe you should tell me the truth *sooner*?"

Obviously I could have. But where's the fun in that?

"Can I point out again that you never technically asked if I was—you assumed. I was going along with it."

She fiddles with the hem of her sweater. "That's the literal definition of lying by omission."

I squint. "Is it, though?"

"Yes!"

I cross my arms, leaning back into the cushions like I'm contemplating a serious philosophical debate. "I don't know. I feel like omission is more of a gray area. It's not like I *lied* and said 'I'm the king of the fucking woods.' I just didn't correct you." I give my nonexistent beard a scratch.

"Does Annabelle know?"

No. "Obviously not. She's too busy trying to run the event to notice. Plus, she's not exactly hovering over me, watching my every move. I suspect the dudes who actually work for the company have figured out I'm a fraud."

Though none of them have busted me. Or they obviously don't recognize me. Or don't give two shits about football. Or they've got a betting pool on how long it takes before I injure myself.

"I'm sorry, but this whole thing is blowing my mind. Of all the things to fake—why didn't you tell her you have no clue what you're doing?"

Is Lucy being serious? "Have you ever tried to back out of something after showing up day one bragging that you know what you're doing?" I chuckle. "It's a lot harder to admit failure when you've already committed to the bit." All the peacocking around I did . . .

She rolls her eyes at the ceiling. "That ego of yours is bigger than I thought it was. I'm shocked you fit through my door."

I clutch my chest dramatically. "Ouch. You wound me, Lucy."

She smirks. "You'll survive."

Her prissy little pout is so fucking cute. So sexy.

I want my mouth on her again.

"What if I told you I'm faking something else right now too?"

Her smile fades; curiosity fills her expression. "What do you mean?"

I lean in, dropping my voice. "I'm pretending that sitting this close to you isn't driving me insane."

Lucy scoffs. "What if I'm mad you lied to me?"

"I would say: Let me make it up to you."

"How?"

She knows how.

Her eyes flick to my mouth, and I can see the gears turning in her head. She's pretending to be mad, but the way her breathing changes gives her away.

I smirk, closing the distance between us inch by inch. "I'm thinking we skip the part where you stay mad and go straight to the part where I . . ."

"Where you what?" she whispers, her voice barely above a breath.

I kiss her, slow at first—just a soft press of lips, though it doesn't stay gentle for long. Her fingers curl into the front of my shirt, and the second she tugs me closer, I'm done holding back.

I cup her face, deepening the kiss, and she sighs against my mouth, the sound making something hot twist low in my stomach. Her hands slide up my chest, fingers exploring like she's memorizing every inch of me. I groan softly, and when her nails graze the back of my neck, I lose the ability to think straight.

"Still mad?" I murmur between kisses, nipping gently at her bottom lip.

She laughs breathlessly. "I don't know. Maybe I should stay mad more often if this is how you apologize."

Her fingers slide under the hem of my shirt, grazing the bare skin of my stomach, and I swear my brain short-circuits for a second. I pull her closer, my hand slipping around her waist, fingers splaying against her lower back as I guide her into my lap.

She straddles me without hesitation, her knees pressing into the couch on either side of my thighs, and the heat between us kicks up a notch. "I should have known you guys are all professional athletes. The signs were all there." Lucy pauses. "You're so . . ."

"Big? Manly? Huge? Strong?"

She laughs. "Yes."

I capture her lips again. Her hips shift against mine, and the friction makes me groan into her mouth. Her hands tangle in my hair, tugging and sending sparks shooting down my spine.

I want her—no, *need* her—and judging by the way she's clinging to me, she feels the same.

Her shirt rides up as my hands explore, and when my thumbs brush the underside of her bra, she arches into me. I trail kisses down her neck, taking my time, and when I reach the spot below her ear, she lets out a soft moan that makes my self-control hang by a thread.

"Strong enough to lift you in one motion and carry you to the bed."

Lucy's breath hitches, and her laugh is soft as she nuzzles my neck. "I don't doubt that for a second."

Before she can say another word, I hook my hands under her thighs and stand, lifting her off the couch like she weighs nothing.

She gasps, her arms wrapping instinctively around my neck as she clings to me.

I'M STRONG, GODDAMMIT.

ME CAVEMAN.

"Show-off," she whispers, but the smile on her face says she's not complaining.

I start walking toward the hallway, each step slow and deliberate, making sure she feels every bit of my strength holding her securely against me. Her legs tighten around my waist, and the friction sends another jolt of heat straight through me.

I gently press her back against the doorframe for a moment, my lips finding hers again in a kiss that's deeper, hungrier than before.

Her fingers tug at my hair, and I groan, the sound rumbling between us as her hips shift against mine again.

"Bed," she murmurs, her voice barely audible between kisses.

The soft mattress dips beneath us, and she pulls me down with her, her body molding perfectly to mine. My hands slide up her sides, pushing her shirt higher until I pull it over her head and toss it aside.

"God, you're beautiful," I whisper, taking a moment to admire her, my gaze trailing from her flushed cheeks to the soft curve of her waist.

She bites her bottom lip, her eyes dark with desire, and it's all the encouragement I need.

Her hands find the hem of my shirt, and she tugs it upward, like she can't wait to feel my skin against hers. I pull it off in one motion and toss it to the floor before leaning down to kiss her again. Her fingers trace the lines of my chest and abs, her touch light but electric, making my muscles tense under her fingertips.

"You're so hot," Lucy breathes, dragging her nails down my stomach.

Her hips lift, pressing against mine, and I groan, the friction almost too much to handle. My hands move to her waist, fingers slipping under the elastic of her leggings. I pause, looking up at her, giving her a chance to stop me.

"Is this okay?" I ask, my voice rough with restraint.

Her gaze meets mine, and she nods, her voice soft but sure. "Yeah. More than okay."

I slide her leggings down, leaving a trail of kisses along her thighs as I go. She's trembling beneath me, her breathing shallow, and I can't help but smile, knowing I'm the reason for it.

When I finally return to her lips, she pulls me closer, her hands roaming over my back as if she can't get enough. Her legs wrap around my waist, and the feel of her pressed against me has my control hanging by a thread.

"You're making it really hard to take things slow," I murmur against her mouth, my hands gripping her hips.

She grins, her eyes sparkling with mischief. "Who said I wanted slow?"

Her words are like gasoline on a fire, and I crash my lips against hers, my movements growing more urgent as the last of my restraint slips away. Her hands explore every inch of me, and I do the same, memorizing the way her body responds to my touch.

"I've wanted to get you naked since the second I saw you at that coffee shop."

"Really?" Lucy hesitates. "I was wearing yoga clothes."

"I know." I nod. "So hot."

She laughs. "You have terrible taste."

"Not even a little," I counter, kissing the corner of her mouth. "You looked like trouble. The kind of trouble I knew I wanted to be in."

Lucy shakes her head, still grinning. "You're ridiculous."

"And you love it," I tease, trailing kisses down her neck, savoring the way her body arches into me.

"I'm considering it," she whispers. Her nails trace lazy patterns down my spine, leaving a trail of heat behind them.

I'm considering it . . . What does that mean?

This isn't a fling, but it's certainly not a forever thing.

Is it?

Lucy's breath brushes against my neck, pulling me back into the moment. Every soft touch from her feels like a brand, a reminder of how badly I want this, even if I don't know what *this* is supposed to be.

Maybe it's complicated. Or maybe it's simple right now—two people who can't seem to stay away from each other.

Her lips graze my collarbone, and I shiver, my hands tightening on her hips instinctively. I tilt her chin up so I can meet her gaze, and for a moment, neither of us says anything. It's like we're both holding our breath, waiting to see who will speak first, who will say something that pushes this moment past the point of no return.

"What are you thinking?" she whispers, her voice soft but searching.

I could lie. I could say something smooth and simple that keeps the mood light, keeps us exactly where we are. But the way she's looking at me—like she's trying to read my mind—makes me hesitate.

"Honestly?" I exhale, brushing a strand of hair away from her face. "I'm thinking about what you meant when you said you're considering it."

Her brow furrows slightly, like she wasn't expecting me to ask. "Ah."

"Yeah." I offer a small smile, hoping I'm not ruining the moment. "Are you considering liking me, or are you considering where this is going?"

Lucy bites her lip, and for a second, I think I've overstepped. But then she sighs, her fingers stilling against my back. "Maybe both."

My heart does a weird, hopeful lurch. "Okay," I say carefully. "What do you want to do about that?"

She hesitates, her gaze flicking between my eyes like she's trying to figure out what I'm thinking. "I don't know."

At least she's being honest.

And. At least I know she likes me for me—not because I make a shit ton of money and play football on national television.

I press a kiss to her lips, taking a moment to think. "We don't have to figure it all out tonight."

Her body relaxes. I take that as a good sign.

"You're right," she murmurs. "We don't."

I don't hesitate. I close the space between us again, capturing her lips in a kiss that's deeper, more deliberate than before.

I groan, the sound low and rough. When I reach the hollow below her collarbone, her body shivers beneath me, and I smile against her skin, proud that I know exactly how to get this reaction out of her.

Her hands are everywhere—my chest, my shoulders, my hair—like she's trying to feel as much of me as possible.

My hand slips under her bra, cupping her breast, and when my thumb brushes over her hardened nipple, her body arches into me. I trail kisses down her neck and across her chest, taking my time, savoring the way she responds to every touch, every kiss.

Her breath is shallow, her fingers tightening in my hair as I slide her bra straps down her shoulders and unclasp it. The fabric falls away, and I take a moment to look at her, completely captivated.

"Perfect," I murmur, brushing a kiss over the swell of her breast.

She gasps softly, her back arching as I trail my mouth lower, my lips and tongue teasing her until she's squirming beneath me. Her hands tug at the waistband of my jeans, and I chuckle against her skin.

"Impatient, are we?"

"Yes." She shoots me a playful glare, her breath hitching when my fingers skim her waist. "Take them off."

I don't need to be told twice.

I kick off my jeans, and her hands are back on me in an instant, exploring the bare skin of my hips and thighs. The heat between us is unbearable now, and when her hips grind against mine, the thin barrier of fabric between us feels like too much.

I slip her thong down her legs, my hands trembling slightly as I toss them aside . . .

Ease my way down her body, crawling down, kissing her stomach along the way.

Her hands are in my hair, fingers scratching my scalp.

Encouraging me.

Chapter 17

Lucy

It starts slow.

The way his lips move across my stomach, leaving a trail of warmth, making my breath hitch as I stare down at him. His hands are steady now—no more trembling like before, when he slipped off my thong. Now they're confident, gliding over my thighs like he's been waiting to touch me like this forever.

I'm not used to this. Not used to someone taking their time, savoring every second like I'm something worth worshipping.

He looks up at me, his dark eyes locking with mine, and for a moment, I forget how to breathe. There's something in his gaze that's deeper than desire. It's admiration.

Devotion, even.

I bite my lip, watching as he presses a kiss above my hip bone, his stubble grazing my skin in a way that sends shivers down my spine. My hands are in his hair, fingers threading through the soft strands, and I can feel him smile against my skin like he knows exactly what he's doing to me.

God, he's good at this.

It feels like ecstasy.

My breath comes out in a shaky gasp, my back arching off the bed as I give in to the feeling, to him. My fingers tighten in his hair, and he groans against me, the sound vibrating through my body like an electric current.

Oh God . . .

I want to come so bad.

But I don't. I want him to be inside me when it happens. I want . . .

To come together.

Feel his body racking with his own orgasm.

But the sight of his head between my legs . . .

"Oh God."

So fucking hot. Sexy.

I watch as he sucks my clit, close to double vision. Intoxicating.

Finally, I push at his shoulders, needing him closer. Wanting his dick to fill me up. "Harris . . ."

He shakes his head.

"Please!" I push at him again. "Fuck me."

He hesitates. Moves, using my thigh to wipe his mouth before climbing back up my body, hard dick brushing against my leg.

Yes, yes, yes . . .

"Condom?" His rough voice wants to know, and I tilt my head toward the bedside table, pleased with myself for being prepared. A Girl Scout.

I pant as he tears the package open and slides it on. Giddy with anticipation. Mouth watering with need.

So hungry for his dick.

Greedy.

I almost laugh, but hold it in.

Harris presses a kiss to my collarbone, then my jaw, before finally reaching my lips.

"Still mad at me?" he murmurs, his breath warm against my mouth.

"No." My own breath is a whimper, slipping out as he shifts, hitting that spot that has me seeing stars.

His lips curve into a delicious grin, teeth grazing my bottom lip before he bites down, just enough to sting.

"Good girl," he says, his voice a rough, sinful rasp. "Because I'm not even close to being done with you."

Good girl.

The way he says it—low and dark and dripping with arousal—makes my whole body clench around him, heat pooling low and tight as he starts to move again . . .

He pulls back just enough to meet my eyes, his thumb tracing along my bottom lip. "You like that, don't you?"

"Yes." So much.

Harris rocks into me, *deeper*, *harder*, making me gasp. "I know you do."

If this is how he plans on apologizing, he can piss me off any time he wants.

Chapter 18

Harris

The first rays of morning light filter through the curtains, casting a soft glow across Lucy's bedroom. I blink awake, momentarily disoriented, until the events of last night flood back.

She lies beside me, her hair a tousled halo on the pillow, her breathing steady and peaceful.

Naked.

I lean toward her and press a kiss to her nipple, tempted to suck on it.

My stomach rumbles, settling that debate.

Careful not to wake her, I slip out of bed and pull on my boxers. The floor creaks under my weight as I make my way to the kitchen, intent on surprising her with breakfast. I rummage through the fridge, finding eggs, milk. Some random vegetables. Tomato. Mushroom. And a bag of shredded cheese.

Omelets it is.

As I whisk, my mind drifts.

Last night was so fucking hot—but it was more than the physical connection. I've always been the guy who keeps things casual, never letting anyone get too close. But with Lucy, it's different.

I pour the egg mixture into the heated pan, watching it sizzle. As I finish setting the table, I hear the soft padding of footsteps behind me. I turn to see Lucy standing in the doorway wearing my T-shirt, eyes still heavy with sleep.

Sexy as fuck.

"Morning," I say, offering her a warm smile.

She looks at the table, then back at me, a surprised expression on her face. "You made us breakfast?"

I shrug, trying to play it cool. "Figured it was the least I could do after . . ."

"After fucking me three times?"

My eyes go as wide as my grin at her use of foul language. "You sore?"

"Yes, obviously." She laughs. "I limped out of bed."

"I didn't hear you complaining last night."

"What can I say? I like orgasms." Lucy gives me a teasing glare, but her lips twitch like she's fighting back a smile. "But I also think you should be held accountable for any damage."

I raise a brow, leaning across the table and brushing her fingers with mine. "Accountable, huh? Should I apologize or double down?"

Her laughter bubbles again, filling the kitchen. "Oh, I think we both know you'd double down."

"Guilty," I admit. "But for now, breakfast and recovery." I tilt my head. "After that? Who knows?"

She narrows her eyes, playful suspicion lacing her tone. "You planning on ruining me again?"

"Only if you ask nicely," I tease, then take a bite of my omelet like I didn't drop that line.

Her cheeks flush, but she doesn't shy away. "I'll think about it," she says, her gaze dropping to her plate before flicking back up to mine. "In the meantime, what's your day look like?"

I shrug, pretending to think. "No team building, no meetings. I could do whatever I want." Although I should probably go get some more logrolling in—the last thing I want to do is embarrass myself in front of the crowd.

Whatever. I'll worry about that later.

"And what do you want?" She arches a brow, already knowing she's the focus of that answer.

"You," I say simply.

I lean back in my chair, watching her take another bite of her food. The way she's so comfortable, sitting across from me in her blanket, with no makeup, hair still messy, has me wondering why this feels so easy.

Natural.

Like we've done this a hundred times before.

She shifts the focus. "So, what's next for you after this team retreat?"

I finish my toast, brushing off my hands. "We head right back to work. It's going to be a grind."

"And after that? What does offseason look like?"

"Usually pretty quiet. I do some traveling, visit family—maybe work on endorsements," I explain, watching her reaction carefully. "Why? Planning to pencil me in your calendar?"

I like the direction this is going.

Lucy gives her head a tiny shake. "Just curious what your world looks like beyond football."

Oddly enough, I'm disappointed in that answer. It would have been cooler if she'd been like *I totally want to spend time with you in Arizona!* Or wherever.

I'm not picky—I could chill with her in town a weekend or two.

"My life outside of football . . ." My voice trails off as I consider this. "Uh. Staying in shape. I like keeping my hands busy. Woodworking, sketching, trying new recipes in the kitchen."

Her eyebrows lift. "You actually enjoy cooking?"

"Yeah. But it's not like I'm a pro." Not even close. "I like experimenting. My specialty right now is homemade pizza dough. I've mastered the crust—crispy on the outside, chewy on the inside."

"Okay, now I'm impressed."

"I'll make you some," I offer, the words slipping out before I realize I'm making future plans. "If I survive this lumberjack thing."

Lucy's smile softens, and I feel something shift again. More than the easy conversation—this is comfort. The kind that sneaks up on you before you can protect yourself from it.

"I'll hold you to that," she says.

Interesting. "Is this you admitting you like having me around?"

A slow nod. "Maybe."

Her *maybe* hangs between us, soft but heavy enough to knock me off balance. I grip my fork, leaning toward her as I watch her, trying to read the layers beneath that answer.

"Careful, Lucy," I say, my voice low, teasing. "Keep saying shit like that, and I might show up uninvited."

She arches a brow. "Uninvited, huh? Just make sure you're not climbing up the lattice and knocking on my window in the middle of the night."

I make a mental note of that for future reference.

Lucy sets her mug down and rests her elbows on the table. "So, if you weren't doing the lumberjack thing, what would you want to do instead?"

Easy. "I'd take you somewhere," I answer without hesitating.

"Where?"

"Someplace chill," I continue. "We'd hit a local farmers' market in the morning, grab coffee, and then drive with the windows down. No plans."

"Well, dang," Lucy says. "That sounds kind of perfect."

For a second, I wonder if I'm imagining the shift in her expression. It's like we've skipped past the "what if" and fallen straight into "when."

"Yeah. It's too bad I'll be swinging an axe." *And trying not to kill myself.*

Lucy laughs softly, the sound warming the space between us. "You've got this. Think of it as a workout. You love those, right?"

Not necessarily. But it comes with the territory and is a necessary evil.

I run a hand through my hair. "There's a difference between lifting weights and pulling a Paul Bunyan."

"You're not giving yourself enough credit." She rests her chin on her hand, meeting my eyes. "You're built for this."

The way she says it makes my pulse hitch for a second. Compliments from Lucy hit different. She's not trying to inflate my ego—she's not full of shit.

I could sit here all day trading lines with her, but the trash bag waiting by the door is starting to bug me, like a reminder that even perfect mornings have mundane tasks.

I rise from the table and grab the bag. "Hold that thought—if I don't chuck this out, it's going to drive me nuts. Be right back."

"Earn your keep, Lumberjack," she teases, tilting her head back so I can peck her on the lips. "I'll be here."

I grin as I head outside.

The air is crisp, the kind of morning that smells like fresh dew and pine. After tossing the trash into the bin, I pause for a second, letting myself breathe. Conversations with Lucy are a strange mix of ease and tension—enough push and pull to keep me guessing.

I'm about to head back inside when a deep voice cuts through the quiet.

"Didn't realize Lucy had someone over."

I freeze.

Turning slowly, I spot a man standing near the driveway, arms crossed and gaze sharp. He's older, with a rugged face and the kind of presence that tells me he's no stranger to making people squirm. Jeans. Flannel shirt pushed up to his elbows. Gray hair at the temples. Bare feet.

Must be her dad.

Shit.

I glance down at myself—also barefoot, wearing pajama pants and nothing else. Not exactly the look of a guy ready to make a good first impression.

"Morning," I manage, offering a small wave like that'll help.

He doesn't smile but states the obvious. "Taking out the trash?"

"Yup." I nod, trying to play it cool. "Making myself useful."

That earns me a raised brow. He steps closer, and I can feel the shift in the air—like this is a test I didn't know I was about to take.

"You from around here?" he asks, like he's already made a judgment but wants to hear what I'll say.

"Not exactly," I admit. "Just visiting."

"Ahh. With that group at the lodge." He nods slowly. "Why do you look familiar?"

"I play football."

He nods again. "Ah. Everyone in town is chirping about the group of giants that have descended upon us."

"Yes, sir."

I have no idea how to talk to dads. It's not the same as speaking to a fan.

I had sex with his daughter, and he knows it.

"You always take out the trash in nothing but pajama pants?" he asks, eyes flicking to my bare chest. Down to my bare feet.

"Only when I'm trying to make a good first impression," I deadpan.

He stares at me for a second, then lets out a bark of laughter. "Well, at least you're honest. Ya look like a guy who escaped a house fire."

Translation: You look like a guy who sleeps naked and decided to throw something on quick out of decency.

"I *feel* like I've escaped a house fire."

Lucy's dad snaps his fingers. "Wait a minute. Now I know who you are. Harris Bennett."

I give him a nod, standing a little taller. "That's me."

He grunts, unenthused. "Yeah, I've seen you play. Not much of an Arizona fan, though."

Oh.

Well.

My dick shrivels at his humble praise. He's not easy to impress, but I respect it.

"Why is a linebacker from Arizona doing chores for my daughter?"

Because we're friends seems like an idiotic thing to say to his face, given my state of undress.

"Lucy doesn't bring men home," he continues without waiting for my answer. "Not often, anyway."

There's a weight to his words, one that makes my spine straighten despite the fact that I look like I just rolled out of bed. His daughter's bed, ha ha.

"I know," I say honestly. "She told me as much."

He grunts. "All right, well. It was nice meeting you. Now go put on a damn shirt before my wife catches a glimpse of you through the window and decides to leave me for a younger man."

I blink. "No threats? No 'hurt my daughter and I'll bury you in the backyard' speech?"

He shrugs. "Eh. I'm getting old. Besides, you're bigger than me and could kick my ass. Seems like a waste of breath to lecture you."

I raise an eyebrow. "That's it? I pass?"

He squints at me like he's reconsidering. "Do you *want* me to threaten you?"

"Not exactly," I say, shifting on my feet. "It feels like there should be more. Like a lie detector test in a secret room or have the police chief run a background check on me."

He stares at me. "You watch too much TV."

Guilty.

Her dad chuckles. "Relax, kid. If I thought you were a problem, you'd already know."

"Phew." I let out a sigh. "That's a relief."

"If you screw up," he goes on, "I won't have to do a damn thing—Lucy will handle you herself."

I nod, because: fair point.

"She's got a good head on her shoulders," her dad says. "She doesn't put up with nonsense. So if you're still standing here, I'm sure that means you're doing *something* right."

"She really *doesn't* put up with nonsense. I've seen it firsthand."

Her dad eyes me for another second, weighing his next words. "You seem all right, but I've seen plenty of 'good guys' turn out to be anything but. I reserve the right to change my mind at any time."

"Noted." *Sir.* "I'll try to keep my approval rating up."

We share a few more words before I turn toward the steps and make the climb back up to Lucy's apartment, find her still in the kitchen waiting for my return.

"What was the holdup?" she teases. "Was there an animal rooting around in one of the cans down there?"

What? Animals root around down there, and she didn't give me advance notice?

"No. I met your dad by the trash cans."

Lucy blinks at me over her coffee mug. "The *trash* cans?"

I drop into the chair across from her. "Yup. Real bonding moment. Nothing says boyfriend material like taking out the garbage half dressed."

She bites her lip, trying not to laugh. "And? What's the verdict?"

I rub the stubble along my jaw. "The verdict is—I *think* he likes me. Or at the very least, doesn't actively want to murder me for sleeping with you."

Lucy raises a skeptical eyebrow. "That's a good thing."

"I'll take what I can get." I gesture toward the back door. "He basically said I *seem* all right but reserves the right to change his mind at any time."

"Love that for him."

Wow. She is seriously something else . . .

Cutthroat.

"According to your dad, you're the real threat. If I screw up, *you'll* handle me—not him."

She laughs. "That sounds accurate."

"And he told me to put on a shirt." I let out a long, dramatic sigh. "Basically I'm on thin ice forever."

Lucy winks. "Welcome to dating me."

"At least he didn't give me any rules to follow."

Lucy taps her chin, pretending to think. "Hmm. Rules might be a little *formal*—but I *do* love the idea of a penalty system."

I arch an eyebrow. "Penalty system?"

"Yeah," she says casually. "Like, if you put on a shirt again, you owe me a back rub. And if you ever try to mansplain football to me, you owe me dessert." Mansplain? I would never. "If you say something cocky, you have to . . ."

"Go down on you? Deal. Where do I sign?"

Lucy chokes on her coffee, coughing as she sets the mug down. "Wow. You agreed to that a little too quickly."

I grin, completely unapologetic. "Trying to be a *team* player."

She wipes a stray drop of coffee from her lip, eyes twinkling with amusement. "You do realize penalties are meant to discourage certain behaviors, right?"

I shrug. "Sounds more like positive reinforcement to me."

Who wouldn't want to go down on her? Her pussy is sublime.

Speaking of which . . .

I push back my chair and stand, then round the table before she has a chance to react.

"What are you—" she starts, but I don't let her finish.

I scoop her up effortlessly, one arm under her knees, the other around her back. She lets out a squeal of surprise, smacking my chest.

"You *cannot* pick me up whenever you want."

"Pretty sure I can," I say, grinning down at her. "It's part of the penalty system. Immediate consequences."

She laughs, looping her arms around my neck. "Oh, so now you get to decide punishments?"

"Absolutely," I murmur, shifting her weight easily as I carry her toward the nearest surface. "You make the rules. I'm the enforcement plan."

Lucy narrows her eyes playfully. "And what exactly is my penalty now?"

I smirk, lowering my voice. "You're about to find out."

She doesn't protest—doesn't tell me to put her down. Instead, the little minx tilts her head, lips curving into a challenge.

I accept.

Chapter 19

Lucy

To say things with Harris are amazing would be an understatement.

Blissful.

Exciting.

Fun.

Much better description.

I tuck the phone between my ear and shoulder as I stir the simmering pasta sauce on the stove. The air is thick with the scent of garlic and tomatoes, warm and homey, but my mind is miles away—specifically, the times I've spent in bed with Harris Bennett and when everything felt less complicated.

Annabelle's voice crackles through the speaker. "You sound *suspiciously* happy. Like, glowing-skin, smiling-to-yourself, post-good-sex happy."

I grab a handful of cherry tomatoes and slice them in half with a little too much force. "No comment."

"Lucy," she says, voice sharp with accusation. "That's basically a comment."

I sigh, tossing the tomatoes into the pan. They sizzle instantly. So satisfying . . .

I nudge the fridge door shut with my hip, then snatch a handful of fresh basil from the counter. "Look, all I'm saying . . ." I trail off, stirring the sauce again, letting the words linger.

Annabelle makes a knowing noise. "When are you going to admit out loud that you're developing feelings for him?"

I freeze, wooden spoon hovering midair. "I have feelings about a lot of things. Sunshine. Good coffee. Pasta."

"Harris."

"Yes, him too."

The second the words leave my mouth, my stomach *plummets*.

My eyes widen. My hand slaps over my mouth. "Did I admit that out loud?"

"Yes!" Annabelle screams. "Holy shit! You said it out loud!"

I frown. "I am not catching feelings."

She sighs. "You're already *in* the feelings, Lucy. You're *marinating* in them. You're like the saucy sauce on your stove right now. Simmering goodness." She pauses. "I am so fucking jealous of you right now."

I scoff. "Why?"

"'Cause my love life is so boring." Loud sigh. "Can I confess something to you, and promise you won't repeat it?"

I shift the phone to my other ear, lowering the heat on the stove. "Of course. You know you can trust me."

Annabelle hesitates, which is *so* unlike her. "I broke things off with Tim."

"What?" I'm not sure I heard her correctly.

"I ended it," she says quickly, ripping off the Band-Aid. "Two nights ago."

I rack my brain. "Tim?" Pause. "*The* Tim?"

"No, Lucy—some *other* Tim I've been secretly dating behind his father's back," she deadpans. "Yes, *Tim*."

I set my sauce spoon on the counter with a clatter. "But . . . why? You two were—" I stop myself, because they weren't actually much of anything. They weren't *bad* together, but I wouldn't call them soulmates either.

I can hear the exhaustion in her voice. "It wasn't working. I don't know. I kept waiting for that feeling, but it didn't come."

I press my lips together. I *do* know that feeling. Or at least, I think I'm starting to.

I prod her for more details. "And?"

"And . . . he's a great guy. You know all this. He's nice, smart, totally dependable. I felt *nothing*. Like, *zero butterflies*. Zero excitement. It was like dating an oatmeal-flavored protein bar."

Translation: boring.

I shake my head, stirring the sauce again. "So you're done done?"

"Well, yeah—obviously." She says it as if it's the simplest thing in the world to do. "It wasn't fair to him. Or to me. I don't want to be with someone because it makes sense on paper."

No, she wouldn't stay in a relationship that felt stale. Annabelle has always been the kind of person who chooses *more*. More passion, more excitement, more *feeling*. She doesn't waste time on anything that doesn't set her heart on fire.

"Besides," she goes on. "It was mostly sex anyway. It's not like Tim was taking me on dates."

True. Tim had always been a little detached. Routine. The kind of guy who sends *thumbs-up* emojis instead of an actual reply.

"No regrets?" I ask, even though I already know the answer.

She exhales, thoughtful. "Only that I didn't do it sooner."

"I'm proud of you."

Annabelle made a choice. A clean break. She let go of something that wasn't serving her, because why *settle* for lukewarm when you could have something *electric*? I, on the other hand?

I have spent my whole life choosing the safe bet. I cling to routine like it's a life raft, convincing myself that predictable means *stable*. That steady, quiet affection is *enough*.

Simple means *right*.

But Harris?

Harris is none of those things.

And now, with Annabelle's voice still humming in my ear, I realize something terrifying.

I don't think I *want* safe anymore.

I *want* fire.

I *want* electricity.

I want something that shakes me awake, something I *feel* in every nerve ending—something like *him*.

"Are you still there?" Annabelle's voice cuts through my spiral, pulling me back to reality.

I blink, gripping the edge of the counter. "Of course I'm here."

There's a beat of silence before she hums knowingly. "You were thinking about *him* just now, weren't you?"

I exhale sharply, but I don't bother denying it. "Yes."

"So what's stopping you?"

I open my mouth, then shut it.

What *is* stopping me?

On the other end of the line, I hear Annabelle starting what sounds like the bathtub. "Look. I'm not saying you have to marry the guy, but at *least* let yourself have fun."

Marry the guy . . .

Marry.

The word lodges itself in my brain like a rogue splinter. I shake my head, forcing out a laugh.

"I will not be dating him, let alone marry him." I nibble on my bottom lip. "He lives a plane ride away."

Annabelle makes a noncommittal noise, and I envision her dusting her bathwater with lavender Epsom salts. "So?"

"So?" I repeat incredulously. "Hello! Long distance? Have you met me? I can barely keep up with my own schedule, let alone coordinate FaceTime calls across time zones."

She exhales. "God, you're exhausting."

I frown. "Ex*cuse* me?"

"Lucy." Her voice is patient but laced with amusement. "I said *fun*—not *forever*. No one is forcing you to pick out a wedding dress."

Agitated, I aggressively stir the pasta water, staring into it to see if it's boiling. "Then *why* did you put that word in my head?"

She laughs.

"How did this conversation go from you dumping Tim to my relationship issues?"

"Stop projecting." Annabelle huffs. "You don't need a five-year plan. You don't need a color-coded itinerary mapping out your emotional availability. You need to . . . I don't know—do what feels good for once."

I roll my eyes. "I do what feels good all the time. I'm making pasta right now."

"That is *not* the same thing."

I stop stirring. "Annabelle—he is leaving. Why start something when it's going to *end*?"

She goes quiet for a beat, and for a second, I think I've won. But then she says, "Why are you assuming it has to end? Did he tell you he didn't want to see you anymore?"

"No," I admit, gripping the spoon a little tighter. "He didn't."

I've been daydreaming about going to see him in Arizona but know I can't afford it.

My pasta water finally starts to boil, little bubbles rising to the surface, but my thoughts are suddenly nowhere near my kitchen.

"Right. So let me get this straight—he's offering to see you again, and you're over here acting like you two are Romeo and Juliet, doomed from the start?"

I scowl. "That's not—"

"It *is*, though," she interrupts, amused. "You're grieving something that isn't even dead. You're so busy bracing for impact that you won't even let yourself be happy."

Well. When she puts it in those terms . . .

I groan. "This is a disaster."

Annabelle *cackles*. "Babe, this is *romance*."

I roll my eyes and stab at my pasta with a wooden spoon. "If this is romance, it's *stressful*."

The sound of her bathwater sloshing in the background fills the silence. Then, "Love is supposed to be a little stressful. That's what makes it interesting."

Interesting? Ha!

Before I can respond, a thump echoes from the living room.

I freeze. The kind of freeze where your whole body goes rigid, your breath locks in your throat, and your heart hammers so hard it rattles your ribs.

"Annabelle." My voice drops to a whisper.

She doesn't catch on to my fear. "Oh no. Did I break you? Are you having a feelings-induced *crisis*? Because if so, I am so proud of yo—"

"Shh!" I hush her, clutching the phone tighter, straining to listen for more sounds. "I think someone's outside."

Silence.

Then—

"What?" Annabelle is suddenly alert. I hear more sloshing as she sits up in her tub. "What do you mean, someone is outside?"

Another thump—closer this time. A scrape against the glass.

I grab the nearest weapon, which happens to be a wooden spoon, because of course. "I heard something by the window."

"Lucy," Annabelle hisses. "Are your doors locked?"

Panic floods my chest. My front door *is* locked . . . but is it? Did I lock it when I walked the groceries up? My brain scrambles, trying to retrace my steps from earlier.

Another noise. A soft rustling, like someone—or something—is moving outside. A wild animal? A cat?

My grip tightens on the spoon. "Shit. What if it's a murderer?"

"Ya think?" Annabelle practically screeches. "Call the police. Now."

"It's coming from the window."

I inch toward the living room, keeping my steps light, heart *slamming* against my ribs. The curtains are drawn, but there's a faint shadow shifting against the window.

I barely manage to swallow the fear in my throat. "There's definitely something out there."

Annabelle curses. "Lucy, do *not* open the door. Call someone—call Harris for the love of G—"

Before I can answer, a loud bang erupts against the glass.

I scream.

Annabelle screams with me.

And then—

A low, snuffling grunt.

I clutch my chest, heart racing. "*OhmyGod, ohmyGod, ohmyGod,*" I chant.

Annabelle is still screaming in my ear. "WHAT IS IT? WHAT'S HAPPENING? ARE YOU DEAD?"

I suck in a sharp breath and continue forward, my grip tightening on the wooden spoon as if it were a *real* weapon. The shadow outside shifts again, larger this time—less *wild animal*, more *horrifying intruder*.

My stomach plummets.

I reach for the curtain, fingers shaking. Slowly, I peel it back an inch—

And that's when I see him.

"HARRIS?"

Harris is mid-climb, scaling my window like some kind of deranged burglar. His hands are gripping the window ledge, one boot most likely planted in the vine trellis, muscles straining as he tries to—what? Break in?

The second I shout his name, he startles.

And then?

He *falls*.

"OH SH—"

Thud.

I wince as he lands hard in the bushes below with a loud groan.

"Holy shit!" I scream. "Oh my *God*!"

Annabelle is shrieking at full volume in my ear. "WHAT? WHAT HAPPENED? ARE YOU *MURDERED*?"

I don't think. I *move.*

Barefoot, heart pounding, I dash down the stairs, nearly tripping over my own feet in my rush to get to the front door. The second I fling it open, I sprint toward the driveway, phone still clutched in one hand as Annabelle shouts in my ear.

"LUCY?! ARE YOU DEAD? BLINK TWICE IF YOU'RE DEAD."

"I CAN'T BLINK IF I'M DEAD, ANNABELLE!" I screech back, my brain operating at peak useless-panic mode. "FOR THE LOVE OF GOD!"

The garbage cans are toppled over, their contents spilling onto the pavement as if ransacked by a gang of raccoons. And right in the middle of the mess?

Harris.

Sprawled out. On his back. Arms spread. A butter wrapper stuck to his shirt.

I skid to a stop, hands on my knees, breathing hard. "Harris, are you—"

"I'm fine," he groans loudly. He sounds pained. He shifts, trying to sit up, and an empty soup can rolls off his stomach. "Okay, maybe not fine."

Annabelle is still screaming in my ear. "IS IT A BURGLAR? DID HE KILL HARRIS? IS THERE *BLOOD*?"

I press a hand to my forehead. "It's Harris."

Silence.

Then:

"You mean to tell me this entire moment was caused by Harris being a *moron*?"

I roll my eyes. "I'll call you back. My boyfriend needs me."

"NO! Don't hang up!" she begs. "Put me on FaceTime!"

"Bye Annabelle," I singsong, turning my attention back to Harris, who lets out a strained laugh, still lying in the trash pile.

"Boyfriend, huh?" he has the energy to ask. "I like the sound of that."

I gape at him. "You almost died, and *that's* what you're focusing on?"

He blinks up at me, head half buried in a pile of my recycling. It's strewn all over, bottles and cans rolling across the pavement.

Harris closes his eyes, smiling as if he has stars behind his eyelids. "If I go out, I wanna go out hearing you call me your boyfriend."

I make a strangled noise, trying not to giggle. "You are not my boyfriend."

"Not with that attitude."

I pinch the bridge of my nose. "Harris, why were you climbing up the side of my house?"

He winces as he shifts, dislodging a crumpled box from beneath his back. "I thought through the part where I'd surprise you. I miscalculated the execution and the amount of weight that trellis can hold. In theory, I was being romantic."

I blink. "In theory?"

"Yes." He begins pushing himself up by the elbows. "In execution? Less romantic. More . . . mildly concussed."

I stare at him.

Harris stumbles to his feet, brushing debris off his jeans before straightening to his full height. Too close. The smell of his cologne, mixed with a hint of cedar and—yesterday's leftover pizza and expired condiments—wraps around me.

Holy crap does he stink.

"For the record, I *knocked* first."

I raise a brow. "And when I didn't answer, you thought, 'better climb the house'?"

He flashes me that easy, infuriating grin. "What can I say? I'm committed."

I gawp up at him. "Committed to making me lose my mind?"

"Committed to seeing you," he corrects smoothly.

My stomach flips as I step back. "You scared the crap out of me."

His expression shifts, something softer edging into his amusement. "Sorry." He rubs the back of his neck. "Didn't mean to freak you out."

Harris exhales and takes a tentative step toward my porch. That's when I notice the slight hitch in his stride.

I frown. "Are you limping?"

He scoffs. "Me? Pfft, no."

A second later, he stumbles.

I arch a brow.

"Fine. Perhaps I'm limping a little."

I sigh, stepping forward. "Come on, garbage boy. Let's get you inside before you actually break something."

He grins, and I don't miss the way he leans on me for support as I hook an arm around his waist. He's solid, his body radiating warmth and a strong smell of—I gulp—*trash.*

Harris glances down at me. "You're strong for someone your size."

The moment we're inside, I shut the door behind us and drop my keys on the counter.

"Bathroom," I announce, already steering him in that direction.

He gives me a lazy grin. "Trying to get me naked already?"

"Trying to get you *clean.*"

I guide him down the hallway, push open my small bathroom door, flip on the light. Harris steps inside, glancing around as I cross my arms.

"Clothes off," I order.

"Oooh." His brows lift. "Daddy like."

My eyes roll. "You reek to high heaven."

Harris grins, pleased with himself. "Aw, come on, babe. You don't find my *Eau de Garbage* rugged? Manly?"

I make a face. "If you don't get in that shower right now, I will drag your ass outside and hose you down for all the neighbors to see." And by *neighbors,* I mean my parents, who—thank God—are not home at the moment.

He chuckles, reaching for the hem of his shirt. "Kinky."

His grin is wobbly as he lifts his shirt, peeling it off in one slow motion. The fabric clings, damp and dirty, before he finally drops it onto the tiled floor.

I inhale through my nose, regret settling deep in my chest as I get a proper look at him.

His ribs are faintly bruised from the fall, a smudge of dirt streaking along his side. He's favoring one leg slightly, and now that his adrenaline is fading, I can *see* the stiffness in his movements. The way he exhales a little too hard, like breathing itself is painful.

I press my lips together.

"You're hurt," I murmur, stepping closer. I place a hand on his chest, feeling for his heartbeat. Playing doctor.

He stills instantly. I don't know if it's because of the touch or because he *knows* I won't buy whatever tough-guy nonsense he's about to sell me. Either way, his smirk falters.

I exhale softly, smoothing my hand over his ribs, careful but searching. He tenses slightly under my touch.

"Does this hurt?" I ask quietly, pressing lightly over the faint bruising.

His jaw tics. "Not really."

I look at him.

He sighs. "Okay, maybe a little."

I shake my head, guilt curling in my stomach. "I shouldn't have yelled at you."

His brow furrows. "Sure you should have. I scared the shit out of you."

I frown, fingers still absently tracing his side. "Yeah, but now you're *hurt*, and I feel like an ass."

Harris chuckles, but it's softer this time. "Sweetheart, you're the opposite of an ass."

I flush at his easy use of the endearment, then clear my throat, nudging him toward the shower. "Come on, big guy," I say gently. "Let's get you cleaned up."

He doesn't argue, lets me guide him a step closer to the shower stall, body moving slow and careful. He reaches for his zipper, fumbling slightly, and I realize his hands are shaking.

I step forward to help. I undo the buckle carefully, then slide the button through the loop, my fingers brushing against his waist. Harris stays perfectly still, watching me, something unreadable in his gaze.

When I finally tug the zipper down, I murmur, "Can you handle the rest?"

His throat bobs. "Sure."

I nod, stepping back and grabbing a towel. "Take it slow, okay? If anything hurts too much, I have ice packs."

Harris tilts his head, smiling slightly. "Nurse Lucy. I like it."

I turn to leave so he can have privacy, but before I can step out, a whimpering little murmur reaches my ears. "Wait."

I pause, hand on the doorknob, bracing myself. *Here we go.*

"What if I fall?"

I stare at his bare chest. "Hmm?"

He gestures toward the shower, expression that screams earnest—and *I am full of shit.* "I'm injured, Lucy. What if I lose my balance? Slip? Hit my head?" He lets out a pitiful sigh. "You'd never forgive yourself."

I gape at him. "You expect me to believe you *suddenly* lost your ability to stand upright?"

He is somber when he says "Tragic, I know."

I watch as he presses a hand to his ribs, wincing—not enough to be concerning, but enough to guilt-trip me into oblivion.

"Nurse Lucy," he whimpers. "Are you really going to make me suffer alone?"

Yes, I was planning on having him shower alone. I press my lips together, determined not to fall for his act. "You made it up my stairs fine. You'll survive a five-minute rinse off."

"Seriously? You would abandon me in my time of need?"

I glare. "Your time of need?"

He nods solemnly. "Vulnerable. Helpless. *Soapy.*"

I *hate* that a tiny, *traitorous* part of me is picturing it—*me* stepping into the shower, warm steam curling around us, his body pressed close, soap-slicked skin under my hands—

But then he *shifts*, his ribs clearly bothering him more than he wants to admit.

I exhale slowly. "Fine."

His brows lift, clearly surprised. "Fine?"

I cross my arms tighter, forcing myself to remain calm—like this is a logical choice and not an emotionally reckless one. "I'll help."

Harris grins like he won the damn lottery. "Well, well, well. Looks like I am the favorite patient after all."

"No screwing around. If you fall because you're trying to get handsy, I won't be able to lift you."

"Oh, I'm definitely getting handsy," he promises, stepping into the shower first, groaning as the hot water hits his skin. He braces a hand against the tile, rolling his shoulders under the spray, letting it soak into his muscles.

I should give him a moment of privacy—should *not* stare, should definitely not notice the way steam clings to the glass, blurring but not *entirely* concealing the way his silhouette moves.

But when I shift my eyes to his face, his gaze is on *me*.

Watching.

Waiting.

Through the fogged-up glass, Harris tilts his head, eyes dragging lazily over me like he has all the time in the world. He doesn't speak—leans into the water, expression unreadable but unmistakably aware of my impending nakedness.

A slow prickle of heat creeps up my neck.

Tentatively, I reach for the hem of my shirt and tug it over my head in one smooth motion. His eyes track the movement, following the drop of fabric to the floor.

I try *not* to let this striptease affect me.

I try *not* to feel the weight of his attention, lingering, waiting as I unbutton my shorts and slide them down my legs.

But I do.

Chapter 20

Harris

This was not on my bingo card for the night.

Standing in Lucy's shower, hot water sluicing down my back, I watch transfixed as she steps inside and makes room for herself—wet, naked. Yeah, I definitely didn't see this coming . . .

I am absolutely *not* complaining.

Steam curls around us, thick and hazy. Every single inch of her is on display, dewy and slick from the water, her skin glowing under the dim bathroom light. I try to be subtle about it.

I *fail.*

Gorgeous tits? Check.

Rosy nipples? Check.

Slick, wet thighs? Check, check.

Water beads along her collarbone, slipping lower, trailing between her breasts before making its way down the dip of her stomach. I swallow, my throat *dry*, which makes no sense, considering I'm standing under running water.

Lucy doesn't seem fazed by any of it. If she is, she's doing a damn good job pretending otherwise. She reaches for the soap, movements slow and deliberate, lathering it between her palms before stepping closer.

Taking her sweet time.

My breath locks in my chest as her hands meet my shoulders, smooth and slick with soap, gliding over my skin. I tilt my head back under the water, exhaling through my nose, forcing myself to focus on my dick not getting hard.

Jesus Christ it feels good.

Her nails scrape lightly over my collarbone, a soft, barely there touch, but enough to send a sharp bolt of awareness straight down my spine. The tenderness of it—the care she won't admit she's giving—hits harder than her teasing did.

I stay quiet, watching as she works, the water sliding between us, steam wrapping our bodies in warmth.

I don't think I've ever wanted someone like this.

Not just *physically*.

Emotionally too.

She's quiet. Intentional. I *feel* her attentiveness in every slow stroke of her hands. Like she knows exactly what she's doing to me but won't let herself acknowledge it. At least not out loud.

Or. Maybe she's waiting for me to crack first.

I give. "You always take your job this seriously?" I murmur, watching her lather up her palms again before smoothing them down my chest.

Her fingers hesitate for a second before resuming their path, gliding lower, enough to make my breath catch. "I thought you said you needed help. Suddenly it seems like you have an ulterior motive."

"An ulterior motive." I chuckle, leaning in, my voice dipping lower, brushing the shell of her ear. "Who, me?"

She laughs.

My hands twitch at my sides. I haven't touched her once, but I *want* to.

Lucy doesn't say anything for a moment, keeps lathering soap over my stomach, her eyes very pointedly avoiding mine.

"You're quiet," I note, watching her. "Something on your mind?"

She huffs out a laugh, betraying herself by sounding nervous. "God, you are so—"

She doesn't finish.

I grip her waist, fingers pressing into her slick skin, and I swear to *God*, if she's trying to drive me insane, she's doing a damn good job.

I tilt my head, voice dipping lower. "Say it."

Her eyes bounce to mine, something flickering in them that wasn't there a second ago.

Worry.

"Annoying," she whispers, pressing a kiss into my chest.

"Try again." I force her to meet my gaze, and damn—she's enjoying this power she has over me.

Her lips part, like she's about to fire something back, something sharp and cutting, but then—

She thinks better of it. Changes the rules on me.

Her fingers slide lower, skimming the sharp dip of my hip bone, and I *swear* my entire body locks up.

"Oh," she says, voice all fake innocence. "Were you expecting me to say something else?"

Fucking hell.

Of course I was expecting more. To play with her tits, perhaps?

My jaw clenches, my entire body wired with so much tension I could snap in half.

She knows it.

She *thrives* on it.

And when I think she's about to put her hand on my cock—the way I'm wishing she would—she steps away. She reaches past me, twists the water off, and turns to face me, her expression unreadable. And then, without *one single ounce* of hesitation—

She steps out of the shower.

Naked.

Dripping wet.

Bare ass.

I drag a hand down my face, exhaling slowly, trying to shake the chaos in my head before stepping out of the shower. My towel is barely secure when I push open the bathroom door, scanning the hall for her.

I hear the soft shuffle of feet, the creak of her bed.

Bedroom.

My towel hits the floor somewhere between the bathroom and her bedroom, but I don't even register it.

All I can think about is *dick*.

Mine.

Inside her.

I brace a hand against the doorframe, inhaling deep, willing some kind of rational thought back into my body.

It doesn't work.

She's leaning back against her pillows, sprawled out. "You lose something?"

My jaw tics. "You know damn well what I lost."

Her eyes roam down my chest, to my cock. "You came chasing after me."

"As if I wasn't gonna? You're fucking *naked*!"

Lucy laughs, tipping back her neck, water dripping onto her bedding. She does not care. Shimmies forward on the bed, legs hanging off the edge . . .

I step up, pulling her forward, standing between her thighs. My hands trail up, slow, deliberate.

My grip tightens, and I drag her closer until our bodies are flush. Until the head of my dick is at the entrance of her heat. The scent of her shampoo, the fucking smug glint in her eye—I should make her beg me to fuck her. Should make her chase me . . .

But I'm desperate for her.

When she lifts a leg, wrapping it around my hip, I'm gone.

She smirks. "You love being teased."

I nod in agreement. "You love pushing your luck."

Her fingers trail up her stomach and over her own breasts. "What are you gonna do about it?"

"*Fuck* you."

I don't wait. Don't hesitate.

Her gasp is swallowed by my mouth as I lean down to claim her, her back arching, hands gripping my shoulders. Her nails bite into my skin, dragging, *demanding*, pulling me in deeper.

"God," she breathes, head tipping back as I thrust, slow at first . . . to make her squirm . . . to hear the little whimper she makes when I go deep inside her.

I could make her wait longer. Draw this out. But I'm barely holding on myself.

"Not so smug now, huh?" I murmur against her throat, my lips trailing lower, tasting the salt of her skin.

She fists a hand in my hair, tugging me back to meet her gaze. Lust drunk, hazy, and completely unguarded.

"Shut up," she whispers, voice rough with need. "Don't stop."

I grin, my grip tightening as I pull her impossibly closer. "With pleasure."

Her body arches beneath me, her breath breaking in a gasp that sends a shiver down my spine. I drag my lips over her collarbone, lingering at the pulse point beneath her jaw, feeling the way it pounds in time with mine. She's warm and pliant in my hands, her skin damp.

Lucy buries her face in my neck, her lips brushing my skin, a quiet moan spilling against my throat. I swear it's the most intoxicating sound I've ever heard.

"Jeez, you feel so fuckin' good," she whispers, voice barely audible, but I feel the plea in the way her body moves against mine.

Her hands slide down my back, fingers digging in as I move, as I press her deeper into the mattress. She meets me with equal fervor, breath sharp, gasps ragged, body molding to mine like we were made to be together.

I'm braced above her, forehead resting against hers as we move together while the heat builds and builds and builds . . .

"Look at me," I murmur against her lips.

Her eyes flutter open, heavy lidded, pupils blown wide. And damn if that sight alone doesn't undo me.

When we finally shatter, it's together.

I collapse against her, burying my face in the crook of her neck, my breath coming in uneven pants. Her fingers comb through my hair, slow and gentle, grounding me.

Finally, she exhales a breathless laugh.

"Well," she murmurs, voice hoarse. "I'm so glad you're not a murderer."

"Nope. Just murdered your pussy."

My body buzzes, oversensitized, and hers trembles slightly as she exhales. The air in the room is sticky with the smell of sex and shower gel and wet bodies.

I prop myself up on my elbows, peering down into her flushed face.

Beautiful.

Freckles.

Brown hair.

Strands of it stick to her damp forehead, and her lips are swollen from my kisses. Lucy looks like she belongs here, tangled in these sheets with me.

She blinks up at me, eyes still half lidded but sharp. "What are you thinking?" She smiles. "Sorry—I know guys hate when women ask that."

Do they?

Lucy stretches, arms above her head, affording me the opportunity to lean forward and suck one of her nipples in my mouth.

Pink.

Perfect.

She inhales sharply, fingers threading through my hair before she seems to remember herself. Her hands slide down to my shoulders, pushing gently. "You need rest."

I groan against her skin. "I need you more."

She huffs out a laugh, shifting beneath me. "I'm serious."

"I'm thinking that . . . I'm going to be a mess at that logrolling bullshit."

Lucy's eyes go wide as she bolts upright. "Oh my God, you're right." She presses a hand to my ribs, gentle but firm, and winces. "The bruise is getting worse."

"Well, I'm not going to no-show. Annabelle would kill me."

Lucy shakes her head, lips pressing into a line. "No, she wouldn't—she was on the phone with me when I thought a lunatic was breaking into my house. She'll understand."

I shake my head too. "No. Not doing that to her."

Her fingers trail along my side, cautious but curious. "Harris—"

"I'm fine." I catch her wrist and squeeze, not enough to stop her but enough to make her pause. "It's not that bad."

She doesn't look convinced.

"Besides," I add, tipping my head back onto the pillow, "I already know how this is going to go. I'll show up, do the damn logrolling, probably fall on my ass a few times, and then Annabelle will yell something about teamwork before letting us all get drunk at the bonfire."

Lucy hums, sliding back down beside me, her bare leg curling over mine. "And what if you wake up tomorrow and can't move?"

"Then I'll crawl there."

She smacks my chest lightly, the corner of her mouth twitching. "Stubborn."

"Determined."

"Same thing," she murmurs, tracing patterns on my skin. "You should get a tattoo here."

I glance down, watching as she draws an invisible design on my rib cage, beneath the worst of the bruise. "Oh yeah?"

She nods, her head resting on my shoulder now, her lips barely brushing my skin as she speaks. "Something tough."

I huff out a laugh. "You don't think I'm already tough?"

"You are," she says, tilting her head to meet my gaze. "But this would make you even tougher."

I smirk. "And what exactly would make me tougher?"

"No idea." She bites her lip, then grins. "Maybe a bunch of trees—a tree line and mountains, to commemorate your time in my little town." She pauses, eyes glinting mischievously. "And my vagina," she adds, giggling.

I choke on my breath, caught between shock and laughter. "Oh yeah?" I slide my hand down her back, fingers tracing slow, deliberate circles against her hip. "You want me to get a tattoo of your pussy on my body?"

"That is so gross," she laughs, smacking my shoulder.

I chuckle, pressing a kiss to her shoulder. "Would you ever get a tattoo?"

Lucy shrugs, staring up at the ceiling. "I've thought about it a few times but have no idea what I would ink on my skin."

I tilt my head, watching her. "Nothing at all?"

"Well . . ." She stretches, her body shifting against mine. "I like the idea of something small. Maybe meaningful. Except every time I think I've found something I might want, I talk myself out of it."

My thumb brushes her wrist. "I think tattoos should mark a moment."

Lucy exhales, eyes searching mine. "Like . . . the moment you leave?"

Ouch. That was a sharp dig.

Still, I hesitate. The truth is, I don't know.

I don't know what happens after I'm gone.

I don't want to think about that.

I want to exist here, in this bed, with her.

So I tighten my grip on her hip, pulling her closer. "We'll figure it out."

Her lips part, like she wants to argue, like she wants to demand an actual answer, something tangible she can hold on to as I smooth my hand up her spine, feeling the warmth of her skin, the steady rise and fall of her breathing.

Neither of us speaks.

Neither of us moves.

At some point, she shifts, her forehead tucking under my chin, her breath ghosting across my collarbone.

"Lucy?"

"Yeah?"

"My back is killing me."

Chapter 21

Lucy

This is not how I imagined the scene when Harris Bennett met my mother.

No. She didn't catch us in the act.

She didn't barge in unannounced.

She's here because she's the only person I could think to call with a level head; we already know Annabelle is zero help during an emergency. Obviously, the only logical thing to do was call my parents over—moms usually know what to do, and I'm fairly certain my father's back has been jacked up a time or two.

Yes. They'll have the answers.

They're standing over Harris—giant hunk of a man—like two field medics assessing a patient, fussing over his bruises.

Dad stares down at him, Harris's lower half covered by my comforter. I couldn't get a T-shirt on him without causing more pain, so his chest is still bare, bruises and all.

"Well, hello, young man," Mom says, clasping her hands together as she gives Harris a slow, assessing look. "I'm Liz—Lucy's mom."

Harris, for all his usual confidence, visibly swallows before shifting his arm off his forehead and attempting to sit up a little straighter. "Uh, hello, Mrs. . . ."

He doesn't even know my last name.

Oh God. Could this get any more embarrassing?

"LeBrandt," my mother supplies, glancing at me over her shoulder, brows raised as if to say *Seriously, Lucy?*

I shrug.

Harris clears his throat. "Mrs. LeBrandt."

He shifts again, like he's trying to sit up properly, but then immediately winces and gives up, sinking back into the pillows. It does nothing to improve the situation. If anything, it makes all this look so much worse—because he looks like some wounded knight in a romance novel, battered and bare chested and in *my* bed.

"Have you taken any ibuprofen?" Mom asks Harris, pressing her open palm to his forehead. She smooths his hair back as if he were a feverish toddler, giving him the same sympathetic expression she once reserved for me all the times I was sick or injured.

"No."

She gives me another disapproving look. "Luce—can you grab three?"

As I leave the room I glance at them again. Harris Bennett, a literal football-playing tank of a man and wannabe lumberjack, leans into my mother's pampering like he *is* indeed a feverish toddler.

Kill me.

Kill me now.

Dad, who has been standing silently through this whole exchange, finally sighs. "Liz, stop babying him. Look at him, he's huge."

Mom scoffs. "He's hurt."

"He fell into a garbage can."

"Poor thing," my mother goes on. "And after all that, Lucy made you climb the steps up here instead of driving you home?"

I whirl around. *"Excuse me?"*

NO, SHE DID NOT!

"I felt fine after the fall, Mrs. LeBrandt. I was trying to be romantic."

I groan, digging through my medicine cabinet, one ear on the conversation in my bedroom.

"Romantic?" Mom repeats, and I can hear the *interest* in her voice.

Oh no.

No, no, no!

I knock over the ibuprofen bottle in my panic, pills spilling everywhere as I rush to grab three.

"I tried to surprise Lucy," Harris continues, voice dripping with pure, undiluted theatrics. "Climbing to her balcony, like in the movies."

Dad snorts. "What movie? *Jackass?*"

I hear Harris grinning as I shut the cabinet. "I was going for *Romeo and Juliet*, sir."

Mom actually swoons. "Oh, how sweet."

I grip the bottle tighter. "It was not sweet, you guys," I mumble weakly, already losing control of the narrative, setting the pills into Harris's open palm.

He shrugs his bare shoulders, looking far too pleased with himself. "I miscalculated."

Dad raises a brow. "You think?"

Mom is still smiling, like this is the most adorable meet-cute she's ever heard in her entire life. She loves a good romance novel. "Luce, why didn't you tell me about Harris?"

I feel *all* the blood drain from my face.

Harris—the absolute menace—turns to me, expression one of lazy amusement. "Yeah, *Luce*. Why didn't you tell her about me?"

Murder. Cold blood.

Right here. *Right now.*

I clear my throat, shifting awkwardly on my feet near the doorway. "It never came up because he flies home on Monday."

A beat of silence follows my words, my mother's delighted expression falling off her face as she processes this new information. "Monday?" she repeats, her gaze flicking back to Harris. "Where is home?"

"Home is Arizona. I was here with some of my teammates to get a little rest and relaxation." He stretches, then immediately winces, his face tightening as he drops his hand back to his side. "That part hasn't worked out so well."

Dad nods. "That's what happens when you scale the side of a garage and break half the trellis."

"I wasn't thinking straight."

"What were you thinking?" my mom asks.

"I—"

Before he can finish, the front door swings open with a dramatic crash, and Annabelle's voice slices through the tension like a chain saw. "Lucy! Harris! I'm here—help is on the way!"

I squeeze my eyes shut. *Of course* she would arrive at this moment, when things couldn't get any more awkward.

I'd briefly forgotten that in addition to my call to my parents, my bestie knew about the marooned hottie in my bed, and of course she wants to be involved. I should have known she'd come over.

Annabelle appears in my bedroom doorway seconds later, a hot tea in one hand and a cookie in the other. She takes one look at the scene—Harris still bare chested in my bed, my parents standing over him like doctors, and me, looking like I'd rather *die* than be here—and grins.

"Oh," she drawls, stepping inside like she owns the place. "This is even better than I imagined it. No worries—I brought ice packs, Band-Aids, and snacks."

"I'm sure you did."

Annabelle holds up the cookie, breaks off a chunk, and pops it into her mouth, chewing like she's savoring the moment. Like *this moment*—one when I'm dying of embarrassment—is the best evening entertainment she could have possibly hoped for.

I groan, dropping onto the edge of the bed and pressing my fingers to my temples. "Annabelle, why are you here?"

She lifts her cup and sips from it. "Moral support. I was worried."

Dad snorts. "She's gonna need it."

Annabelle grins. "Phil and Liz—just so you know—I happen to *love* Harris. I give him my stamp of approval."

Mom sighs dreamily. "He *is* very charming."

Harris beams at them both. "Thank you, ladies."

He raises his arms above his head like he's going for a casual stretch, but the second his muscles tense, his face twists in a grimace.

I glare, crossing my arms over my chest. "You don't get points for winning over my mom and best friend—they don't even know you."

I'm never telling Annabelle anything ever again, I swear!

Mom, thrilled by this disaster, hums. "We know *enough.* He's delightful, persistent, and—" She gestures toward his shirtless, rugged, hot body. "Very dedicated."

I pinch the bridge of my nose. "Mother!"

Dad sighs, rubbing his temples. "Are we actually going to stand here pretending climbing her trellis with the intention of breaking in was some noble, romantic gesture?" He levels Harris with a stare. "The man fell onto my garbage cans."

Harris nods solemnly. "I'd do it again, sir."

Mom actually gasps.

Annabelle clutches her chest. "Such a heroic thing to do."

I shoot Harris a look. "Would you please stop flirting with them?" He is not doing me any favors.

Harris shrugs, all easy confidence. "Can't help it, Luce. I'm just a guy doing romantic shit and making all of y'all swoon."

I want to smother him with a pillow. Who is this guy? He's hurt! What man turns into a total wicked flirt when he's laid out on his back? HE IS LEAVING. HE HAS NO RIGHT TO CHARM THE PANTS OFF MY MOTHER.

Mom sighs wistfully. Annabelle fans herself, playing along, winking at me to let me know she's teasing.

Then—when I think things cannot get any worse—there's a loud, insistent knock at the door.

Annabelle perks up, her face none too innocent.

I narrow my eyes at her. "Why do you look guilty, Annabelle?"

She swallows, lifts her travel mug as if she's making a toast, and adds, "Just let his buddies from yoga know that Harris was gravely injured. Plus Wally, Bill, and Kyle, but they're not as concerned."

I hate her so much sometimes.

My mouth opens—ready to unleash the full force of my outrage—but before I can get a single word out, the front door swings open with zero hesitation.

Two massive bodies storm into my apartment like it's a damn police raid, heading straight for the bedroom with determination.

"Where's Bennett?"

The deep, booming voice comes from none other than Miles, a guy I recognize from morning yoga—though he looks ten times more imposing indoors than he does on the beach.

"Oh." He looks down at me. "Hey, hot yoga instructor. What are you doing here?"

"I live here."

Behind him, another one of his teammates—Deshaun?—follows, scanning the room like he's ready to assess the damage and take command of the situation.

They barely spare me another glance before their eyes land on Harris, lounging shirtless in my bed, looking like some kind of hunky fallen gladiator.

Miles's brows shoot up. "Damn, bro. You look *rough*."

Deshaun steps closer, arms crossed. "We heard you almost died."

Almost died? I shoot a glare in Annabelle's direction.

Harris lets out a groan, bearing the burden of a great and noble tragedy. "Honestly, guys, it was touch and go for a while."

Mom gasps, eyes wide with concern. "Nobody told me it was *that* serious!"

I throw up my hands. "Oh my God."

I give up.

Harris's teammates take up most of the oxygen in the room simply by existing, their giant frames hovering over the bed as we all stand idly by, watching. "Wait." Miles scratches the back of his head. "Why are you here? And not in the hospital?"

Harris waves him off, like this is some minor inconvenience and not a series of truly terrible life choices catching up to him. "Because I'm fine."

Deshaun doesn't believe him. "Sure. *Okay.*"

Miles still looks unconvinced. "Nah, man. We need the full story."

Harris gives them the rundown, starting at the part where he was trying to be romantic, lost his footing, got startled when I got startled, and ultimately crashed and burned in a flaming pit of trash.

Deshaun and Miles exchange glances, slowly turn to me, then back to Harris. Finally, Deshaun asks the question everyone has clearly been dying to ask. "Bruh—are the two of you *seeing* each other?"

I choke. "Can we please focus? The man fell out of a second story window!"

Miles crosses his arms. "Yeah, but *why*?"

Deshaun nods. "Dude—what the fuck have you been up to these last couple days? Is she the reason you've been a no-show for the team activities?"

The team activities? "What team activities?" I blink, the pieces clicking into place. "Oh my God—yoga was a team activity, wasn't it?"

Miles and Deshaun exchange glances, then both turn to Harris, who suddenly finds the ceiling very interesting.

"Uh . . . I showed up for the *mandatory* ones," Harris offers, scratching the back of his head.

Deshaun raises an eyebrow. "But you've skipped almost everything else."

Harris shrugs, attempting nonchalance. "I've been busy."

I decide now is a fantastic time to throw Harris under the bus and tell his friends what he's actually been up to. "You all know he's been moonlighting as a lumberjack, right? For the fall festival?"

There.

Take that!

Both teammates turn to Harris. "We thought Lumberjack was just a sexy nickname." Miles blinks. "Do not tell me you were being serious. Dude, do not."

Annabelle decides to chime in. "Yes, gentleman, he's serious. He's a flannel-wearing, axe-swinging logroller. You know—a lumberjack."

Deshaun's mouth drops open. "Why the fuck would you do that? What did I tell you, man! You cannot afford an injury!"

Harris nods in my direction. "I did it to impress *her*."

Miles and Deshaun turn to me in sync, slowly, waiting for me to confirm or deny their friend's madness.

I shrug. None of this was my doing.

Meanwhile, my mother claps her hands together in absolute delight. "That's the most romantic thing I've ever heard!"

Dad groans. "Liz, *please*."

"Oh, hush," she scolds him, beaming at Harris like he's Prince Charming. "He's been chopping wood for my daughter! She needs to marry this man!"

"Mom!"

Harris smirks at me. "You heard her, babe. Guess we better start ring shopping."

Annabelle is laughing. "I call maid of honor, and obviously I'll be planning the wedding."

"There is no wedding!" I throw my arms in the air, patience slipping away along with my dignity.

My father, who has had enough of this conversation, clears his throat. "So, to summarize—this idiot falls out of a window, nearly concusses himself, is also a lumberjack, has apparently been skipping team-building activities during a retreat . . . to flirt with my daughter?"

"I wouldn't say *skipping*," Harris argues, readjusting himself against the pillows. "More like prioritizing."

Miles shakes his head. "Damn. The man has fallen in every sense of the word."

"Him landing in a trash can was symbolic," Deshaun deadpans.

Harris laughs. "Fuck you guys." He glances at my mother. "Shit. Sorry, Mrs. LeBrandt."

Dad stands, exhaling like this entire experience has aged him ten years. "All right, I'm done. I need coffee. And silence. Preferably both at the same time." He gestures at me. "Lucy, don't let this idiot climb your house again."

Mom rises to follow, patting Harris on the arm. "Take care of yourself—and we'll be across the driveway if you need anything."

Annabelle takes another drink from her cup. "Welp, I think that's my cue to leave." Her loud sigh is one of contentment. "This has been the highlight of my week." She glances at Harris. "Get some sleep, Paul Bunyan. You have a big day coming up."

I feel my eyebrows rise. "Big day? Look at him—he can't chop wood anytime soon!" The man is a mess!

"We are not going to miss this asshole in some logging-timber show," Deshaun says. "He's going to suffer through it for my entertainment."

Harris rubs a hand over his face. "Lucy is right—maybe I shouldn't do the logging competition."

Annabelle grins, moving forward to pat him on the leg. "It's so cute that you think you have a choice."

"I'm injured!" he argues.

Deshaun clucks his tongue and crosses his beefy arms. "Nah, bruh—you're fine. Worst-case scenario, you swing with one arm."

I glare at them. "That's not how axes work."

Miles hums thoughtfully. "Dude. You'll earn extra sympathy points from the crowd if you struggle. People love a wounded warrior."

He's not wrong.

"You can't seriously expect me to compete like this," Harris says from my bed, staring up at her. Still bare chested. Still slightly bruised. Still giving her puppy dog eyes.

Annabelle bats her lashes. "Babe, I don't *expect* it—I'm counting on it. It's going to be great. You're a fighter, you'll be fine." She stretches.

"All right, losers, I'm heading out. Harris, make sure you wear that flannel shirt I ordered you, with the suspenders."

My best friend breezes out my bedroom door.

"And then there were four." I give Deshaun and Miles a pointed look.

Deshaun leans back against my dresser, entirely entertained. "Man, I don't know what's funnier—the fact that she had to order you a lumberjack outfit or the fact that you're going to be forced to wear it."

Harris scowls. "I'm not wearing the damn suspenders."

"Sure you are."

"Would you please leave?" He crosses his arms over his chest, still very much shirtless, still very much sulking. "I have no idea why you're even here."

Deshaun smirks. "'Cause your new boss down at the log yard tracked us down and said you broke your back. Little bitch ass."

Harris rolls his eyes. "Shut the fuck up—I'm fine."

Miles gestures toward the bed. "Then why haven't you gotten out of this bed yet, eh?"

Deshaun shakes his head. "Yeah, bro. You're stalling."

Miles crosses his arms, amused. "You scared of putting weight on those little bitty legs, big guy?"

Harris scoffs. "I carried an entire log over my shoulder yesterday, fucker."

Deshaun snickers. "Yeah, and then you carried yourself straight into a trash can."

Miles snorts. "A hero's journey."

That makes me laugh. These three are quite adorable, and I almost feel bad for Harris. Almost.

He groans, tilting his head back to glare at the ceiling. "I should've stayed unconscious in that damn trash can."

"You weren't unconscious," I remind him with a giggle, sitting myself on the bed where my parents were. Glance behind me at his friends and say what I've been wanting to say since their arrival: "Okay, guys. Time to go. I have to nurse this guy back to health. He has a big day coming up."

Deshaun smirks, not ready to leave. "You're nursing him back to health? That what we're calling it now?"

Miles grins. "You need us to bring you anything? Ice packs? Crutches? A *priest*?"

Harris groans again, dragging his hands down his face. "For the love of God, fucking leave."

"Text us if he cries."

Harris flips them the middle finger as they exit, their laughter trailing behind them. The moment the door clicks shut, he exhales heavily and slumps back against the pillows.

I tilt my head, watching him. "You okay, Paul Bunyan?"

He glares at me. "No."

I smile sweetly and pat him on the stomach, letting my fingers linger above his belly button. His abs tense under my touch, and I swear I see his jaw tighten. "You will be. After some rest, hydration, and maybe some mild humiliation this weekend."

"You're enjoying this way too much."

"Duh." I swirl my fingers in a small circle against his skin before pulling away, to mess with him.

He mutters something about regretting every life decision, but I grin as I crawl in beside him and turn off the light.

The spectacle is going to be *amazing*.

Chapter 22

Harris

I know my rib cage is sore, but I've fared worse.

Nothing is going to stop me from going out with a bang or giving her one last perfect date before the festival and before I leave.

It's a day of grand gestures.

And this date?

Is going to be the coolest.

I pull into her driveway, eager to give Lucy one perfect date if it kills me.

And so far, it almost has; getting dressed was painful, and bending to tie my boots was worse—but we're powering through in the name of a good time.

Also: Fuck my teammates, who have given me endless shit about all the time I've been spending with Lucy when I should have been bonding with them. In fact, they're probably at dinner right now, talking more shit—*all the shit!*—schmoozing with coaches and talking strategy. But what's more important than prioritizing the people we care about most, new as the relationship may be?

So no.

I don't care about dinner.

Not even a little. I will catch up with them tomorrow.

Scout's honor.

The guys can roast me all they want. They can call me whipped, soft, distracted—all three things are true. Say what they want, they're not the ones leaving someone behind they already can't stop thinking about. I am.

Now? Now I'm making damn sure Lucy knows exactly how impossible it will be to leave her, and I want to show her what she means to me. I have a plan for one last ridiculous adventure lined up, meant to impress. Earlier, I texted her three simple instructions:

Wear boots.
Pack snacks.
Bring your sense of adventure.

What I didn't text: We're going Bigfoot hunting!

Goddamn right, we are! Fun surprise, am I right?

I cannot wait to see the look on her face.

Dex was regaling us with the Bigfoot lore the night we arrived—something about sightings in the woods, enormous footprints on the Ice Age trail—and the tale of a man who claims Bigfoot stole his fishing pole and left behind a turd in a granola bar wrapper.

I was like, *Dex, bro, that's not Bigfoot. That's your cousin Greg.*

As usual, he was not amused.

Equipped with a tackle box full of what I'm calling *expedition supplies* (read: trail mix, two flashlights, a hand-drawn trail map, and some beef jerky), I ease to a stop and throw the truck into park.

Sit back for a second, surveying the same trellis I tried—and failed—to climb, giving it a respectful nod. "We meet again, old friend."

As if on cue, the side door opens. She steps out onto the porch, looking suspicious and amused all at once, wearing jeans, hiking boots, and a sage green sweatshirt that reads *Namaste in Bed*.

I watch as she descends the stairs, looking hella fucking gorgeous and already apprehensive. She rolls her eyes and hops into the passenger seat. "If I die, you're the one who has to explain it to my mother."

From the dash, I pull out a camo ball cap that says *SQUATCH SQUAD* in neon-orange letters and tug it down over my head. It's amazing.

She stares at it—then at me. "Where on earth did you get that?"

"The hardware store." Obviously. I reach back and feel around the seat. "I have one for you too."

"Whatever is about to happen, I regret it already."

I grin. "Adventure awaits us, babe!"

She sighs, but I catch the twitch of a smile as she buckles up.

I crank the engine, the truck rumbling to life, and we head in the direction of the trailhead, to the spot where all the locals say to go. It's a scenic drive, the road winding up into the woods, trees thick and golden with late-afternoon light.

Lucy side-eyes me. "You're enjoying this way too much."

"Incorrect," I say, flipping down my visor and fixing my hat. "I'm enjoying this *exactly* the appropriate amount."

It takes fifteen minutes before we pull into the lot. I step out, plant my feet wide, and tip my head back to take it all in. The air is crisp and sharp, filled with the scent of pine sap, fresh earth, and a faint curl of smoke from some distant campsite. The old wooden trailhead sign stands weathered, carved with decades of initials and hearts—proof that plenty of people have passed through here chasing adventure.

"Ahh, nature." I point at my chest. "Me outdoorsy. Me like forest."

Lucy snorts as she climbs out of the truck behind me, eyeing me like I've completely lost it. "You are *so* weird."

I flash her a grin. "Weird and prepared."

I grab the tackle box—which, frankly, looks more suited for fishing than tracking a beast—and hand her a tall, handcrafted walking stick.

She stares at it. "Did you *make* this?"

"Pfft, I wish," I say. "Bought it at the hardware store, along with all the other stuff."

"Other stuff?"

I pop open the tackle box with dramatic flair. "Ta-da!"

Lucy's laughing so hard she has to sit down. "You brought candy to bribe Bigfoot?"

"Everyone loves peanut M&M's. You don't?"

I let her look around at the supplies before securing the tackle box and pulling the cross-body strap across my chest.

The path stretches ahead of us, winding through towering evergreens, the forest floor soft with fallen pine needles and speckled sunlight. Birds chirp somewhere above us, and every now and then, a breeze rustles the leaves, making the whole forest sound alive.

"All right, Squatch Squad," she says. "Lead the way."

I tap the map, squinting into the tree line dramatically. "We follow the ancient markings of our forefathers."

She groans but follows me into the woods—right where I want her. The trail crunches under our boots as we walk, sunlight filtering golden beams that make the place feel almost magical. Or possibly haunted. Hard to tell.

Two minutes in, I stop dead in my tracks and point with great authority at a *suspiciously* large mound of dirt. "Evidence," I whisper.

She glances down. "That's a molehill."

I shrug. "Bigfoot's mole."

Lucy shakes her head, laughing, and grabs my hand, dragging me farther down the trail.

We walk on, and every now and then I pause dramatically to point out another "clue," and every time she meets me with pure, unfiltered sarcasm.

Honestly? She is goals.

Following the winding trail, she teases me with every step. I of course pretend to take this mission deadly serious.

I stop again, holding up a hand like a park ranger. "Shhh."

"Oh God—*what* now?"

I point to a low-hanging branch that looks freshly bent. "New break."

Lucy gives me a shove as we move along the trail. "You're such a goofball."

When we make it to a little clearing that Monty McNair—owner of the hardware store—told me about, I set the tackle box down on a stump with great ceremony.

"Time to bait the legend!" I announce, pulling out a handful of M&M's and sprinkling them dramatically in the grass.

"Is this considered littering?" She glances around nervously, as if waiting for the actual park ranger to jump out of the woods. "I don't think we're supposed to feed the animals."

I pop one in my mouth and roar, "I am the animal!"

Lucy groans, but she's smiling, that kind of smile that crinkles her nose and makes me want to kiss her senseless.

Before I can make another ridiculous proclamation, there's rustling in the underbrush.

Her eyes go wide. "What was that?"

I halt, holding the bag of M&M's midair. More rustling.

Lucy freezes. "If this is one of your teammates in a gorilla suit, I swear to God I'm slashing your tires."

More rustling. I square my shoulders, ready to take on a mythical beast.

Out strolls . . .

A deer.

Trepidatiously. Tentatively. It blinks at us curiously, one foot in front of the other, walking toward my carefully placed M&M offerings. It steps forward, daintily sniffs the candy—and promptly starts eating.

"Holy shit. I almost crapped my pants." Lucy has her hand on her heart and is breathing heavy. "I thought we were about to die."

Honestly? Same.

The deer flicks its tail.

Lucy collapses onto the grass, still laughing. Her hair spills around her, fanning out and framing her face like a halo. "I cannot believe you dragged me out here for this."

I flop down beside her. "You love it."

"I do," she says, turning her head toward me, nose crinkled, eyes shining. "You're ridiculous. It's perfect."

She takes my hand as we gaze up through the clearing in the trees. The sky is streaked with shades of pink and orange, the last light of the day filtering through the evergreens like something out of a postcard.

The breeze rustles the branches above us, and somewhere off in the distance, an owl hoots. "I feel like we're in a nature documentary," she whispers.

"Have you ever done this before?"

"Bigfoot hunting? No."

I shake my head. "Hiking."

"Sure—of course."

Our gazes find the sky again. For a moment, neither of us says anything. The forest settles around us, crickets chirping, the air cooling as night sets in.

Her voice drifts over. "Can I ask you a serious question?"

"Always."

"What would you have done if you had found Bigfoot?"

Shit my pants. Run.

But I clear my throat and say, with as much dignity as I can muster, "I would've offered him candy and taken a selfie. Obviously." I roll onto my side and prop my head up on my elbow. "Okay. Your turn."

She raises an eyebrow.

"If you'd actually seen Bigfoot tonight," I ask, "what would *you* have done?"

She considers this for a long, long moment. Grins. "Asked him if he's single."

"Ouch!" I clutch my chest dramatically. "Betrayal."

She shrugs. "He's tall, mysterious, and elusive. What's not to like?"

I grin and lean in closer. "I'm tall, mysterious, and only elusive when I'm trying to avoid press conferences."

She hums, pretending to consider. "Close second."

I tackle her with a playful growl, and she squeals, laughing beneath me, her smile wide and real and perfect. Pinning her hands gently above her head, I gaze down at her.

Her chest rises and falls with laughter, but there's something softer in her eyes now—something that makes my breath catch.

Her smile is slow. Sweet. "I don't even know what to do with you anymore."

"Good," I say, mouth dangerously close to hers. "You're stuck with me."

"Bigfoot would approve."

Her lips part to say more, but I kiss her.

It starts playful. Light. Quickly deepens.

Lucy's hands twist out of my grip and thread through my hair, driving me the tiniest bit crazy. She pulls at it . . .

Tugs . . .

The forest and everything around it melt away.

All I can focus on is the soft gasp she makes when I nip her bottom lip. The way her legs shift, cradling me between them. The warmth of her body beneath mine, even with the earthy earth we're laying on.

My hands slide under her sweatshirt, fingertips skating over the warm skin of her waist. She arches into me with a content sigh that shoots straight to my head. Her hands slip beneath my shirt, palms running over my back, nails dragging lightly.

I groan against her lips. Trailing my kisses down her neck, I nip at her collarbone—I swear I could spend hours mapping out every spot that makes her squirm. Moan.

"Still think Bigfoot's your type?" I murmur against her skin.

She lets out a quiet laugh that turns into a groan as I find a sensitive spot below her ear. "You're doing a strong job of convincing me otherwise."

"Should we tear off our clothes and fuck in the woods?"

Lucy pulls back a bit so she can see my face. "I wouldn't suggest getting naked in a forest full of bears."

"Fuck bears," I boast. "Fuck Bambi over there."

The deer lingers but has ambled closer to the tree line, leisurely strolling back into the thicket.

I press my forehead to hers. "I would do it, you know."

She blinks up at me, a little dazed. "What?"

"Fight bears for you."

Lucy goes still. Tilts her head back and lets out a loud, echoing laugh. "You're just saying that to get into my pants."

"Little late for that . . ."

"You brat," she teases, grabbing the front of my shirt and pulling me so close our noses bump. Her breath is warm, her smile lazy. "For real, though. That's still the most romantic thing anyone has ever said to me."

I lower my mouth to her neck, kissing beneath her ear, where her pulse thrums quick and steady. Her laughter dissolves into this soft, breathy gasp that makes my blood heat.

She arches against me, breathing shallow, lips parting . . .

She wants me to kiss her there.

I lift my head to say, "We're definitely scaring away all the wildlife."

"Maybe Bigfoot is watching."

I chuckle, leaning down to plant kisses in the valley between her breasts. "Lucky bastard."

Together, we tug her sweatshirt off completely, toss it aside. I pause to look at her because—why wouldn't I? I love the sight of her tits, her chest heaving up and down, and the smooth expanse of her stomach.

She's beautiful. Flushed cheeks, messy hair, eyes bright and full of mischief.

Her lips curve into a shy smile, and she hauls me back down. "Less staring, more kissing."

I trail kisses down the slope of her neck, over her collarbone . . . lower, until I reach the swell of her breasts. I kiss along the lace, nipping gently, and she lets out a whimper that gets my dick hard.

She arches up into me, hands sliding into my hair . . . towing me closer. I happily oblige, savoring every last bit of her.

The impatience.

The excitement.

Her hands tug at my waistband, and I don't stop her. Let her undo the button of my fly, pull down my zipper . . .

It's a frenzy—partly because we're desperate, partly because it's cold . . .

Lucy drags the sweatshirt over my head, palms roaming over my bare skin, over my bandage, fingertips tracing round and round my hard nipples.

"Let me kiss your boo-boos and make them better," she whispers, running her fingers over my rib cage. "Poor baby. You're so strong."

"Me lumberjack."

We roll until she's on top of me, her knees bracketing my hips, hair falling like a curtain around our faces.

She grins down at me, breathless, cheeks flushed. "You look like one." She leans down, her tits brushing against me as she plants a whisper of a kiss on my mouth that leaves me chasing for more.

She obliges, deepening it until we're both lost in it again—mouths warm and eager, hands wandering without hesitation. We pull down my underwear . . .

Pull aside her thong . . .

Lucy does all the work, lines herself up and slides onto my rock-hard cock, stifling a moan once I'm buried deep inside her, and we find a rhythm that suits us both.

Goose bumps cover my flesh. Hers.

Back and forth . . .

Back and forth . . .

More feverishly this time.

"I'm so close . . ." she whispers to no one. Me. The birds.

"Same," I answer back, fingers gripping the flesh of her butt, ignoring the stinging in my side.

I want to smack her ass, driving deeper into her as the dirt and pine cones and grass and plants dig into my bare ass. A rock jams itself into my thigh, but I don't care.

I never. Want.

To stop.

Fucking her.

When we finally collapse, tangled and breathless, she rests her head on my chest, tracing lazy circles over my skin.

I press a kiss to her temple. "Best day ever."

She hums in agreement, her fingers lacing with mine.

We lie there in the clearing, under the stars, not ready to move yet—soaking up every last second of the night before Monday rolls around.

Chapter 23

Harris

The lakefront is buzzing, the air thick with the scents of sawdust, sweat, and maple-fried donuts. Children perched on parents' shoulders, waving miniature axes—harmless replicas sold at the makeshift concession stand. Caramel apples. Sizzling bratwursts. Mulled cider.

I stand at the edge of it all, hands on my hips, stomach twisted in knots. Laughter and chatter are almost drowned out by the country song blasting from the loudspeakers—and the hired lumberjacks taking practice swings on logs nearby.

For the first time all week, I feel like a fraud.

A phony. Fake.

I am, without a doubt, the worst lumberjack in this entire lineup and have no business being here.

Not to mention: I'm injured! The ache in my ribs is a dull, persistent reminder that I shouldn't be doing this.

Instant regret.

Abort mission.

I step forward, rolling my shoulders, bracing myself for Annabelle's pep talk before the day begins, eyes scanning the crowd.

Lucy has taken a spot among all the people, and I smile to myself.

She's perched on the edge of her seat, her hands wrapped around a coffee cup, and I can see her grin from here. Unlike the rest of the spectators, who are here for the spectacle of burly men chopping wood, she's here for *me*.

Probably to make sure I don't kill myself—or keel over.

She's so damn adorable. I wish we were still snuggled in her warm cloud of a bed. It smells like her, feels like her . . .

"Excuse me." Annabelle clears her throat, stepping around me to the center of our little lumberhuddle. She's chipper, sporting red lipstick as sharp as the axe she's holding, which she brandishes like a pointer as she paces in front of us.

Kind of like a general in the army . . .

"Listen up, you fine specimens of flannel-clad manliness. You've been training for this moment your whole lives," she announces theatrically. "Some of you have been conned into this under questionable circumstances—and little white lies."

When her gaze flicks over to me, the guys chuckle.

I scowl.

"Guys, it doesn't matter how you got here—all that matters is four out of eight lumberjacks are here. Warm bodies." She twirls the axe. "In less than five minutes, you're all gonna be up there, chopping logs for the glory of the Fall Fest. *Some* of you will impress the crowd, earning thunderous applause. Some of you will look like absolute morons. And some of you"—she grins at me—"will make a certain yoga instructor swoon."

I roll my eyes. Cheesefest.

"Here's the deal," she says seriously, all business. "Don't cut off any fingers—we don't have liability insurance for contracted labor. Don't embarrass yourselves. And most importantly . . ." Her voice trails off. "Give the people what they came for."

Bill whoops. Wally slaps my back so hard my ribs scream. Kyle and I high-five.

"Game faces, gentlemen!" Annabelle announces, thrusting the axe at me.

The crowd buzzes with anticipation, the announcer's voice booming over the speakers, hyping up us "lumberjacks" for the Fall Fest Wood-Chopping Challenge. Wally and Bill begin stretching nearby like this is the damn Olympics, and my eyes trail Annabelle as she walks off, soaking up the energy, waving to the crowd with both hands.

"Harris!"

I glance up, following the sound of my name.

Lucy is halfway down the bleachers, weaving through the crowd, dark hair tied into a high ponytail that bounces with each step. As always, she's got a determined look on her face as she beelines toward me.

Fantastic.

I need a hug.

Full frontal, if possible . . .

I shift the axe to my other hand, steeling myself as she skids to a stop in front of me, breathless, her cheeks flushed. It's a cold morning, and the air is chilly, the smells of cinnamon and hot tea tease my nose the closer she gets.

"You okay?" she asks, gaze dropping to where I'm cradling my ribs.

"Peachy," I deadpan, unable to lie. I woke up slightly sore, and she gave me a few ibuprofen to take the edge off, but they haven't kicked in yet.

Lucy tilts her head, studying me. Reaching out, she places her palm lightly over my chest, right above my racing heart. "Ready for all this?"

I swallow hard. For all her teasing, all her sass, there's something about the way she's looking at me—*like she actually cares*. Like she sees, through all my grumbling and joking around, that I'm doing this for her.

To impress her.

"Ready as I'll ever be." I swallow again. "This is more nerve racking than the Super Bowl."

Her brows go up. "You've played in the Super Bowl?"

This is no time for her teasing. “Are you fucking with me right now?”

She bites her lip, a twinkle in her eyes. “Yes, but your reaction was worth it.”

I huff out a laugh, shaking my head. “Unbelievable.”

“Oh, come on! I’m teasing.” She bumps into me gently. “If you can handle three-hundred-pound giants trying to crush you on a football field, I think you can handle log chopping for a few minutes.”

Up in the announcer’s stand, a microphone crackles. *“All right, folks! Who’s ready to see some real lumberjacks in action?”*

The crowd cheers, and my stomach drops.

Lucy notices my expression; her smirk softens into something gentler. She steps closer, lowering her voice. “You’ll be fine.”

“Sure,” I mutter. “If by *fine* you mean humiliated in front of half the town, then yeah. I’ll be fine.”

“You got this,” she says softly. “This started as fun—so go out there and have fun.”

I let out a slow breath, my grip tightening around the axe handle.

Fun. That’s what all this is about—the whole week, actually. This is what our coaching staff had in mind when they sent us to Star Lake. Comradery. Team building. Bonding.

Fun.

I scan the crowd for more familiar faces—sure enough, Miles, Deshaun, Dex, and a few others stick out like sore thumbs, the families around them seemingly oblivious to the larger-than-life figures among them. They’re here for a show!

Lucy steps in front of me, resting her hands lightly against my chest.

My pulse spikes.

“You know . . .” she muses, voice dropping flirtatiously. “You might need some *extra* luck.”

“Oh yeah?” My throat goes dry. “How extra?”

“Very extra.” Her fingers flex against my black-and-red flannel shirt, the smallest movement, but I feel it everywhere. Then—I watch transfixed as she rises on her toes and presses her lips to mine.

It's not a quick peck, not some playful good luck peck on the cheek.

Nope.

It's slow. *Lingering.*

The kind of kiss that has me gripping the axe tighter, fighting the urge to drop it and pull her against me completely. The kind that makes my ribs ache for an entirely different reason.

The kind of kiss that makes my dick hard.

Lucy finally pulls back, lips curling into a satisfied smile. My brain? Scrambled. My grip on the axe? Wobbly. My entire body? Tense in a way that has me wanting to scoop her up, carry her off, and bang her in the bed of my pickup truck.

And, judging by the eruption of laughter from behind me, my lumberjack coworkers appreciate it too. Kyle lets out a low whistle. "Somebody's got a serious case of morning wood—and it ain't me."

The guys erupt into laughter.

I shoot Kyle a glare. "Jesus Christ. Be a damn gentleman—there are ladies present."

He smirks. "What I meant was, we're all about to chop wood."

Wally waggles his brows. "If I got a kiss like that before competing, I'd be swinging too hard."

Kyle snickers. "Or not hard enough."

"Enough." Annabelle claps her hands, interrupting us—thank God. "Rein it in. We have an audience, and I refuse to let you ruin this event before it starts."

"We're playing to the crowd." Kyle grins. "You told us to give the people what they want . . ."

"You know what people *don't* want?" Annabelle counters. "To hear you two rambling about your lack of wood while they sip cider with their cute families. Now, enough innuendos—axes up!"

Then she gives Lucy a tiny nudge. "Luce—time is up. You've sufficiently flustered Harris." Annabelle waves her hand toward the bleachers. "Shoo, shoo—off you go. Let the man do his job."

Lucy grins at her best friend but follows her directions, taking a step back. "You're going to do great," she tells me. "Do your best."

Do my best?

I laugh as she kisses me one last time before jogging back up to the stands, ponytail bouncing.

The announcer's voice crackles over the speakers. *"Ladies and gentleman! It's time for the first round of the standing block chop! Let's hear it for our competitors as they step up in position!"*

The crowd erupts, a mix of cheers, whistles, and a few good-natured boos from my teammates, who are clearly enjoying the spectacle of Harris in flannel, pretending to be a lumberjack.

Kyle elbows me as we step up to our respective logs. "You look like you're in a goddamn Hallmark movie."

"Was that a compliment?"

He grunts.

As I'm adjusting my grip on the axe handle, the announcer's voice crackles once more. *"Well, well, well, folks! I've been informed we've got ourselves a special guest competitor in today's competition!"*

I freeze.

Oh shit.

The last fucking thing I want is more attention on myself.

The mood shifts, murmurs of curiosity rippling through the stands. The audience members crane their necks.

My stomach drops into my ass.

"*Now, I don't know if y'all noticed,*" the announcer continues, dragging out this pronouncement, savoring every damn syllable. *"But chopping wood isn't the only thing this guy does. You might recognize him from Sunday Night Football because standing right here in front of us, ready to take on some good old-fashioned timber, is none other than Harris Bennett from the Arizona Sentinels! And he's brought along a few of his friends."*

Silence.

For half a second.

Then—absolute chaos.

The bleachers *erupt.*

When I raise my hand—and axe—to wave, the roar of the crowd crashes over me, my nerves disappearing. Poof, gone.

If they want a show, *I'll give them a damn show.*

I adjust my stance as if I'm about to play a round of golf, roll my shoulders, lift my chin, letting the moment sink in.

I've played in stadiums packed with seventy thousand screaming fans, but there's something about *this*—a small-town festival, flannel-clad families cheering like I just walked onto the Super Bowl field—that hits *different.*

I flash a slow, easy grin and raise my axe into the air.

The crowd absolutely loses their freaking minds.

Kyle groans, shaking his head. "Great. Now he's *feeling* himself." He laughs. "Is that stadium strength any match against *real* lumberjack muscle?"

The announcer is still hyping the crowd, his voice booming over the speakers. *"Who's ready to see if Harris Bennett can chop more than just offenses?"*

I grip my axe tighter, glancing over at Kyle. "Hope you're ready to lose, old man."

He laughs, shaking his head. "We'll see about that."

Annabelle raises a hand. "Axes up!"

I roll my shoulders one last time, plant my feet, and get into position.

"Three . . . two . . . one . . . GO!"

I swing hard, the first strike biting deep into the wood with a satisfying THWACK. The force reverberates up my arms, but I don't stop to feel it—I keep going, correcting my angle, swinging again.

Beside me, Kyle is a machine. His axe hits in rapid succession, each swing throwing up wood chips, the log splitting in slow, deliberate destruction.

But I'm faster.

Perspiration forms on my forehead as I push through, bringing the blade down again and again. My ribs ache from the impact, but the adrenaline overrides it.

The crowd is going *wild.* Every time my axe hits, they *feel* it. Each crack of splintering wood fuels their cheers.

Sweat beads between my pec muscles. I don't stop. I can't. The adrenaline is pumping, my muscles are screaming, and I've got an entire crowd losing their damn minds every time my blade makes contact with the wood.

The energy is *electric.*

The cheers. The heat. The sweat dripping down my back.

I swing again—THWACK, THWACK—the log splintering beneath my blade. The crowd eats this shit up, an unyielding wave of hoots, whistles, and screaming.

I *should* be focused on winning. On chopping more wood than Kyle.

But then I hear a voice from the stands . . . loud. Clear.

"TAKE IT OFF, BENNETT!"

Take it off, take it off, take it off . . .

It's not a horrible idea. Give the ladies what they want!

I step back, gripping my axe with one hand, and with the other—

Grip the front of my flannel and rip it open.

Buttons go flying.

The crowd *loses their collective minds.*

Well. Maybe the dudes don't, but the moms sure do.

"*He's possessed by the lumberjack gods, folks—look at him go!*" the announcer shouts. "*He may indeed be the winner—at least in the hearts of the fans here today.*"

Kyle wipes sweat from his brow with his sleeve, glancing over at me, disgusted. "I can't compete with this!"

I grin, whacking away. "Damn right!"

But then—

CRACK!

His log splits.

Mine? Still standing.

Shit.

"*Time!*" the announcer bellows. *"And the winner . . . is . . . KYLE! Give it up for* Kyle, *everyone!"*

The second the announcer declares Kyle the winner, the crowd detonates again, breaking into thunderous applause, roaring with approval. Kyle lifts his arms in victory, grinning as if he's conquered Everest. I clap him on the shoulder, giving him his moment. He *earned* it. The guy is a maniac!

Then—

"BOOOOO!"

Dex is standing on the bleachers, cupping his hands around his mouth to amplify *the* most dramatic booing I've ever heard—and I've heard a ton of booing. Comes with the job.

Deshaun joins in. "RIGGED! THE *HOTTEST* LUMBERJACK SHOULD'VE WON!"

"THE MAN SACRIFICED HIS SHIRT!"

That's what pushes Annabelle over the edge.

"*Enough!* This is a family show—put your damn shirt back on!" she bellows at me, stomping over with the authority of an irritated kindergarten teacher. She jabs a finger in my direction. "You absolute menaces need to get moving before this turns into a full-blown riot."

"Don't blame me." Kyle holds up his hands in surrender. "I haven't done anything!"

I grab my flannel off the ground and sling it over my shoulder. "What's next?"

Annabelle points toward the opposite side of the event space, where several giant logs bob in the water. "The birling competition," she says.

I blink. "The what?"

"Logrolling," Bill clarifies, rejoining us. "We run on a floating log and try not to eat shit."

I hadn't heard them call it that before—I thought it was called logrolling.

I stare at him. "And if we *do* eat shit? Stay in the water? Bob around? Wave?"

Annabelle smirks. "You make a big splash in front of all your adoring fans and, yes, give them all a big wave."

Kyle whoops. "Or. Try not to eat shit."

"Uh—hey, Annabelle, I thought I was log splitting." The last time I tried standing on a log, I fell in within three seconds. Maybe less.

Annabelle levels me with a look. "Oh, you thought you were only log splitting? That's cute—we need all hands on deck."

"I'm serious," I argue. "I didn't sign up for that."

"I don't have time for your cold feet. The crowd has seen you, they know you're here—now they're out for blood or, at the very least, an embarrassing wipeout."

"But . . ."

Annabelle sighs, rubbing her temples. "Look, Harris. You're here. You're famous. Adding lumberjacks to the event has been the most entertaining, profitable weekend we've had in years. Now—you *will* climb onto that log, you *will* attempt to roll it, and if you *do* fall in—" She smirks. "You'll do it with grace and a smile."

I rub my hand down my face. "There's no such thing as *graceful* drowning."

Four massive logs bob in the water, each one slick and spinning lazily with the current. There's no way in hell I'm staying upright—not today.

I exhale sharply, glancing at the water. Then back at Annabelle. Then at Bill, who looks way too excited to watch me suffer.

"You're really making me do this?" I ask, stalling. "I'm injured."

"Lucy told me you were out traipsing through the woods hunting Bigfoot. You're fine." Annabelle taps the tip of her boot on the ground. "Let me ask you this: Do you want to disappoint all your adoring fans?"

I glance at the crowd.

Big mistake.

Huge.

They've shifted toward the water's edge, where separate bleachers are set up, eager for the next spectacle. People are gathering by the shore, pointing. Chattering.

Waiting.

Wally, for his part? Jumps up and down in front of the bleachers, racing back and forth with his hands around his mouth, shouting, "Who wants to see Harris Bennett get dunked?"

Everyone, obviously.

Annabelle gestures to one of the logs. "Hop on, boys."

Bill steps up first, moving with the confidence of a man who has done this before. He balances with one foot, then the other, and stands on the log, changing his stance like he was born to do this. 'Cause he was.

I look down at my log. Then at the water. Then back at Annabelle.

"Hypothetically," I start. "What happens if I *don't* get on?"

She gives me a *look*. "Hypothetically? I will personally shove you in."

Chapter 24

Lucy

"What's the most ridiculous thing a man can do?" I ask Annabelle, crossing my arms and staring at the water. "Hop on a log he has no business being on to show off for a crowd."

Full disclaimer: I haven't decided if this is a turn-on or a turnoff.

Because on one hand, Harris looks ridiculous. He's flailing like a baby deer standing on its legs for the first time, his arms pinwheeling as he tries to steady himself. Harris is wobbling so hard, the log might as well be a trampoline. It's embarrassing, kind of. Like *secondhand cringe.* I can feel my face heating up just watching him.

On the other hand . . . those abs.

Those shoulders. That cocky smirk that would be so much easier to ignore if he didn't look like he just walked off a *Sports Illustrated* cover shoot for the limited-edition mountain-man issue.

In my hands is a thick, gray towel, ready to dispense the second he falls ass over teakettle into the water. Because he will. And I will be ready for him when he emerges.

Annabelle nudges me, standing close as we watch the chaos unfolding on the water with wide eyes. "I don't even know how to thank Harris. Seriously. If he hadn't stepped up to help me, this whole thing could have gone down in flames. Word has gotten out, and we can officially call the weekend a huge success.

"You're lucky, you know that?" she goes on, not taking her gaze off Harris. "The way he looks at you? The way he keeps trying to impress you? I'm not saying I would kill for a guy like that, but I might be willing to commit a petty crime."

I smile.

She's right.

He is pretty freaking amazing.

Looking at him, I have an ache in my chest now and an itch on my boobs with an unattractive rash on my ass.

I scratch, doing my best to leave it be.

"Honestly, Lucy, I've been a little jealous. The past few days, watching you two . . . it's like you're living in some kind of romantic comedy. And I'm just over here trying to make sure this festival doesn't implode."

I look at her, surprised. "Jealous? Of Harris?"

"Of you!" She swats at my arm. "Your meet-cute is with the hottest guy in town. Meanwhile, I'm running around making sure Wally doesn't hack his fingers off with an axe, which hasn't been easy." Annabelle sighs. "Maybe some hot, muscular lumberjack will just come strolling through, dripping with sweat, carrying a log, and sweep me off my feet."

"It could still happen," I say, nudging her back. "Harris's teammates are still in town—not sure if all of them are leaving. Stranger things have happened."

My gaze goes back to Harris, who continues to flail.

Still, he seems to be hanging on.

"My God—his ribs must be so sore," I muse with sympathy. "He is going to be such a mess tomorrow."

"Poor bastard. He's taking one for the team."

I give her another look. "You know he's here today because he respects you. It has nothing to do with me." I slide my arm around her waist, pulling her close. "You did this—all of this is amazing because of you. Yeah, they're nice to look at, and it's fun. But they wouldn't be here without you."

"Stop. You're making me blush."

But I don't stop. She obviously needs to hear it. "I'm not kidding. You're running the show. You're a badass, and someone is going to sweep you off your feet if you don't beat them to it. It just won't be with a log."

Annabelle scrunches up her nose. "You think?"

"I know." I squish her. "It's going to be your antihero: tall, dark, handsome."

"*Ohh*, a Viking would be perfect."

Before I can say more, there's a loud splash from the lake, followed by a chorus of shouts and laughter.

Both our eyes go wide, and my hand goes over my mouth. "Oh God, that looked horrible!"

Harris bobs in the water, sputtering, hair plastered to his forehead; he looks more like a drowned rat than a man who's doing a massive favor for my best friend while injured.

"Bless his heart, he stayed on an entire forty seconds."

"You think it's been that long?"

"Let's give him the benefit of the doubt." Annabelle giggles, then glances at me with a smirk. "Look at you, ready to run over there with that towel like a doting wifey."

I shove her, but I'm already moving toward him, towel in hand as Harris hefts himself out of the water to the roar of the crowd, dripping wet and grinning like he just won an Olympic medal.

So hot.

He ignores the outstretched towel I'm offering him. One arm hooks around my waist, the other under my thighs, and suddenly, I'm being carried under protest. My squeal echoes across the bleachers as he hoists me up against his chest, my legs flailing as I cling to his shoulders.

"Harris, put me down!" I shriek, laughter bubbling up as cold water from his soaked shirt seeps through mine, chilling my skin. "You're getting me wet!"

"Don't get mad," he says, his grin wicked, eyes glinting with that familiar, dangerous mischief. "The crowd is gonna love this."

Then he's charging toward the water's edge, gripping me tightly as I try to wiggle free, screaming the entire way. "Harris, no!"

He holds me close, muscles tensing beneath my hands as he takes a running leap off the dock.

And then we're airborne.

My stomach flips. Lurches from the jump.

Water rushes to meet us, and we hit the surface with a splash so loud it drowns out the cheers and laughter echoing from the shore.

Glub . . . glub . . .

Glub.

Cold water engulfs me, rushing up my nose and filling my ears. Free from his arms, I resurface, sputtering, my once cute hair now plastered to my face. Harris bobs up beside me, water streaming down his face, grinning like a maniac.

I want to strangle him.

He kisses me as if we were the only two people around.

As if the entire town wasn't watching from metal bleachers.

It's messy and wet and tastes like lake water, and I want to be furious, but I can't! I can't seem to care! His hands slide up my back, pulling me against him as the water ripples around us, waves lapping against our bodies.

They love it.

I love it.

And honestly? I think I love *him*.

I must.

Nothing else can explain the way he makes me feel.

Chapter 25

Lucy

What I want to do is spend the evening at home, where it's quiet. Where the lighting is dim. Where I can sit in my pajamas in front of the TV and have Harris massage my feet . . .

But that's not what happens.

Because Harris is famous—and so are his friends—and once he became the belle of the festival? Well. The only logical place to spend the evening is up at the big, fancy lodge, being roasted and toasted by his friends, the locals—and the tourists.

The moment he ripped his shirt open like a freaking romance cover model, I *knew* the night would spiral into chaos.

So now here we are, crammed inside the Lakeside Resort, packed with way too many people, all of whom have only one goal: to ensure Harris or his teammates stay as long as possible.

The man of the hour groans, rubbing his temples as yet another round of applause—and another round of shots—breaks out. "I swear, these people are acting like I personally chopped down the entire forest with my bare hands."

I nudge his side gently. "I mean, you *did* tear your shirt open like some kind of woodsy superhero. I think that earned you the title of Lumberjack Linebacker for life."

He gives me a deadpan look. “That was not intentional.”

I snort loudly. “Tell that to the thirsty divorcées at table six.”

A trio of women, each armed with a fresh martini, are brazenly eyeing him like he’s the dessert menu.

“Please.” He reaches for my hand. “Save me.”

I arch a brow, feigning innocence. “It would be *rude* to leave now.”

His fingers tighten around mine, lips ghosting near my ear as he leans in. “I will do *anything* if you get me out of here.”

The way he says it—low and promising—sends a shiver through me. “Tempting,” I murmur, letting the words drag out just to watch his expression shift. “So tempting . . .”

Before he can retaliate, a commotion near the bar catches our attention. A giant bear of a man is hoisting himself onto the bar top while the bartender struggles to remove him, raising a beer stein high above his head and shouting, “TO THE LUMBERSEXUALS!”

The entire bar erupts, laughter echoing off the wood-paneled walls.

“I swear to God, if one more person uses the word ‘lumbersexual’ in my presence . . .”

I bite back a grin, smiling above the rim of my glass. “What’s wrong, *babe*? Not a fan of your new title?”

He levels me with a flat look. “I play football. I am not a lumberjack.”

I glance down at his flannel-covered chest, then up at the thick scruff lining his jaw. “Mmm. Debatable.”

Before he can argue, another cheer erupts as the bear of a man on the bar top jumps off, slams his beer stein down, and bellows, “SOMEONE GET BENNETT AN AXE!”

More drunk cheers. More drunk chanting: “*Axe! Axe! Axe!*”

I’m mid-sip of my drink when a stranger shoves her phone in my face, her grin wide with mischief. “Lucy,” she shouts over the noise, calling me by name. “What was your reaction the moment Harris ripped his shirt open? Be honest.”

I lower my glass slowly, dragging out the moment for dramatic effect. “Well.” I tap a fingernail against my cocktail glass. “I didn’t *hate* it.”

Harris's eyes darken a little as a roar of approval erupts from the group, someone clapping him on the back like he's won an actual championship.

And suddenly, *the game has begun.*

Again.

Harris leans back in his chair, one arm slung casually over the backrest, his drink loose in his other hand. But his eyes? Yeah. Those are locked on me now, sharp and *interested*, like my words flipped a switch in his brain, simple as they were.

The bar is loud, buzzing with energy, but I'm suddenly all too aware of him. The way his jaw tics slightly. The way his fingers drum against his glass, slow, deliberate. The way his eyes settle onto *me*.

Dex whistles. "Ohhh, she didn't hate it, boys."

Miles claps his hands. "Yoga teacher gave a love confession."

They are such idiots.

"He made a scene—now he has to live with the consequences." I roll my eyes. "When he ripped his shirt open, I was somewhere between mildly entertained and—seriously confused."

Harris's smirk grows. "Mildly entertained?"

I sip my drink to hide my smile. "Sure."

He tilts his head slightly, watching me. "You weren't impressed?"

I raise a brow. "Do you *need* me to be impressed?"

The table erupts into chaos.

"OH SHIT."

"She's calling *him* out*!"*

Harris exhales, shaking his head, amusement in his expression. "Lucy."

I blink innocently. "Harris."

He leans forward and rests his elbows on the table, closing the space between us. Lowers his voice so I have to lean closer to hear him. "Know what I think?"

I lift a brow. "Please. Enlighten me."

His tone is so low only I can hear. "I think you *were* impressed."

I don't react.

Don't blink.

Don't let it show that he's right. Maybe—just maybe—I was affected by his over-the-top performance earlier. By his bare chest glistening in the sun. His muscles. Broad back. Shoulders.

Six-pack abs.

I tilt my head, matching his energy. "And I think *you* like that I won't admit it. You love it when I'm stubborn."

A Cheshire cat–like grin spreads across his face. "You *love* playing this game with me, don't you?"

I sip my drink, unbothered. *"Clearly . . ."*

His eyes flick to my mouth.

The air between us tightens.

The noise of the bar fades.

It's *just us now*.

I keep my expression neutral, swirling my drink as if I'm completely unaffected. As if I don't feel the heat rolling off him in waves. As if I haven't memorized the sharp cut of his jawline, the way his clean shirt clings to his shoulders.

His lips twitch. "I *knew* you were looking."

I roll my eyes toward the ceiling. "You were standing on a stage. Ripping your shirt open. Everyone within a one-mile radius was looking."

He is so full of himself! Honestly!

My heartbeat picks up as he leans in more, elbows still braced on the table. "You wanna know what I think?"

I feign indifference. "Oh, please. Tell me what's on that *brilliant* football mind of yours."

He's unfazed. *Too* controlled. "I think you're trying *really* hard not to let me know you liked it."

I scoff. "Liked what?"

He tilts his head, voice dipping lower. "Me."

"I think we've already established that I like you. I wouldn't be here if I didn't."

"You know what I mean."

Hmm, do I? "I'm not sure I'm following."

"You *like me* like me."

I snort this time. "What are we, five? Of course I like you." I pause. "You're fun. What's not to like?"

The world around us disappears.

Harris stares at me, his jaw tight, his body tense in a way that tells me he's already made a decision—one I don't know if I'm prepared for. He exhales, low and controlled.

One second goes by.

Then another.

And another . . .

Tick.

Tick.

Boom.

Then he moves.

Before I can react, before I can process what's happening, his hands are on me—strong. Steady. *Decisive.*

And then?

I'm off the ground, gasping in surprise.

"Harris—"

The bar erupts the same way they did earlier at the lake today when he jumped into the water with me.

I let out an undignified yelp, my hands gripping Harris's shoulders, my body suddenly pressed against his chest as he hoists me into his arms like I weigh nothing.

I glare up at him. "Harris, I demand to be put down."

He doesn't even hesitate. "Nope."

The door up ahead.

He's headed straight for it.

Behind me, people are banging on tables. "GOING ONCE, GOING TWICE—"

"AND THEY'RE OUTTA HERE!"

If I said this wasn't the most exciting, romantic thing that's ever happened to me, I'd be lying. And the cold night air does nothing to cool the heat simmering between us the second the door swings shut.

Harris doesn't slow down. Doesn't falter. Just keeps moving, his grip firm, his chest *solid* beneath my palms.

I should be fighting this. Wriggling out of his hold, demanding he put me down so I can walk like a fully functional adult.

I *should* demand—again—to be put down. I *should* tell him he's being ridiculous. That he made a scene back there and I'll never live it down. That there is *absolutely no reason* for him to be carrying me bridal-style into the night.

But the truth is . . .

I *don't* want him to let go.

My fingers curl into the fabric of his shirt, my body pressing closer, the traitorous part of me *craving* the warmth of him, the steady strength beneath my hands. Despite everything—the chaos, the spectacle, the way he *hauled* me out of that bar—being in his arms feels *right*.

It's thrilling.

And I . . .

I *belong* there.

I stare up at him, my breath short. "Where the *hell* are you taking me?"

He doesn't answer. Instead, he keeps walking—down the steep steps behind the resort, down the dimly lit path leading toward the lake . . . and the road. The night is quiet, save for the faint rustling of wind through the trees and the distant sounds of festivalgoers lingering in town and at the resort. But here, in the darkened path beneath the pines, it's just *us*.

And Harris is determined.

His grip doesn't falter. His pace doesn't slow. He moves with purpose, his arms firm around me, jaw clenched. He knows damn well where he's going.

I let him carry me farther, past the trees, the thick scent of pine filling my senses. The dirt path narrows beneath us, winding toward the lake, where the moon reflects silver against the glassy surface.

The air is *crisp*, but I barely feel it, wrapped in his warmth.

He shifts his grip, adjusting me slightly, and I try not to notice the way his fingers flex against my thigh or the way my body fits easily against his.

I clear my throat. "You realize this is completely *insane*, right?"

His lips twitch. "Is it? Hadn't noticed."

"No second thoughts? No regrets about *abducting* me?"

His smile deepens. "Nope."

My glance moves from his face to focus on the path ahead as we leave the resort behind and approach the narrow road leading to the rental cottages tucked between the trees. Porch lights glow in the night, soft and warm, casting shadows over the gravel.

So pretty.

So peaceful . . .

Gravel crunches beneath his shoes. He pauses at the edge of the road, glancing left, then right, like we're not in a tiny, peaceful town where the chances of getting run over at this hour are zero to *none*.

I use the moment to collect myself. My pulse is *too loud*, hammering against my ribs, and I can't tell if it's from the way he's holding me or the fact that I *haven't* demanded he put me down.

His little rental cottage comes into view, but he doesn't head for the steps. Instead, he strides straight past it, moving toward the driveway, toward the parked truck. When we reach his truck, he finally slows. With one arm still wrapped securely around me, he reaches out and tugs open the tailgate with his free hand.

The metal creaks, lowering into place. Then—with purpose—he sets me down on the edge of it.

I don't move.

Don't dare breathe.

His hands linger at my waist, his fingers flexing slightly before finally—finally—he steps back. His eyes are dark and unreadable, the flickering porch light catching the sharp angles of his face, his nose. Jaw.

My heart is *pounding*.

Legs dangling over the edge, my breath short as I grip the sides of the truck bed for balance. The night air is so much colder without his warmth wrapped around me, and I reach for him. Spread my legs and pull him between them.

The shift, the sharp inhale, the way his body *tenses* the second my fingers hook into his belt loops, the second I pull him closer.

He doesn't resist.

Doesn't hesitate.

I curl my fingers into the fabric of his shirt. "Harris."

"Yeah?"

He's waiting.

For me to make a move. Guide him along, tell him what to do. But I love it when he's bossy and takes charge—I need someone like him in my life.

I want him to take. To stop waiting for permission and do something about it.

I let the silence stretch. My legs stay spread around his waist, my pulse hammering, my breath short as his hands tighten around the truck bed, holding himself back.

Then—*finally*—his restraint snaps.

His hands find me, gripping my waist, pulling me forward so my body is flush against his, his fingers digging in like he's afraid I'll slip away.

"Tell me you want this," he murmurs roughly.

I stare up at him, heart pounding, skin burning. "Harris—"

His thumb skims along my jaw, slow, teasing, a silent dare. "Say it, Lucy."

The way he says my name—gritty, *commanding*—sends a delicious shiver down my spine. Ugh, so good . . .

I bite my lip, my pulse thrumming. He *knows* I want this.

But he wants to *hear* it.

I exhale, voice barely above a whisper. "I want this."

"You're all I think about, you know," he admits. He sounds almost . . . *broken*. "I-I don't know what to do with that."

My chest tightens. *I'm all he thinks about?*

I take a slow, steady breath, reaching out to touch his face, tracing my fingers along the rough stubble on his strong jaw. As long as we're doing confessions, I might as well admit my own. "I have no idea what to do about it either."

His throat bobs with a hard swallow, his hands flexing at his sides like he's fighting some internal battle. "I don't want to leave on Monday," he reveals. "I don't want to go to Arizona."

"Then don't," I whisper. The words slip out before I can think better of them. "I don't know why I said that—I know you can't stay."

My hands play with his waistband, and he leans forward, nuzzling my neck with the tip of his nose. He exhales against my skin, the warmth of his breath sending a shiver down my spine.

"You make this so damn hard," he says, lips brushing beneath my ear.

"Then don't go," I say softly, like maybe if I say it gently, it'll become possible.

His hands find my hips. "We both know that's not possible. I'll be back at work next week."

Work.

As in: football.

As in: the professional kind.

A big-boy job.

I tilt my head back, meeting his eyes, and the ache in them nearly undoes me. "Then what are we doing?" I whisper.

His thumb brushes the bare skin beneath my shirt, slow and reverent. "Making it impossible for me to leave."

I don't know if that's a promise—or a warning.

His mouth crashes onto mine.

The earth *shatters*.

Heat floods through me, a slow, burning ache curling in my stomach as his hands roam my body. One holds my waist, the other slides up my back, pressing me into him so I'm as close as possible.

And I?

I melt.

Completely, entirely.

I clutch at his shoulders, seeking the warmth of his chest, tilting my head as his lips part, deepening the kiss, tongue teasing against mine in a way that makes my whole body tighten, makes me grip him even harder, makes me pull him *closer* still.

He is not gentle.

It's a *collision.*

A hot, heated collision . . .

Every moment leading up to this—every tease, every push and pull, every unspoken thing between us—pours into this kiss, into the way he moves against me, into the way his hands stake his claim.

He drags his lips from mine, trailing along my jaw, down the curve of my throat, open mouthed and unrelenting. I tilt my head, giving him more, shivering when his teeth scrape against sensitive skin.

"Yes . . ." I whisper, voice unsteady.

A low, rough sound rumbles in his chest, his hands sliding up my rib cage, fingertips teasing beneath my shirt, grazing bare skin.

The wind stirs the pine trees around us.

I shiver.

His body tenses against mine, and then, without warning, he shifts, grabbing the truck bed as he hoists himself up beside me. The movement is fluid—effortless—like he couldn't stand another second of distance between us.

He nudges my legs farther apart, fitting himself between them as he presses me down against the bed of the truck. The metal beneath us is cold, a stark contrast to the warmth of his body, the heat of his hands as they slide over my hips, my waist.

I arch into him, sighing against his lips as his fingers dip beneath my shirt again, tracing lazy patterns against my skin.

"I want to fuck you in the bed of my truck like I'm in high school again," he groans. "Is that what we're doing?"

His groan is low, guttural, vibrating through me as he kisses me again, deeper this time, hungrier.

And I let him.

I let myself fall.

Chapter 26

Harris

The second I climbed into the back of that truck with Lucy—the second she pulled at me with those desperate hands—any rational thought I had in my brain evaporated into the breeze.

Lucy is *everywhere*. Beneath me, around me, in my head, under my skin. She clutches my shirt as if she could pin me down, breath stuttering when I press deeper into her. Warm. Soft. Womanly.

I shouldn't let this go any further, because I'm leaving.

But I will.

Because I'm a selfish bastard.

She shivers because it's not exactly warm outside, and for a brief second, I think she might be shivering because of me as my hands trace the smooth expanse of her stomach, my lips teasing the spot along her jaw. Below her ear . . .

When the wind picks up again, it threads its way through the trees, curling over us. Chilly. Causes Lucy's fingers to twitch against my shoulders.

I smirk, running my hands over the curve of her hips. "So you're using me for body heat?"

She shrugs, all innocence. "Gotta take advantage while I can."

Something in my chest tightens at that. She's teasing—but there's truth buried in her words. While she can? Does she think we have an expiration date?

"If that's the case, we should take advantage, don't you think?" I press a slow, deliberate kiss beneath her ear 'cause that's where she likes it. "Under the stars. Just you, me, and—"

"Bears," she cuts in.

I pull back, blinking. "Bears?"

I had not thought about wildlife since I've been here, not once.

She nods, face completely serious. "You know . . . big, furry creatures? Roam the woods? Have a taste for eating unsuspecting lovers *fucking* outside. That happened once in one of my true crime podcasts."

A grisly chill runs down my spine. I glance over my shoulder, eyes narrowing at the dark tree line, searching for bears. I gulp. "You're messing with me."

She tilts her head. "Am I?"

I try to gauge whether or not Lucy is screwing with me—should I actually be worried about being eaten alive? "You literally just said we might end up on a true crime podcast."

"No, I said I heard a story about two lovers being mauled while they were banging. But that wouldn't happen to us." She mulls this over. "I don't think."

"You don't *think*?"

"Well . . ." She drags her fingers lightly down my arm to distract me, my brain too busy conjuring images of sharp-toothed bears and cougars and badgers lurking in the shadows, waiting to kill me, to concentrate on her light touch. "I mean, we *are* in their territory. And they *do* attack people sometimes. Especially unsuspecting ones."

"What the fuck, Lucy?" I hiss, scanning the woods again like I might see a pair of glowing eyes through the bushes. "You couldn't have mentioned this *before* I shoved my hand up your shirt and got a boner?"

She bites her lip. "I thought you were tough."

"Are you gaslighting me?" I squeak, heart pounding. "I'm not trying to *die* in the middle of the woods with my dick out."

She full-on laughs now, sitting up beside me. "Relax, Harris. It's not like bears are . . . waiting for two horny people to start making out in the woods before they attack."

I stare at her, slack jawed. "Why did you put that idea into my head?" Seriously, what the hell is wrong with her? This is not funny!

"When I said it, I didn't think you would get so worked up about it!" She grins, reaching for my hoodie. "We could always test the theory? See if a bear pops out of the woods?"

"Abso-freaking-lutely not. We are *not* risking my life over this."

"*Your* life? What about *mine*?" Lucy is laughing all over again, giggling as if it's the funniest thing she's ever heard. Then she stops, putting a hand to her ear. "Did you hear that?"

My head whips around. "What?"

Lucy's eyes are wide, locked on to the trees. "I swear I heard something."

A prickle runs down my spine. "Do *not* mess with me right now."

I'm sensitive. Fragile.

An absolute mess of a man.

"Shh." She shakes her head, holding up a finger for me to shush. "Shhh."

I hold my breath to listen, but all I hear is the wind rustling through the branches, whispering through the trees, and then—

A crack.

A very distinct, *not-the-wind* kind of crack.

I stiffen, every muscle in my body tensing up. "What. The. Fuck. Was that?"

My cock deflates, all the blood draining out of it.

Lucy presses a hand to my chest, patting me twice. "It's probably nothing."

"Probably?" My voice shoots up half an octave. "That's *not* comforting. At all."

She bites her lip, like she's debating whether to mess with me or let me suffer. "Could be another deer."

"Or *a bear*!"

"Or a serial killer." She says it nonchalantly, as if she's filing her fingernails—not a care in the world.

"Oh my God." I slide toward the tailgate, already reaching for her, tugging her along with me. "I'm not dying like this. Not naked. Not with you laughing over my dead body."

Lucy tries—and *fails*—to suppress more laughter. "I cannot believe how terrified you are right now."

"Excuse me for having survival instincts!" I hiss, unamused.

Another crack. *Closer this time.*

I grab her arm. "We're leaving. Come on."

I don't wait for another sound. I *haul* her out of the truck like we're in a full-blown horror movie, my survival instincts fully engaged.

Lucy stumbles, half laughing, half protesting as I practically drag her toward the cabin. "Harris—oh my God—are you seriously—"

"Yes! Yes, I *am* seriously! Pick up your feet before I throw you over my shoulder."

Another *snap* of a branch.

I don't look back. I don't want to *see* whatever the hell is out there. I grip Lucy's wrist tighter and *run*.

She's gasping through her laughter. "You—you do realize we're probably running *toward* it, right?"

"Do not say that!" I yell, fumbling with the cabin door. My fingers are shaking far too much to get a good grip on the handle or insert the key.

Lucy leans in, breathing on my neck. "What if it's already inside?"

I stop. My entire body locks up.

She *loses it*.

I whirl on her. "This is *not* funny, Lucy."

She's *crying* with laughter now. "It's a *little* funny. Baby bit."

I yank the door open, shove her inside, and slam it shut behind us, chest heaving, back braced against it. "You are *never* talking me into outdoor sex again."

"Do I have to remind you that we were just getting started?"

"No." I shake my head vehemently. "Not happening. My dick is so flaccid right now."

She bites down on her lower lip to entice me. "Bet I could change your mind."

I scowl, crossing my arms. "Nope."

She steps closer, fingertips dragging along my arm. "Not even if I—"

A loud thump hits the side of the cabin.

I *scream.*

She doubles over, gasping while I clutch my chest like I went into cardiac arrest. "You—" she wheezes. "You *actually* screamed."

Of course I fucking screamed! I'm scared, goddammit! I glare, panting. "I—that was a *manly* yell."

"That's what you're calling it?" She shakes her head, eyes sparkling with mischief. "No, babe—that was a *high-pitched terror* scream."

When I open my mouth to argue, Lucy shocks me by dropping to her knees in front of me, hands smoothing up my thighs. She runs her palms over my jeans, nails tickling me through the denim.

"Jesus Christ, Lucy." I back up so fast I nearly knock into a table. "Now is *not* the time."

My back hits the front door.

"Oh?" she laments. "You don't look very . . . *conflicted.*"

"I am *not* conflicted." I glance toward the window like whatever thumped against the cabin is about to burst inside and eat us alive. "I'm trying to *survive.*"

She bats her lashes. "Or we could make the most of our *last moments* together."

I scowl down at her. "You *suck* at comforting people."

A wicked smirk plays at her lips as she lifts the hem of my T-shirt and presses a slow, deliberate kiss to my stomach, right above the waistband of my pants. "Speaking of sucking . . ."

My brain *short-circuits.*

My breath catches in my throat.

My hands hover uselessly at my sides like my body can't decide if I should stop her or help her along. I am a dude, after all, and my dick loves to do the talking . . .

"Lucy," I warn, sounding so, so weak.

She looks up at me through dark lashes, the picture of sweetness and sin wrapped in one. "Hmm?" Her fingers toy with the button of my pants, the lightest graze of her nails sending sparks through my already overloaded system.

I exhale sharply, tilting my head back. *I am so screwed.*

"Still worried about survival?" she teases, pressing another kiss to my stomach. Navel.

My moan is not subtle. "I *was.* Now I'm worried I might actually die, but for very different reasons."

She hums, hands splaying over my hip bones. "If you do, I promise to give a touching eulogy. Something tasteful."

I tip my head forward so I can look down at her, one brow raised. *"Tasteful?"*

She grins. "*Mostly* tasteful. I might have to mention how you collapsed with a look of pure bliss on your face because your dick was in my mouth."

I *choke* on a laugh, gripping her shoulders.

Lucy tugs at my zipper, fingers working with deliberate slowness, and my head falls back against the front door with a dull *thump.*

"Don't you wish you could resist me?" she wants to know, doing her best to undo my pants.

Resist her?

I *can't.*

Which is the problem.

My hands go to her arms so I can haul her up, ignoring her startled gasp. "Enough of this," I murmur, sliding my arms around her waist and spinning us so *her* back is the one pressed against the door. "You think you're in control here?"

She blinks up at me, a wicked little smile curving her lips. "Oh, honey," she whispers, dragging her nails down my chest. "I *know* I am."

I don't give her a chance to prove it.

I claim her mouth in a desperate, searing kiss, pressing my body flush against hers, feeling every inch of her warmth, every soft curve molding against me. She *melts*, a sigh slipping from her lips as I tangle my fingers in her hair, tilting her head back so I can taste her deeper. Her hands fist in my hoodie, pulling me closer, no space left between us.

And then, *to drive me completely insane*, she lifts one leg, wraps it around my leg, a silent plea to screw her against the door.

I break the kiss with a groan, dropping my forehead to hers. "Lucy," I murmur, breathless. "You're going to kill me."

"Only in the best way."

I shake my head, pressing my hips flush against hers, feeling her sharp inhale. "Bed. Now."

She hums, considering. "Or. We could do it right here."

See? What did I tell you? She totally wants me to fuck her against the door—I wasn't imagining it.

Lucy bites her lip again, eyes sparkling. "I dare you."

"Or." I nip at her earlobe, enjoying the way her fingers tighten against my hoodie. "I drag you to the bedroom and have you under me in five seconds flat."

My hands snake around to her back, drop low, skimming the backs of her thighs. Then, without warning, I lift her, hooking her legs around my waist in one smooth motion.

Lucy gasps, gripping my shoulders. "Harris!"

I grin against her neck. "Told you."

She glares down at me. "I hate how cocky you are."

"Liar." I take a step, securing my hold on her. "You *love* how cocky I am."

She makes a sound in her throat like she's gonna argue as I carry her straight toward the bedroom. "Don't you dare toss me on that bed. Lower me gently."

I laugh, deep in my chest. She's so cute. So bossy.

Her eyes widen as realization dawns. "Harris . . ."

"I love it when you say my name." I kiss her, ready to drop her.

"Harris—"

I *dump* her onto the mattress.

She bounces once, boobs jiggling beneath her sweater as she lets out a startled squeal; then she pushes herself up on her elbows, a mixture of shock and irritation on her face. "You *asshole*!"

I chuckle, yanking my hoodie over my head. "You asked for it."

Chapter 27

Harris:
Done with your class?

Lucy:
Done with the 7AM . . . waiting on the ladies for my 8:15

Harris:
I didn't love waking up to find you gone.

Lucy:
Why are you acting like I snuck out? I kissed you goodbye . . .

Harris:
Guess I'm being greedy.

Lucy:
You could've come to yoga class if you wanted—in fact, there's still time. Coffee delivery is also accepted.

Harris:
Noted. Favorite coffee order?

Lucy:
Oat milk latte with cinnamon. Hazelnut.

Harris:
Adorable. Mine's black. No nonsense.

Lucy:
Interesting . . .

Harris:
Would it make me sound like a pussy if I said this has been the best week ever, of my life?

Lucy:
Why do I feel like that sentiment might be an exaggeration? You've played in the Super Bowl.

Harris:
Yeah, but after you've done it once, doing it a second time doesn't live up to the hype.

Lucy:
You are SO FULL OF SHIT lol

Harris:
I'm offended by your lack of faith in me.

Lucy:
I found a video last night after you fell asleep and watched you eat two dozen pizza rolls straight from the microwave. Don't talk to me about being offended. You have NO taste.

Harris:
Pizza rolls are a sacred post-practice tradition.

Lucy:
Blah blah blah . . .

Harris:
How many people are in your next class?

Lucy:
Anywhere between 8 and 12 people show up, it all depends.

Harris:
Are you going to be glad to be rid of the guys?

Lucy:
I'm going to miss them in class, they're fun. And surprisingly good at yoga.

Harris:
I'm pretty sure Dex's girlfriend makes him practice yoga and Pilates, but don't quote me on that.

Lucy:
I knew it! Dex has perfect balance.

Harris:
So . . . how did the whole festival end yesterday for Annabelle? Did she survive?

Lucy:
Barely. I think she aged five years in one afternoon. She almost lost her shit when the waffle stand ran out of syrup.

Harris:
NOT THE SYRUP!!!!

Lucy:
Lol I know. Like, she had ONE job.

Lucy:
Well. She had a million jobs . . .

Lucy:
She's meeting me later to give me the rundown and I fully expect a meltdown. Or at least a tear or two. RIP waffle stand.

Harris:
Gone, but never forgotten.

Lucy:
Okay, I have to get moving. But I'll let you know if Annabelle combusts.

Harris:
Deal. And Lucy?

Lucy:
Hmm?

Harris:
I meant what I said about this being the best week.

Lucy:
Stop, you're going to have me blushing before class . . .

Harris:
Will I see you today?

Lucy:
It's a small town. See if you can find me.

Chapter 28

Lucy

I know before I even get out of my car that Annabelle is teetering on the edge of a breakdown or applying for a one-way ticket out of town.

She's camped out at our usual booth at Loon Landing Café, clutching her iced coffee, three seconds away from crushing the cup like an aluminum beer can, her daily planner splayed open.

I brace for impact.

She looks up as I slide into the booth, her smile tight and wild-eyed. Annabelle pushes a muffin and coffee mug toward me. "I survived. *Barely.*" She leans against her booth bench, exhausted. "Okay. Do you want good news or chaos first?"

I pretend to think. "Let's build suspense. Hit me with the good news."

She points dramatically at her planner. "We raised eighty thousand dollars."

I nearly choke on my coffee, sputtering over the rim of the mug. "Eighty thousand? Are you freaking kidding?"

"Nope. People really enjoy watching large men chop wood."

I nod knowingly. "Small-town America at its finest."

She nods solemnly. "Harris ripping off his shirt didn't damage my eyes. Once news got out that he was performing, we had to cut the line off and stop selling tickets." Annabelle groans. "May his abs forever fund the community."

Amen. "They deserve a plaque. Maybe their own wing at the community center."

My bestie clinks her cup against mine, eyes half lidded with exhaustion. "I swear, I need to hibernate for a week."

"You deserve it." Understatement of the year. "Are you going to tell me the bad news, or are you going to make me beg?"

She sighs, hand snaking across the table to snatch my muffin. "Someone stole one of the decorative carved bears at the hardware store. It's . . . gone."

I blink. "Who steals a bear statue?" Those things are seriously heavy—carved out of solid wood and probably weighing several hundred pounds. A person doesn't casually toss one in their trunk and drive off.

Annabelle waves a hand, exasperated. "Apparently, someone with a pickup truck, questionable morals, and excellent upper-body strength. Or a group of bored teenagers?"

"Or that." I shake my head. "Welp. I hope they at least gave it a good home." I take a sip of my coffee, letting the absurdity settle.

There's a pause—long enough for me to think we might be done dissecting small-town crimes. "Soooo what was up with you and that guy from last night?"

"The guy at the lodge I was flirting with?" Annabelle tears the top of my muffin off and pops a chunk of it in her mouth. Chews. "He's from Cincinnati and is here kayaking with friends from college."

"And?"

"And—nothing. I couldn't figure out if he was married or not. And too tired to find out the hard way. You know, by sleeping with him, then getting a DM next week from a pissed off wife. No thanks. Hard pass." Annabelle takes another bite. "I haven't gotten laid in weeks—like, I've been dry downtown since *long* before I dumped Tim."

This gets my attention. This is news to me. "You and Tim weren't having sex?"

She shakes her head. "I mean—I take some of the blame. I've been so busy leading up to Fall Fest and planning the Vodgs wedding—and Tim was so busy doing . . . Tim things . . . that we just . . ." Annabelle shrugs.

I lean back in my chair, watching her pick at the crumbly remains of my muffin like it's the last meal she'll ever have. Her confession lingers between us. *Dry downtown.*

I snort quietly into my coffee cup. "You know," I say, swirling the last sip. "Maybe after this weekend is over, you should plan to get out of town for a bit."

She pauses, hand hovering midair with a crumb stuck to her fingertip. "What—like a vacation?"

She says the word *vacation* like it's a foreign word she's only heard spoken in movies.

"Exactly." I sit up straighter, excited about this topic. "A real one. No clipboards, no color-coded calendars."

She drops her hand, brushing crumbs into a napkin with a frown. "Where would I even go?"

"Anywhere," I suggest. "Somewhere warm, with a beach. Cocktails. Sunburns. Cabana boys who can carry your luggage and emotional baggage."

She gives me a wry look. "I have a lot of that."

Don't we both? "Exactly. You need *two* cabana boys."

She snorts, but I can see the wheels turning. Annabelle has always been the planner, the one who keeps everyone else's life in order while hers stays on the back burner. Tim was another project she thought she could fix. And now?

She's running on empty.

I can see it in her eyes.

Annabelle huffs out a laugh. "I wouldn't know how to relax."

"That's exactly why you need to go." I lean forward, resting my chin on my hand. "Seriously. When was the last time you did something for yourself? Not for the town. Not for your brides. Something for you."

Annabelle's mouth opens, but nothing comes out. Her shoulders sag. "I don't remember."

"Babes, I'm not trying to make you feel bad. I just want you to consider being selfish for a second." I pause. "Maybe I'll book a trip for both of us."

Her eyes widen. "Seriously?"

"Dead serious. You, me, cocktails with little umbrellas. We can sit on a beach, complain about men. Eat, drink, have a fling."

Annabelle's smile softens. "Amazing."

I grin. "We'll wear floppy hats that say *Vacation Mode*. I'll read a romance novel and pretend to be shocked by the smut. It'll be great."

We sit in comfortable silence for a moment, the noise of the café buzzing softly around us. I watch her relax and know the cogs in her mind have begun spinning.

Perfect. She needs a break.

I can help her plan one.

"So what do you have going on today?" She changes the subject on me. "Doesn't Harris leave tomorrow?"

I nod. "He does." Swallow. "He's got a team meeting tomorrow about defense strategy or something?" I have no idea what anything is called. A football fan I am not . . .

"And that's it? The two of you are done? Lucy—you can't tell me that whatever is going on between you and Harris is . . . I don't know, a onetime thing. You've been glowing since you met him. And I mean *actual* glowing. It's so irritating."

My heart does this weird little flip. "It was fun," I admit. "He's hot, great in bed. Funny—"

Annabelle makes a gagging noise.

I ignore it. "*And* he's leaving tomorrow. He was *always* going to leave."

She watches me for a long moment. Taps her fingernails on her coffee mug. "So that's it? No deep feelings, no regrets? Just a fun adventure?"

I *want* to nod.

Instead, I pick up my coffee and take a slow sip, stalling for an answer.

Annabelle smirks. "You're hesitating."

I set my cup down with more force than necessary. "I'm not hesitating. I'm . . ." I straighten my spine. "Know what? Maybe *you* should be focusing on your own love life instead of mine."

Her smirk drops instantly. "Low blow."

I lift a shoulder. "You said you haven't gotten laid in weeks. Maybe that should be the priority—and not the fact that Harris is leaving."

She regards me. "Can you be honest with me for a second? Be real . . . Do you have feelings for Harris?"

The question lands like a weight on my chest: period, point blank.

I open my mouth to give her a casual brush-off, to make a joke about how feelings are for people with time for drama—and neither of us have time for that. But my words catch in my throat.

I can't say them, because they are a lie.

Instead, my gaze lands on the table, and I pick at the edge of my napkin, doing my best to ignore the sting behind my eyes.

"Yes," I whisper, barely audible. I clear my throat and say it louder. "Yes. I do." I exhale. "I care about him a *lot*."

Annabelle listens, expression one of tenderness.

"It's crazy, right?" Madness. "I barely know him, but I *hate* that he's leaving. I hate that I knew from the start it was temporary and still let myself fall for him! How stupid am I? Like—I set myself up for this heartbreak."

An idiot.

Stupid.

Selfish.

Annabelle reaches across the table; her fingers wrap around mine. "You're not stupid, Lucy. You're human. And that's why love is hard—our hearts are fickle creatures. They want what they want despite what our heads tell us."

I let out a shaky breath, the tears finally spilling over. "I thought I could handle keeping things casual! I did. I thought I could keep things light. Easy breezy. But uh, Harris is so kind. He listens. He makes me feel . . . sexy. And like I matter." I wipe at my cheeks, raw and exposed, lowering my voice. "I didn't realize how lonely I've been until he showed up. And now he's leaving, and I don't know how to go back to dating the same kind of boring men I dated before."

There.

I said it.

My bestie reaches across the table, fumbling for my hand so she can squeeze it, her own eyes glassy. "You don't have to go back. Maybe this is the part where you move forward."

I laugh bitterly. "Move forward into what? He's leaving tomorrow. He has a life. A career. One I'm not part of."

She tilts her head. "Have you told him how you feel?"

I shake my head quickly. "Obviously not! What would be the point? It's not going to change the situation."

Then Annabelle's expression shifts, eyes going wide. Her lips press together like she's trying desperately not to laugh—surprised? Caught off guard? What is that look on her face? And why is she staring over my head?

"Wait." I narrow my eyes. "Why are you looking at me like that?"

She blinks rapidly, cheeks flushing pink. "Uh. No reason?"

No.

Please no.

He can't be . . .

My stomach flips. I freeze. "He's standing right behind me, isn't he?"

Please don't let him be standing there, please don't let him be standing there, please don't let . . .

"For sure. Yes." Annabelle bites her lip and gives me the tiniest nod. "Totally."

I squeeze my eyes shut and groan. "Of course he is. Why didn't you say anything before I opened my dumb mouth?"

"Why would I?"

Life can never be simple, can it? When life gets dull, I behave like the amateur I am and fall for the first football-playing fake lumberjack that plops into my lap!

GUH!

Inhaling a deep breath, I turn slowly in my chair, heart racing.

Harris stands there, larger than life. Hands in his pockets, crooked smile. His eyes crinkle at the corners in a way I haven't seen before, and I try to translate what the look means. Care? Concern? Is he horrified? Because I am!

"Hi," he says gently.

"Hey," I squeak.

Annabelle is useless to me, muffling laughter behind her coffee cup—no help at all.

I cringe, cheeks on *fire*. "How much of that did you hear?"

He shrugs, still smiling. "Enough." Pause. "Have I told you today how fucking cute you are?"

No. Actually—yes. This morning before I slid out of his bed and headed home to shower so I could change before my classes.

He steps closer, eyes soft. "Why didn't you tell me how you felt? I've been chasing after you like a puppy dog all damn week."

"You have?"

He gawks at me, jaw slackening. "Let me count the ways." Harris holds up one finger, counting. "I lied and said I was a lumberjack to make you laugh." He holds up another finger. "I climbed the side of your house and landed in garbage." He holds up a third finger. "And I drove to four spots to find you because you're not answering my text messages."

I glance at my phone, which is resting on the bench beside me. There are five notifications from Harris. "Oh."

"So why didn't you tell me how you felt?"

I bite my lip, suddenly racked with shyness and nerves. "Because I didn't want to make things harder. You're leaving, and I thought if I kept it light, we wouldn't get attached."

His brow furrows. "And how's that working out for you?"

"Terribly." I laugh, shaky and breathless. "How is it working for you?"

He reaches for my hand and threads his fingers through mine. "Terribly."

"Welp. That's my cue to go." Annabelle stands up, gathering her things. "I'm gonna . . . um . . . go . . . literally *any*where else."

She winks at me and scurries off like a rat. To be honest, I'm shocked she's choosing not to stay and listen to our entire conversation.

Harris slides into the spot Annabelle vacated in the booth, still holding my hand like he's afraid to let go. Honestly? I'm glad he doesn't. I could use his lifeline right about now.

"So," he says softly, glancing around before his eyes land on mine. "What do we want this to look like?"

Do we have to talk about this now? I'm scared.

Harris is afraid of bears. I'm afraid of reality.

Ha!

I swallow hard. "I don't know. You've got workouts, the rest of the season, travel . . . your life is all over the place."

"And you have your life here," he finishes for me.

I nod, staring down at the table. "Right. My studio classes, the yoga schedules, my parents."

Harris squeezes my hand. "Okay, yes—I have football. No getting around that, my career is intense. But! I also have a phone. And a car. And we have planes. And apparently, I have a growing fear of you forgetting about me."

I snort. "You? Afraid I'll forget *you*? You're on national television. I think *I'm* the forgettable one here."

He leans in. "Lucy, I could be standing in a stadium with thousands of people screaming my name, and I'd still be thinking about you rolling your pretty brown eyes at me."

My face flames. "I don't roll my eyes that much."

He gives me a look.

"Okay, fine," I mumble. "I do." Sue me.

He sobers quickly. "Look, I'm scared too. I've never done the long-distance thing. I don't know if I'm going to be good at it. But I do know I don't want this to end without giving it a fucking try."

I worry on my bottom lip. "I don't either."

"Good." We sit in silence for a second, and then he says, "So. Logistics." He pulls out his phone. "We set standing call times," he says. "Even if it's five minutes. We send each other something every day. A text, a picture, a funny meme—something."

I nod, a smile tugging at my lips. "I can do that."

"So. What about Friday?"

Friday? As in, "This Friday? Five days from now?"

"Yeah. Friday. Can I take you to dinner?" The way he's watching my reaction as he says the words, "I'll fly you out. Dinner under the desert sky, you and me."

My jaw drops. "You want to fly me to *Arizona* for dinner?"

IS HE CRAZY? WHO DOES THAT?

Harris shrugs, like it's the most casual thing in the world. And who knows, maybe it is. "I told you—I don't want to wait. And I definitely don't want to say goodbye like this and not see you for weeks."

I press a hand to my chest to temper my beating heart. "You know most guys just FaceTime."

"Most guys aren't me."

"You're insane."

"Only for you." He raises my hand to kiss my palm. "Let me fly you out. We'll have dinner, I'll show you around the city, and you'll see exactly where I am when we talk every day. It won't feel so far."

I bite my lip, heart pounding. "You're serious?"

"Completely." His smile softens. "Come to Arizona and have dinner with me."

Chapter 29

Lucy

The rash has spread.

And it itches worse than it did. Like, full-body, "can't stop squirming," "*this is a nightmare*" itching.

I blink against the soft morning light filtering through Harris's bedroom window, disoriented for a second because it's still so early.

His bed.

His sheets.

The vintage headboard. I had absolutely no trouble falling asleep last night, after lying on my stomach at the foot of his bed, watching him throw the last of his things into a suitcase.

We snuggled on the couch after that.

Took a hot shower.

Climbed into bed and passed out.

The fresh mountain air will do that to a person . . .

I scratch at my arm—then my thigh—then the back of my knee, huffing out my frustration.

Beside me, there's a rustling of sheets. He better be awake.

"Please tell me you're scratching too," I mutter, clawing at my ankle like a lunatic. "I want to scratch my skin off."

Harris moans from his pillow. "I didn't want to say anything, but yes. I think my ass is on fire."

I turn my head to see him dragging his foot up and down the mattress, trying to get relief without using his hands. It's both ridiculous and endearing—and erotic, because we're both completely naked.

And covered in poison ivy.

"Oh no," I say, smothering a laugh. "You've got it too." I roll toward him, tugging the sheets around me. "Do you think there's any calamine lotion here? Or, say—an entire tub of hydrocortisone?"

"Bathroom cabinet," he says. "I'm going first."

He bolts out of bed, scratching his abs on the way, another hand on his butt cheek, itching.

I stare at the ceiling, wondering if it's possible to actually claw one's skin off and if I would, at this point, welcome the relief.

My entire body is on fire.

Every inch of me—from the delicate arch of my foot to places I really shouldn't admit out loud (*vagina*, cough cough)—is consumed by an inferno of itch!

I whimper louder. Impromptu forest sex was supposed to be romantic! Woodsy! Sexy!

Instead, I'm a human petri dish with welts in places no welts should exist.

I hear Harris's expletive from the bathroom. *A thud.* More curses. The medicine cabinet doors opening and slamming.

"Are you okay in there?" I call weakly, nails biting into my elbow for relief.

"I hate this!" he complains. "It itches so fucking bad!"

Tell me about it.

More banging, followed by "How am I supposed to sit on a plane like this?"

Don't know. Don't care.

I have problems of my own!

My butt itches. My stomach itches. My rib cage itches. What fresh hell is this?

Glancing at the nightstand, I grapple for my phone. I reach for it, unlock it, and google: *Can you die from poison ivy?*

The search results are not comforting.

Harris returns, his hot, naked body half covered in pink splotches of calamine lotion; he looks like a walking strawberry milkshake.

"Your turn," he says solemnly, tossing the bottle onto the bed. I grab the bottle and give it a shake to activate the ingredients.

Harris raises his eyebrows. "Need help?"

I blink at him. "Help with what?"

He grins, bending down to swipe his boxer shorts from the floor. "Rubbing it over your tits."

I roll my eyes toward the ceiling and snort. "I am not asking you to rub lotion on my boobs."

He grins wickedly. "But I'm volunteering as tribute!"

"So? I'm too itchy to let you touch me—even if the sight of you makes me horny."

He sits on the edge of the bed, pulling on his underwear. "Why Lucy—that's the most romantic thing a woman has ever said to me."

I laugh, pop open the bottle, and apply it liberally to my right arm, rubbing the thin lotion into my elbow and down my forearm. I groan, trying to twist and reach that impossible spot between my shoulder blades.

Harris watches me struggle for a beat, then holds out his hand. "Please tag me in, Coach. I'll behave."

I hesitate. Behave? He's not capable.

He wiggles his fingers. *Gimme.* "I promise to be professional. No funny business."

I narrow my eyes. "You're incapable of no funny business."

He grins. "Valid point. But also—itchy emergencies call for teamwork."

I hand him the bottle with a dramatic sigh. "Fine. You may apply lotion—but *only* because I can't reach."

He stands next to the bed, turning me so he has access to my entire back, then twists the cap off the pink bottle with an exaggerated motion. Gently runs his cool palms over my back. "Sorry this is cold."

"It's fine." It feels amazing. I nearly melt because it's already soothing my skin. "Marry me."

"So easy to win you over." He nuzzles my ear. "Ask me again twelve months from now."

I roll my eyes. "Never will I ever propose to a man."

Harris laughs, the sound warming my tummy from the inside out. I rest my chin on my arms as he smooths lotion along my spine. His touch is gentle, almost reverent—and if I weren't so miserably itchy, I may indeed be swooning.

When he finishes smoothing the last bit of lotion along my back, I expect him to let me flop forward in my misery—but instead, he hooks his arms around my waist and hauls me right into his lap.

I let out a surprised squeal, legs draped over his thighs. He tucks my head under his chin.

"I cannot wait," he says, pressing a kiss to the top of my head. "For Friday."

Friday is Arizona. Friday is his city, his friends, his house.

I will have to cancel classes, tell my parents I'll be out of town, find someone to open and close the studio . . .

I didn't consider any of these things when I agreed to go. I inhale a breath, reminding myself not to panic.

I can do this.

But Harris feels the tension in my body and pulls back to tilt my chin up. "Hey."

I meet his gaze, my stomach doing somersaults.

"It's going to be fun."

I nod. "What are we going to do?"

"I was thinking we could do an off-roading Jeep tour, and possibly go to the—"

"Oh my God, no. No Jeep tour." I hold out my arms, which are chalky from all the calamine lotion. "Have we learned nothing about your ideas for adventure? You practically broke your ribs scaling my wall, now we're covered in rashes because you wanted to hunt down a creature that doesn't exist."

He goes quiet, deflating like a sad balloon.

I nudge him gently. "I mean, you have a knack for chaos."

He thinks several seconds. "What if we take a hot-air balloon ride?"

Uh. No. "Do you have any idea how many balloons *crash*?" The statistics are mind boggling! Seriously! Google it!

"Oh!" He perks up again. "Indoor skydiving! You wear a jumpsuit. There's a giant wind tunnel, and they have instructors. What could possibly go wrong?"

I give him a warning look. "Harris."

"Fine," he says, dejected. "We'll go swimming in my pool." He sounds so deflated that I laugh. "Mini golf?"

I grin. "I don't hate that."

He puffs out a breath of relief. "And maybe after golf, we eat tacos the size of our faces?"

"Sold!" I shout to the ceiling because who doesn't love tacos the size of their faces?

"Margaritas that come in buckets?"

I kiss his jawline. "You are redeeming yourself so, so quickly."

"I wanted this trip to be amazing for you," he murmurs.

I smile against his chest. "It will be because you'll be with me."

He kisses the top of my head, his breath warm against my scalp, lips lingering. "You're kind of my favorite person, you know that?"

I look up at him, eyes sparkling. "Kind of?"

I can feel him grinning as he says, "Okay, definitely."

My shoulder itches, but I resist the temptation to scratch it, content to be in his arms. I love that he's holding me, this moment is so—

"What about riding a mechanical bull?" he interrupts.

I groan. *"Stop."*

Epilogue

Lucy

I've been in Arizona for exactly forty-eight hours, and here are the important things I've learned:

1. The sun here is not messing around. It will burn you to a crisp faster than Harris can demolish a plate of nachos.
2. Harris's house is . . . massive. Like, "I got lost looking for the bathroom" massive. Like, "I was half convinced there was a wing I wasn't allowed in" massive.
3. His pool is where I now live.

Floating on a giant inflatable donut, I bob up and down on the clear blue water—sunglasses on, hat tilted over my face—while Harris splashes around beside me like an overgrown Labrador puppy.

"I bet you five bucks I can flip you over without using my hands," he announces, wading closer, water dripping down his smooth, muscular chest.

I love that chest. Could stare at it all damn day, especially soaking wet.

"Don't you freaking dare. I will kill you." I've been threatening him all weekend. Another thing I've learned about him (that I basically already knew)? Harris loves making bets—and making things interesting.

It's cute.

Until it's not.

He grins at me, pearly white teeth and mischief, and then—he disappears. Full-on submarine mode.

I freeze. The donut bobbles beneath me, and I tighten my grip, heart racing. "Harris?"

Silence.

The water ripples ominously.

"This isn't funny!" I warn him, squinting over the side of the pink sprinkled tube, peering into the crystal water below me; unfortunately he is nowhere to be seen.

"Oh no," I whisper. *"I swear to God . . ."*

The tube shifts. I squeal.

When his hand brushes my ankle, I shriek overdramatically, flailing as if my life depends on it, desperate to get away from his grasp.

I REFUSE TO GO UNDER!

He surfaces a few feet away, splashing water at me. "You're jumpy."

I glare, pushing soggy strands of hair off my face. "You are so annoying!"

He circles me slowly in the water like a shark, predator-style, shoulders bobbing above the surface. "You look nervous, babe."

Because I am. "Will you leave me alone if I take my top off?" I offer.

He tilts his head, considering it. "No. 'Cause then I'll want my hands on you more."

He goes under again.

I yelp. He wouldn't dare! "Harris! No!"

The water goes still. I whip my head side to side, searching.

Suddenly, my donut lifts—flips—sending me into the water with a melodramatic splash. I flail as if I cannot swim . . . find my footing, and push off the bottom.

When I resurface, I'm sputtering. The dipshit is laughing so hard he's coughing.

"Dead. You are so dead." I launch myself at him, but of course he catches me easily, both of us laughing and breathless.

This has been the best day.

He brushes water off my face. "I couldn't resist."

"I'm going to drown you," I promise, kissing him on the nose. He has freckles in the sun, and I touch one with the tip of my fingers as he cradles me in his arms, walking laps in the shallow end.

Holding me.

It really has been the best few days; neither of us is as itchy as we were when he left Star Lake, and better news? Chlorine from his pool helps take away the itch. *Who knew?*

I rest my head on his shoulder as he keeps pacing slow laps in the shallow end, his arms strong and steady around me. He's holding me like I weigh nothing, his fingers trailing lazily up and down my back.

I trace a freckle with my fingertip. "You have freckles."

He smiles softly. "I get them in the summer. You like?"

"Love."

"You love my *freckles*?" he asks gently, curiosity also lacing his words—like he's hoping I'll say more.

I swallow, heart hammering. "I love everything about you."

His arms tighten around me. "Lucy."

"Hmm?"

"You love my *freckles*?"

I roll my eyes but can't help laughing. "I just said that."

He arches a brow. "That's not the same thing as saying you love me."

I blink at him, feeling my heart do a ridiculous little flip. "Harris . . ."

He waits. I bite my lip, nerves suddenly clogging my throat. I want to say it. I really, really do. But he stares me down, smug as ever, as if he's going to make me squirm for it.

I narrow my eyes. "You're trying to make me say it first."

He shrugs, clearly unbothered. "I like winning."

I open my mouth—then shut it.

He leans in, brushing his nose against mine. "C'mon. Admit it."

I stay stubbornly silent. Because it has only been two weeks since we've met. People can't possibly fall in love in that short amount of time.

Can they? It's not possible. Is it?

I look at him—really look at him. His wet hair sticking up like a rooster, those ridiculous freckles dusting his nose and shoulders, the way his mouth twitches at the corners like he's fighting back another joke.

God help me. I'm completely, stupidly, head over heels in love with this man.

My brain tries to talk me out of it—rattling off logical arguments like some overly cautious life coach in my head. Too soon. Too crazy. Too unrealistic.

But my heart is standing there with a giant foam finger, screaming "TOO LATE, LOSER."

Harris nudges my cheek with his. "I can see it, you know."

I blink. "See what?"

"That you love me." His grin softens into something vulnerable. "You're trying to logic your way out of it, and it's adorable."

I open my mouth to protest, but he cuts me off.

"It's okay," he says happily. "I wasn't expecting it either. But here we are. Floating in my pool, still covered in poison ivy, with a bruised rib from your trellis—and I've never been more happy."

I exhale, laughing and sniffling at the same time. "Why are you like this?"

"Like what?" He blinks at me innocently.

"So . . . infuriating." UGH!

"Why can't you say the words?"

My throat tightens, tears pricking the corners of my eyes. I press my palm against his heart, feeling it beat strong and steady beneath my hand.

"I love you," I whisper.

He lets out a long breath and holds me tighter, kissing the top of my head. "I knew it."

"Shut up."

"Oh my God." He laughs, tipping me back in his arms so he can look down at me. "You are *so* obsessed with me."

Before I can retort, he suddenly drops me—lets me go—and I splash beneath the water with a shriek. When I surface, sputtering and pushing wet hair out of my face, he's already climbing onto one of the giant inflatable donut tubes.

He grins down at me like a kid who found the cookie jar. "Race you. Donut to donut."

I'm not in the mood to race him. I have better ideas.

Reaching around my back, my fingers find the hook of my bikini top and unclasp it, letting the straps hang.

Harris bobs on his donut tube, perched on top of it like a pirate, watching me like I'm a stick of dynamite with a lit fuse. "Why the hell would you do that?" he asks, affronted. "That's cheating."

I shrug. "You wanted a race. I'm leveling the playing field."

One of my straps falls.

Harris freezes. His donut tilts dangerously as he leans forward. "You're bluffing."

Am I, though?

I tug the top free and twirl it around one finger before tossing it to the pool deck with a casual flick. Off it goes . . .

He blinks.

I grin.

"Game over," he mutters, sliding off his donut and swimming toward me like a shark on a mission.

I squeal, trying to backpedal—but he's faster. Strong arms wrap around my waist, pulling me flush against him in the water.

"You're evil," he murmurs into my ear, kissing me. Hands splaying up my backside, along my spine.

"I'm resourceful." I tilt my head up and kiss his jaw, feeling him shiver against me. "Girlies do what they have to do."

He pulls back to look down at me. His gaze is warm and hungry and full of affection all at once.

"Marry me," he says, dead serious.

He is out of his damn mind!

I splash water at him. "You can't propose while we're both half naked in your pool!"

"Well. When *can* I propose?" He's pouting now, but joking.

"You said give it twelve months. So I'll see you in twelve months." I swat at his hands as they reach for my boobs beneath the clear water.

He catches my wrists easily, pinning them playfully against his chest. "Twelve months? That's cruel and unusual punishment."

I raise an eyebrow. "You'll survive."

"I might not." He leans in and kisses me again, this time slow and teasing, like he's trying to convince me otherwise. "And in the meantime . . ."

Harris's giant hands have me by the waist, and he hoists me up, setting me on the pool deck, palms spreading my legs. Up my rib cage. Over my breasts.

I lean back on my elbows, the sun warming every inch of my skin as Harris stands between my legs, water dripping from his body onto the stone deck. He looks up at me with that devilish grin that makes my toes curl.

"You know," he says, fingers circling my nipple. "I could ask again tomorrow. Or the day after that. Maybe every day for the next twelve months until you cave."

I roll my eyes, but my smile betrays me. "Persistent much?"

He shrugs, hands sliding down to my thighs, thumbs flirting with the hemline of my swim bottoms. "I'm a linebacker. Persistence is my job."

When he nips at my skin, I gasp.

The sun beats down on us, the sound of the pool filter humming in the background, and for the first time in a long time, I feel completely, ridiculously happy.

"Ever had sex in a pool?"

I shake my head. "No—and I don't think it's a good idea."

He leans forward and licks my nipple. "Why?"

"Chlorine up my vajayjay? We have horrible luck."

He chuckles, pressing a wet kiss to my sternum. "Nah. We have excellent luck. We found each other."

I melt a little. Sometimes he says the sweetest things . . .

He slides his hands under my thighs, pulling me to the very edge of the deck, my calves resting on his broad shoulders. "I think we should test the pool theory," he declares. "Or. I can do this . . ."

He dips his head between my thighs, finger hooking my swimsuit bottom and pulling it aside before putting his mouth there, lips on my pussy in the spot I love most. Nothing is more erotic than watching him with his face on my clit, but still, I tug him upward by the hair and press my forehead to his.

"Twelve months," I whisper.

"Nine," Harris bargains.

"Ten."

He groans, throwing his head back. "Fine. Ten. But I'm proposing in the most embarrassing way possible."

I grin. "I'd expect nothing less."

Epilogue 2

Annabelle

Lucy was right.

I need a break.

If one more person tells me I "look tired," I'm going to scream.

But. I do look tired. Because I *am* tired. Because running the Lakeside Fall Fest was basically like hosting a royal wedding, the Super Bowl, and a three-ring lumberjack circus all rolled into one, minus the helpful minions and with way more syrup emergencies.

The funny thing is—and by *funny,* I mean cruel—after it was all over and we'd counted the $80,000 we raised (I'm still suspicious someone added a zero), my first thought wasn't relief.

It was *I need a vacation.*

A real one.

One where no one calls me at six a.m. asking if they can bring their cousin's boyfriend's dog to the pancake breakfast. One where I don't have to talk to the fire marshal about whether or not axe throwing constitutes a "controlled hazard." One where I don't have to hear the phrase *Are we out of syrup?* ever again in my natural life.

But I can't take a real one because THERE IS NO TIME.

I text Lucy to complain, thumbs flying across the screen like a woman possessed: I need a vacation. I need three vacations. Possibly a sabbatical. Maybe early retirement. How do I make this happen without abandoning the town or faking my own death?

I stare at the chat bubble, waiting for those three glorious dots to appear.

Nothing.

I hate how impatient I am, waiting for her to reply. I hate how envious I am that she left for Arizona without me, because Harris freaking Bennett swept her off her feet like some kind of romantic comedy hero with biceps carved from marble.

She deserves it.

Obviously she does . . .

But also?

RUDE!

I'm here, running on caffeine and stress fumes, my hair in a bun that hasn't been undone in four days, answering emails about lost and found jackets, backpacks—and whether or not we can *make the lumberjacks come back for Christmas tree lighting in the square.*

I tap my phone impatiently. Still nothing.

I let out a dramatic sigh, leaning my head back against the porch railing, staring at the gray sky. Even the weather is judging me.

My phone dings.

Lucy:
Omg. Stop. Come to Arizona. Get
on a plane. DO IT.

Come to Arizona?

I stare at the screen, wanting to reply with a resounding "YES! Yes, you're right! I'm on my way! Free place to stay! Sunshine!"

My thumbs hesitate over the keys.

Except . . . I can't.

There's a pancake-breakfast meeting on Tuesday. And the Christmas committee kickoff on Wednesday. And Lindsey Vodgs and her fiancé are coming to tour their wedding venue on Tuesday afternoon, and her parents will finally be in town.

Annabelle:
You know I would love to, but I can't.

Lucy:
There are always going to be reasons not to do something. I shut down the studio to fly here, because I couldn't get anyone to cover for me. Sometimes we have to make sacrifices for our mental health, for example . . .

I sigh. She's not wrong—there is always going to be a reason not to do something. Still, that doesn't mean I can drop everything and fly out of town.

I am not like the new, carefree Lucy.

I am not spontaneous.

I don't live on the edge.

I stare out the window, in the direction of the lake. Yes, I live in a resort town. No, my apartment isn't anywhere near the water. Too expensive.

But that's me in a nutshell, isn't it? Practical. *Predictable.* Sensible to a fault. I make grocery lists and stick to them. I budget down to the penny. I plan vacations twelve months in advance and still double-check hotel confirmations the night before. I don't wake up one morning and decide to book a flight somewhere on a whim. I've never been that girl.

I wonder what it feels like to be that girl.

To act first and figure the rest out later.

To leap without worrying if the net will appear.

Lucy:
What about a staycation? Go to the lodge and relax! Let them pamper you! Hang out with the tourists . . .

Annabelle:
The lodge is the least quiet place in town. What I need is peace and quiet and not to stare at the white walls in my apartment, day in and day out . . . UGH!

Lucy:
Okay. What about one of the cottages? I had never been in one until I was inside Harris's and they are SO DARN CUTE. You would love it.

I chew on my bottom lip, staring at her message. Spontaneity? No, thank you. That's how you end up lost, sunburned, and accidentally eating something you're allergic to.

But . . . What if?

What if I *did* take a staycation?

What if I closed my laptop, threw some clothes in a bag—no, not even a bag, just . . . whatever I can grab in ten minutes.

Annabelle:
Wouldn't that be weird?

Her reply comes in instantly.

Lucy:
No! It's self-care. You're treating yourself. Like a mini-retreat!

I glance down at my to-do list.

I glance at the pile of forms on my kitchen table.

I glance at the bottle of wine I forgot to open last night because I passed out fully clothed at 8:30 p.m. Which reminds me: I have to finish doing my laundry!

My phone dings again.

Lucy:
You would be working—but at least you'd be on the lake.

Lucy:
You deserve this. Seriously.

I hesitate. Then pull up the reservation site.

And what do you know? There's a cancellation. This weekend, Friday through Sunday. Quaint cottage with a screened-in porch, fireplace, and—my favorite part—a hammock. What? I'm going to sit in that hammock, sway like I don't have a care in the world even though I have a million problems. Relaxing won't be one.

Before I can second-guess myself, I book it and text Lucy: Booked the cottage. You're a terrible influence. Never stop.

I'm going full cottagecore.

I guess there's only one thing left to do: Pack. Snacks. Sweaters. Bug spray.

And maybe I'll pack a little less anxiety. Because this weekend?

I'm not bringing my to-do list.

I'm bringing marshmallows and vibes, and I'm not wearing a swimsuit when I sunbathe on the pier.

Who even am I?

Acknowledgments

I've always been a daydreamer. Used to stare out the window anytime I was in the back seat of my parents' car, thinking up all the stories I wanted for myself. But I was awkward and a bit shy, and it took me many years to grow into myself . . . Diaries turned into journals turned into stories, which turned into my first real novel.

I learned so much about myself through my work.

I grew.

I am who I am today because of my writing.

To my cute, clever, and supportive readers—I love an escape as much as you do. We love romance, we love learning through words. And I had SO MUCH FUN with this novel! I'd always wanted an accidental mistaken identity to happen to ME; one second I'm writing an athlete—and the next thing you know, Harris pretending to be a lumberjack to flirt with a girl . . .

Sigh . . .

To Jeff, *my fiancé*—you're literally the best support system a girl could ask for—thank you for cheering me on, helping create plot twists. Taking me for cute dates, and dressing up, and smelling *so, so good.* You're truly amazing.

To my family—my incredible kids—you are everything. Thank you for being patient with me those weeks I disappear into my writing for hours at a time, often on weekends, so I don't miss my deadlines.

To Logan Adams, who runs my social media and is fiercely creative, and Hailey, the new young woman in my life who's doing her best to keep me semiorganized. We're learning and growing together! Shauna at the Author Agency, who sends me reminders about almost everything and also: pictures of her new dog, Chloe.

To my agent Michelle Wolfson at Wolfson Literary. You're the best. Maria Gomez and the entire Montlake crew, who make publishing magic happen every single day. Mackenzie and Anthony, your edits are SPOT ON. Perfection. Chef's kiss . . .

Y'all are the reason I get to live my dream. You pick up these books, fall in love with these characters, and let me keep doing what I adore most: writing love stories.

Thank you for being part of this one.

Cannot wait for more daydreams.

xx Sara

About the Author

Photo © Lauren Perry

Sara Ney is an Amazon and *USA Today* bestselling author of new adult college and adult romance, notably the How to Date a Douchebag and Campus Legends series. Her books have been translated for many foreign markets, including Germany, Italy, Brazil, and Israel. Sara lives alongside her partner Jeff in a blended household overrun by four independent teenagers. She enjoys a weekly Cute Date Night, where she and Jeff discuss TV shows they're bingeing and plot new novels together—something he is freakishly good at. Sara also loves traveling, because it's the only time she has the bathroom to herself. For more information about Sara Ney and her books, visit www.authorsaraney.com.

About the Author